the Fool's Girl

the Fool's Girl

CELIA REES

SCHOLASTIC INC.
New York Toronto London Auckland
Sydney Mexico City New Delhi Hong Kong

For Rosemary

First published in Great Britain in May 2010 by Bloomsbury Publishing Plc.

ISBN 978-0-545-38731-6

12 11 10 9 8 7 6 5 4 3 2 1   11 12 13 14 15 16/0

Printed in the U.S.A.   40

First Scholastic printing, September 2011

I

'What country, friends, is this?'

London, 22nd April 1601

VIOLETTA

Have you seen a city under sack? Have you seen what happens there? Have you seen the blood, heard the screaming, smelt the smoke on the wind?

I stood on the battlements and watched them coming. Venetians and Uskok pirates, the scum of the sea, combined together to attack our fair city. I saw the red flash of the guns, the white smoke, felt walls shudder. I saw ships rammed; blown to splinters. I saw tall galleys spew fire that spread over the decks in a blazing carpet, turning men into torches and sails into ragged flags of flame. The burning ships ran on, setting fire to others until our fleet was nothing but smoking hulks set to spin in the powerful current like blackened walnut shells.

Still they came on. Platforms built on towers above the prows of the leading galleys brought the invaders level with us on the battlements. We kept up a hail of stones and arrows but the big ships came in a long line, each platform linked with its neighbour. You could run from one end of the fleet to the other. Those Venetians are clever. The ships rammed against the walls, grounding themselves on the rocks, bringing their forces eye to eye with ours. Men leaped off the platforms and on to the battlements, letting rope ladders down to be caught by those below. Soon men were crawling up the walls in black swarms.

From the landward side, balls of fire rained down on the city, destroying houses and churches. The roofs were obscured by rolling smoke; flames shot upwards and tiles fell in a dreadful scurrying clatter, muffling the screams of those caught inside to burn alive.

The city's walls were breached. The gates lay open. Enemy forces poured in, driving the people up the Stradun. The wide central thoroughfare was already jammed with all those trying to escape the ring of trampling booted feet, the swing and slash of the sword blade. The crowds were forced into the main piazza, caught like fish pursed up in a net. They would find no sanctuary in the cathedral. The great west door lay in splinters. Vestments were strewn about, defiled and discarded. Pages of sacred texts blew around and stuck in the crooked streams of blood that were trickling down the steps to pool on the white marble pavement. Once the piazza was full, the killing began. The separate wails of grief, sobbing and pleading became one constant scream.

FESTE

I took her. I dragged her from the battlements. She wanted to stay, to fight to the end, but her father the Duke ordered her away. He knew that there would be no mercy. He did not want to see his daughter raped in front of him until they put out his eyes. He sent his page, young Guido, with us, not wanting to see the same thing happen to him.

We went down into the cellars. From there I hoped to take one of the tunnels that led out to the ramparts, but from the direction of the walls came the rumble of rolling barrels. The vermin were already down there. Sappers, busy with gunpowder, getting ready to blast their way up into the tower.

I led them up into air thick with the smell of burning flesh and ash falling like snow. The fight had moved on, the streets were deserted, but they were not empty, if you get my meaning, and there was no way for me to shield her. She's seen sights that no girl of her age should ever have to see. There's a madness takes men over. No one had been spared. Men cut down where they stood, women raped and left for dead, children and babies chopped and butchered. Only the animals were still roaming about, and the less said about that . . .

We couldn't get out of the city. We were trapped like rats in a granary. Ever seen terriers sent in to clear them? They kill until they are staggering, then they kill some more.

In the east, a woman's high keening stopped abruptly. In the west, the sky glowed with more than the sunset. The Duke's palace on fire. There were still shouts and screams, but they were becoming scattered and sounded distant. There was a lull while the Venetians and pirates got busy looting or broke open barrels in the inns and taverns, but the looting would finish when there was nothing left to steal, and then they would be out on the street again, this time drunk, and the slaughter would go on until there was nothing left to kill.

We went through the narrow twists of the streets

and up crooked flights of steps slippery with blood. We went to find Marijita, but she was dead with all her birds about her. She had been weaving her own shroud.

VIOLETTA
How did this come about? To understand that, I have to take you back to the very beginning . . .

2

'So full of shapes is fancy'

Master William Shakespeare, poet, player and sometime mage, had been on his way home from the theatre after seeing a particularly poor performance of one of his plays. The crowd had been slow to settle, churlish and sullen, given to outbursts of insults, mewing and hissing, accompanied by a certain amount of peel and bottle throwing. And who could blame them, when those whom they had come to see were stiff-limbed and leaden-footed, late to arrive on stage and slow to leave it? The heroine needed a shave, and her male counterpart was more wooden than the twigs and branches of the 'forest' he wandered. There was sickness in the company, some of the best players laid low, but that was really no excuse. Why did he bother to write at all, when any addle-pated actor thought he could prattle out the contents of his empty head?

Will had left before the end. He knew how that would be, the epilogue rushed to give way to a prolonged bout of energetic, over-exuberant jigging, whether the play warranted it or no. Even though the present production was a comedy, it would not benefit from a lot of antic prancing. The thought of it put him even more out of temper as he went past the sharp animal reek of the bear garden. Here the crowd roared at every deep snarl of fury and sharp yelp of agony.

The animals were earning more applause than their human counterparts at the Globe.

He walked on, eyes down, picking his way over the turd-studded ground, making for his lodgings, close by the Clink Prison. As he turned the corner hard by the church of St Mary Overie, a throng of people stopped his further progress.

A bearded man who looked like a Spaniard strummed a cittern and a blackamoor beat on a row of upturned buckets, but these two were not the focus of the crowd's attention. Every head was turned; every eye was on a small, thin man. He stood, stripped to the waist, his legs encased in black hose, his white visage a blank mask of concentration as his head wove this way and that, trying to balance a motley collection of objects on his forehead: a wooden pole, a painted box, a chair on top of that. His bobbing sideways motion had the crowd weaving with him, as if their sympathetic movement could strengthen his.

He gave a slight nod and the crowd gasped, sure that the whole lot would tumble, but it did not. The clown righted the swaying edifice and his assistant, dressed in the white baggy costume of a Commedia dell'arte *zanni*, threw a puppet high into the air. All eyes turned upwards as the puppet flew, seemed to hover for a moment then fell down, settling on the seat of the chair. The crowd clapped and roared their appreciation as the puppet's tiny head nodded to them and its hand seemed to stir in acknowledgement. The clown gave a violent toss of his own head and the whole lot went skyward, each object falling to the ground arranged neatly around him, the puppet still seated on his chair. The clown picked up the puppet, a black-clad replica of himself, and set it to bowing and waving and accepting the applause.

Will stayed to watch, as did the rest of the crowd, and others joined them. The clown had created a great space out of nothing, a scrap of paving where two roads met. Each successive trick seemed more dangerous, more outrageous, doomed to inevitable failure. That was what held them. They were all waiting for the moment when the clown would falter and the objects he was juggling or balancing would tumble about him. But they never did. Full-size chairs flew through the air like children's toys.

One act followed another. He wriggled out of locks and chains heavy enough to crush him. Fire did not scorch him. Swords and daggers left him without a scratch. He took the crowd with him like the tide pulled the river's flow. Will had long ago left watching what the clown was doing; he knew he would not fail in it. He was watching his face. Terror, fear, relief, humour, happiness and sadness rippled over his expressionless features like water over stone, running out to the crowd who mirrored each emotion, entirely unaware that they were doing so. Will knew that he was in the presence of a master, a great clown, perhaps the best he had ever seen. When the show was over and the crowd applauded, he joined in, throwing a coin into the hat the *zanni* was passing. The clown held the puppet behind his back and they both bowed low, the clown turning to take in all of the circling crowd.

His audience began to disperse into the surrounding streets and alleys, but Will stayed behind.

'What is your name, master?' he asked.

The clown affected not to hear. He pulled a black tunic over his sweating body, his pale torso corded and knotted, his arms like twisted rope. He wiped his face with a rag, revealing a pale countenance almost as white as the paint that had covered it. Will watched as the man walked about collecting the chains, clubs and sticks and various bits he had used, throwing each one into the battered box that had been part of the balancing act. He could have been any age and no age. Will liked the look of him. A thin clown, a lean clown, a clown with no spare flesh on him, the kind Will admired, quite unlike that fat fool prancing about on the stage of the Globe. He was yesterday's clown.

The man picked up the puppet, removing the rudimentary arms and legs like a suit of clothes to reveal the central shaft of a folly stick. The head was hewn from a natural burl of wood, the contours carved into his own features, with a twisted mouth and a sharp, curving nose. Shiny black stones gleamed from lids half closed, sly and knowing, beneath the swirl of a jester's cap.

'My name is Feste.' The clown cradled the folly stick to his chest, twisting its face away to avoid further scrutiny. He turned to welcome back his companion. 'This is Violetta.'

The white-suited *zanni* had slipped away to use a nearby alley as a tiring room and returned as a maid, wearing a low-cut bodice under a soft blue gown. She shook out her dark hair as she came towards them. She wore it loose, with no covering cap. Around her neck hung a pendant charm of branching silver sprigs and strands of coral as delicate as a baby's fingers.

Will stepped forward, intending to introduce himself.

The clown held up his stick, as if in warning. 'We know who you are, master,' he said.

'My compliments to you both,' Will replied. 'You pleased the crowd. But performing is hard work. You must be hungry . . . thirsty. Would you accompany me to the Anchor? It is close by here. We could share a jug of wine and take some supper. It would be my treat.'

Violetta nodded and the clown shouldered the box. The take had been good, but an offer of food and wine bought by another was not to be passed up. Will turned to make sure that they were following after him and led the way to the inn by the river. They were strangers, that much was clear, but more than that, there was a strangeness about them. A Fool who was no man's fool, and his boy who was really a girl. He'd felt the old pricking sensation running through him. He'd sensed a story here, and he was seldom wrong.

3

'I am all the daughters of my father's house,
and all the brothers, too'

VIOLETTA

It began when my mother came to the shores of
Illyria. I am named for her: Violetta, meaning
little Viola. My mother arrived in my country as
much a stranger as I am here. I remember the story
from when I was very young. I remember it from
when I was lying in my cradle, watching the
shimmering light from the sea play like shoals of silver
fish across the ceiling, while the charms hanging above
me seemed to turn to the music and laughter twisting
up the stairs from the great hall below.

In my mind, my mother became mixed with the
heroines of other legends, the stories so woven
together that I could not work out where their stories
ended and hers began.

When I was a child of about four or five I would sit
at my window, watching the ships come and go from
the harbour below – long galleys with their oars
stretched like insect legs; sturdy little carracks, the
wind billowing their slanting sails – and I would
wonder: did my mother come on that kind of ship, or
that? Sometimes I would mount the steep, worn steps
to the Tower of the Eagles, pulling myself up by the
thick rope looping between great iron rings set into
the wall. I would look out from the battlements and

my mind would take flight like the eagles that nested on the topmost turrets.

I would look down at the sheer cliffs, the white waves curling beneath, the tiny coves and lonely inlets with their crescents of pale grey beach, and I would wonder: where did she first come to shore?

I would see the great ship founder: sometimes with a splaying tangle of splintering oars, sometimes with a sturdy hull split asunder – the crack of a tall mast, the rending of canvas, the wild flapping of fallen sails. I would see the cargo spill. Among the casks and barrels I saw bodies floating, arms outstretched, hands and faces livid in the blackness. My mother was among them, her eyes closed in her white face, her pale hands floating upwards, her dress billowing, her hair flowing about her, moving like the weed in the harbour. She hung there, suspended between brightness and darkness, until I was sure that she was dead. Then she pushed upwards, making for the shifting glimmer above her, her head breaking the surface like a sleek seal.

She bobbed there for a moment, looking about her, before breasting the tumbling waves and striking for shore. She was a strong swimmer, my mother. She rose from the water, emerging from the foam like Aphrodite; coming out of the waves like some mysterious mer-creature, stepping on to the sand like a lost princess, spared by the sea to pursue her destiny. Behind her, day had become night. The storm raged and between sky and water there was no margin, only inky blackness. Then a single flash of lightning forked from the firmament, stitching heaven and earth together, and she stood illuminated by the sudden violent brightness. Although yellow was a colour that I never saw her wearing, she was wearing a yellow dress. When I told her this, she smiled and pulled me to her.

'Yes. That is how it was! A yellow dress, exactly. How could you know? You clever, clever child!'

This was her story. How she told it to me. She emerged from the water to find people standing on the shore, attracted by the storm or the chance of a wreck. Her appearance was so sudden, so miraculous, a splash of yellow against the blackness, that they looked behind her, to see if her feet printed the sand. Among them were sailors, lately washed up. Their number included the captain of the ship.

'What country, friends, is this?' she asked.

'This is Illyria, lady,' the captain replied.

She enquired about her brother, Sebastian, who had been travelling with her. He was last seen clinging to a spar, but there was no sign of him on that shore. The captain's words gave her hope, but his eyes denied it. The truth would be too much to endure.

The news took the last of her strength and she shivered. A man started forward to cover her with his sheepskin coat. She was taken to a cabin, a stone's cast from the beach. There was an upturned boat outside, spread with fisherman's nets. The walls of the cabin curved inwards, the beams keel-shaped, made from the timbers of wrecked ships. In the middle of the room a large square grate contained huge drift-wood logs crumbling to ash. Various pots and pans lay lodged in the embers. A toothless crone ladled fish soup as space was made at the hearth.

My mother sat down to share a simple meal with them. She was grateful and courteous. She had charm and grace, a way of making people like her. She was the sort of person that people want to help.

She refused nothing. Although she knew that they were giving her the best of their meagre store, food likely being saved for a wedding or a feast day, she was careful not to proffer any reward. Hospitality was a sacred duty. A holy obligation. To offer money in exchange would be an insult. These were superstitious people. They lived by the old ways, ancient and unwritten. She looked about and saw the glass disc, a milky white circle surrounding a blue iris and black pupil, that hung above the door to ward off the evil eye. In a little niche in the wall a candle burned before the shining icon of the local saint. He was always shown holding the holy relic. It had been brought to these shores in a wreck, just like she had been. She did not know it yet, but that was why these people regarded her with such awe.

After she had eaten, she supped tiny cups of thick, sweet coffee and threw back thimbles of fiery spirits that tasted of bitter mountain herbs. She enquired as to the nature of the place. Who ruled here? The country was small but prosperous, governed by the Lord Orsin. Respect mixed with affection as the people told her about him: a kindness here, a generous gesture there. Although his word was law, he was fair and he kept the coast free from pirates and other marauders. From the way they spoke of him, she could tell that he was a benevolent ruler, good to his people, so she resolved to go to his court in the morning and offer him her service.

Once the meal was over, she began to prepare. She cut off her hair, stained her face with walnut juice and begged a suit of clothes salvaged from the wreck. For ease of travel and the sake of concealment, she had decided that it would be better to go to Lord Orsin's court disguised as a boy.

❖➤◆❖

She went striding along the narrow coast road, a staff in hand and a bundle over her shoulder. The storm had gone. The sea was calm, only a faint swell bearing witness to the fury of the night before. The day was bright, warm with the promise of early summer. She sang as she walked, her voice strong and pure, and gathered flowers: white wayside lilies, asphodel, blue and purple fleur-de-lis.

Presently she turned a corner and saw a large bay before her. On a promontory, a town lay like a curled fist, strong stout walls circling the red-roofed buildings and the small harbour. She stood for a moment, taking in the town, and then started down the winding road to the Eastern Gate.

It was a still day, sound travelled far, and from his terrace in the Tower of the Winds Duke Orsin heard her singing. He loved music of all kinds and had rarely heard a song so hauntingly lyrical, a voice so sweet and high. He sent for the singer. His servants found her by the fountain, just inside the gate, and took her to the palace. Once in his presence, she bowed low and presented him with her flowers.

Within days she was strutting with the other young men in the Duke's service, dressed from head to toe in his livery, one side red, the other side blue, from her round cap to her pointed shoes. She wore the short doublet and long hose of a page in the Duke's service.

What she lacked, hidden by a proud codpiece. What she had, bound close to her body with strips of cloth. She had given herself a new name – Cesare – and no one guessed her true identity. A slender steel stiletto dagger dangled from her belt, elegant as a jewel.

She quickly became the Duke's favourite, going about the town on errands for him, and was soon so deep in his confidence that he entrusted her with a special task. He was sick with love for the Countess Olivia, but the lady would have none of him, so Cesare was sent to woo her. The Duke thought that the boy would make the perfect proxy lover, being prettily handsome, silver-tongued and full of wit but too young to prove any kind of rival. Or so Orsin reasoned. He did not consider that the Lady Olivia might have other ideas.

In her dusty pink palazzo, as grand as anything in Venice but without the canal, the Contessa presided over a household as unruly as the Duke's was ordered. Everyone there seemed infected with some kind of madness, from the Contessa's drunken kinsman and his foolish friend to her pompous, posturing steward. All except Feste, the Lady Olivia's Fool, who seemed to see through everything, including my mother's own disguise.

The courtship of Lady Olivia took place in the garden: a hidden, sunlit space shaded by overhanging pine, studded with statuary, cooled by an ornamental fountain. As the two wandered there they spoke of love, and somewhere between the statues and the fountain the lady lost her heart. The garden faded in a golden haze and all she saw was this beautiful youth. She scarcely heard the honeyed words that he had rehearsed. Instead she watched the movement of his mouth, the fullness of his lips, the line of his jaw, the curve of his cheek, the dark wing of hair falling over eyes the exact same shade as the flowers on the rosemary that she had plucked as they walked. He talked on, berating her for her heartlessness, and she smiled, all the while admiring the graceful sweep of his long neck, the hollow at the base of his throat, overwhelmed with such a strong desire to kiss the place where the delicate collarbones met that she had to turn away to hide her blushes. She cared not a fig for Orsin's suit. She trailed her fingers through the water, looking at her own reflection agitated by the fountain, her mind on ways of keeping this youth with her.

Cesare returned to the Duke and reported that the courtship had gone well.

'But by then I knew,' my mother would say to me. 'The lady was mistook, and I, poor wretch, was in love with your father.'

It was a pretty pass, and my mother was at a loss to think how it might work out, until her brother wandered into town, saved from being drowned by one Antonio, a renowned pirate and enemy to the Duke. Brother and sister were like in looks, very like. The same dark hair, eyes the same shade of blue, the same set of the mouth and curve of the lip that the Lady Olivia so admired. At a distance they would have seemed identical, although Sebastian was slightly taller, broader built, with a peppering of stubble on jaw and chin that could never have belonged to his sister.

When the twins met, all became clear. It seemed all

prayers were answered. Man was revealed as maid; the Duke could marry his page. The Countess was free to transfer her affection to the other twin, and Sebastian most happy to receive it.

The couples were joined in double celebration. It was a golden time. But as you well know, sir, few stories end at the happy ever after.

4

'For the rain it raineth every day'

Violetta broke from her telling, eyes blinking, caught by the feeling of returning into light from darkness, or swimming up from deep immersion to the surface of her tale. Back in the present, watery grey light leaked in from the windows that gave out on to the river. Tankards clattered on tables, men's voices rumbled in conversation, tobacco smoke drifted under the low ceiling and the air was filled with the sour reek of sweat and beer.

Will smiled. 'A tale well told.'

'Ach, I've heard it before.' A small rusty-haired man with a pointed beard spoke from a seat nearby. He had been listening to their conversation. 'Filched from another story. The Italians call it *Gl'Ingannati* – The Deceived. An apt title for what's gone on here.' He gave a creaking, wheezing laugh.

'You have big ears, master,' Violetta glared at this man who dared to eavesdrop on her and then call her a liar. 'I do not remember you being invited into our company.'

'What's it to you, anyway?' The clown's small black eyes fixed upon the red-haired man. 'Are you saying she lies? Cannot life imitate art? Does not art imitate life? I can tell by your fingers that you are a writer, and by the fraying of your coat cuff not a very good one. Since you were listening, perhaps you could learn a thing. Like this one.' He pointed a long finger at Will.

'Who are you?' The eavesdropper scratched at his rusty beard and scowled at the clown.

'I am Feste. Either a character in a story, or flesh and blood.' He lunged forward, fast as a striking snake, his dagger under his antagonist's chin. 'Well, which is it to be? If I do not exist, I cannot hurt you. So why do you start back? I'm warning you.' He pulled one of the man's ears out from the side of his head and brought the edge of the blade to the fleshy lobe. 'Stop these from flapping, or you might lose one.'

Will moved to separate them. 'True or not, what does it matter? It is a good tale, Riche. You have to admit that.'

'So good I've used it myself.' Riche got up to leave. 'Perhaps word thieves are like magpies, often seen together. In that case, you have found the right company.'

'Who was that insulting fellow?' Violetta asked.

'Barnaby Riche.' Will watched as the little man shouldered his way to the door. 'He is a disagreeable man, quick to quarrel. It's best not to rile him too much. He has been a soldier and is almost certainly a spy.' He turned to Violetta, his eyes keen and bright. 'I am curious to know how such mayhem and destruction came about. *That* is not in Riche's story.'

Violetta glanced towards the window. Rain was splattering the glass and it was getting dark.

'We must go,' she said. 'We've been away too long already.'

'Where are you staying?'

'With my aunt's kinsman, Sir Toby. He gave out that he was a great man here, but he has fallen on hard times. He is also very ill.' She shook her head. 'I fear he took the news we brought very hard.'

'Where does he live, this Sir Toby?'

'The Hollander.'

'The Hollander?' A lift of the eyebrows expressed his surprise.

'An inn and a brothel I know. Like I said –' Violetta sighed – 'he's fallen on hard times. He lives there with his wife, Maria. She was my aunt's maid.'

Violetta pushed her hair away from her face. She was tired. The performance, telling the story, had drained her. Had she said too little, or too much? Impossible to know. She'd learnt to live by her wits. Feste had taught her to read the marks who gathered to watch and wager while his quick fingers moved the cups or spread the cards: who had money, who hadn't, who would move on, who would continue to play, who would turn nasty, when to run. She went by clothes, face, hands and eyes. Sometimes she was better than Feste, but this one gave nothing away. He was wearing a dark jerkin and breeches, but was hardly a puritan. His fine linen shirt had lace on the collar and a gold earring glinted in his left ear. He was dark-complexioned with a neat beard clipped close to the skin. He appeared to be approaching his middle years; his hairline was beginning to creep back from his high forehead, although his dark curling hair showed no grey. He had a pleasant face, with a straight nose and broad, strong brows. A face it would be easy to forget. His large, slightly hooded eyes were a deep brown, almost black. Their expression was generally mild, amused, even kind, but ever watchful, and it was hard to tell what thoughts might be passing behind those dark, reflecting eyes. He was a man who spent much time watching people: their faces, their expressions, reading the inner drama from the outward play. He kept his hands very still.

'I must go too,' Will stood up and dropped some coins on the table. 'I have work to do.' He turned to Violetta, then to Feste. 'Your tale was most affecting and you show rare skill. Perhaps we will meet again.'

Feste had taken out a pack of cards and was sending them rippling across the table from one hand to the other. He extracted three cards and placed them face down.

'Find the Lady?' He moved the cards about. 'Care for a wager before you go?'

Will pointed to the middle card. Feste turned it over. 'Queen of Cups. She's a lucky one.' He flipped a coin up to him. 'You win.'

Feste folded the cards thoughtfully. He was a master of this game and he hadn't even meant to have her in the spread. Violetta raised an eyebrow at him. Feste never gave the Queen away. She could tell by his face that he hadn't meant to this time either.

◆◆◆

As he was leaving, Will met Dr Simon Forman. They went out together into the wind and spitting rain. Will was not one of Forman's patients, but the two men knew and liked each other well enough. They used the same alehouses and Forman attended the playhouse as often as he could. He liked to talk to Will about his work, and the talk soon spilled into other subjects.

Forman was interesting company, a great collector of things, stories and people. He was an astrologer and magician as well as a doctor of medicine. He was frequently in trouble with the College of Physicians, but he did less harm than many of them, as far as Will could see. Some of his cures even worked. He was a great gossip and his calling brought him into contact with any number of people from the highest to the lowest. He was a useful person to know.

'Too crowded in there,' the doctor said as he pulled on his gloves. The inn was filling up with river men, sailors from the docks, young blades come south of the river for various kinds of entertainment. 'I'm off home. There's more comfort in my own parlour. The night is chill.' He drew his heavy woollen cloak close. 'Jane will have a fine fire going, sea coal from a captain I know, a good supper on the table and I have some excellent Malmsey – a present from a patient. I'm still practising north of the river, but I've just bought a new house in Lambeth. There is work to be done, but Jane's made it comfortable enough. Perhaps you would care to join me?'

'I'd like to.' Will was genuinely tempted. His own room was sparsely furnished, lacking in cheer. He had no wife there to light the fire and make his supper. 'But I have work to do.'

'A new play?' Forman asked, eager to hear more.

'Yes.' Will nodded. 'But it needs cutting.' He did not intend to say anything else. He did not like to talk about his work until it was finished. 'And I have some rewriting to do before tomorrow's performance.'

'Those two you were talking to,' Forman said as they walked along by the river, 'Feste and the girl –

I've seen them at the Hollander. *Sir* Toby!' He snorted. 'That's a good one. He was at the Elephant for years. Until he was thrown out for debt. He was a great toper in his day. Paying for it now. I looked in on the noble knight this very morning, so swollen with the dropsy he can hardly move. But here's an odd thing. His wife, Maria, wanted a forecast done. Not much point, but I did one anyway. It doesn't do to upset a customer, but it was odd. Very odd. Not what I expected to see at all.'

'When did they arrive, Feste and the girl?' Will asked, bringing the doctor back to what interested him. Forman had a tendency to run on from one subject to another. It was sometimes difficult to turn the conversation back. Significant facts were passed over and lost, like pebbles tumbled along in a stream.

'A week or so ago,' Forman replied. 'Turned up of a sudden, looking for Sir Toby.'

'It must have been a disappointment for her,' Will commented. 'To journey from a distant land, suffer who knows what hardships, and then to have her hopes dashed so quickly must have been a cruelty.'

Forman shrugged. If he felt any pity, he did not show it. He was not a sentimental man.

'It was a shock to Sir Toby all right. You'd have thought he'd seen a ghost. Very agitated he was. I had to dose him with enough poppy to fell a horse. They are an odd pair,' Forman said after a while. 'There's more to those two than is seen at first glance.'

'She says she's the daughter of a duke. Do you think it's true?' Will asked.

'She's got the look about her, the manner.' Forman laughed. 'I thought *she* was going to rip Riche's ear off, never mind Feste. But it *is* true, and much else besides. I have it from another source. One Doctor Grimaldi has some interesting stories about the time he spent in Illyria. Deranged dukes and mad contessas, murder and suicide . . .' Forman laughed again. 'Just up your street, I'd say!'

◆➤◼◄◆

As Will left by one door, a young man came in through another.

'I am looking for Master Shakespeare,' he said as he came towards Feste and Violetta. 'I have a message for him.' He waved a note, folded and sealed. 'I was told he was over here.'

'He's gone, I'm afraid,' Violetta said.

The boy was an actor. He wore the flying swan insignia of Will's company and, from his lack of beard and the smoothness of his skin, Violetta guessed that he played the parts of women. His cheeks were washed with delicate colour, and his expressive pale blue eyes were fringed with dark golden lashes.

'My name is Tod, Tod Brook,' he said, snatching off his green velvet cap to show a tangle of blond curls. 'I'm an actor,' he added as he bowed low.

'I thought you might be.' Violetta smiled up at him. 'I am Violetta.'

He took her hand and kissed it, looking up at her through his long lashes. He had the air of one who knows his power to attract. Some of the serving girls were staring in frank interest, and one or two of the men were casting covert glances his way, but as soon as Violetta smiled he had eyes only for her.

'And this is Feste.'

'Nice to make your acquaintance.' Feste had spread his cards out again. 'Find the Lady. Best of three. Want to try your luck?'

'Not me.' Tod laughed. 'I'm not much of a betting man.'

Feste shrugged and looked around. 'Others might be interested –'

'No tricks here.' Violetta trapped the movement of the cards. 'Put those away. We are leaving.'

'Which way do you go?' Tod asked.

'To the Hollander.'

'In that case, it might be better to travel in numbers. The Hollander is not in the best of areas.' Tod drew his cloak aside to show that he was wearing a blade. 'I will come with you.'

'Thank you,' Violetta said, 'but I have Feste. He is protection enough.'

'Even so . . .' Tod was not going to be deflected as easily as that. 'I can help carry the box.'

'I can manage that.' Feste folded his cards.

'What about the note for Master Shakespeare?' Violetta asked.

'That can wait.' Tod stuffed it into his breeches pocket.

'Very well.' Violetta smiled. 'We will be glad of the company.'

She took his arm as they left the tavern, ignoring Feste. He was scowling now, his brow kinking into just the same expression that Little Feste always wore on his wooden features. The boy's chivalry had sparked his jealousy, which could make him argumentative. He had been drinking steadily and Violetta could tell that his mood was about to tip into morose and melancholy. He could be trying company. The boy would make a pleasant diversion.

'Well, come on if you are coming!' Feste staggered slightly as he shouldered the box. Tod reached to help him, but he shrugged the boy off. 'Leave it! I can manage fine, I said.'

'You are not from hereabouts, are you?' Tod said as they walked ahead of the struggling Feste.

'No.' Violetta laughed. 'That we aren't. We are from a little country swallowed by a larger one. We were forced to flee. First to Italy, then to here.'

Tod nodded. It was a common enough tale. London was full of people who had come from somewhere else, either fled or been expelled. Each had a story to tell.

'I've seen you, over by the church. Or I've seen him.' He jerked a thumb at the sweating Feste. 'I didn't realize t'other one was you. Is that how you make your living?'

'Aye. Tricks and tumbling.'

Tod shrugged. It was odd for a girl to do it, but he was a player and that's how they all survived. It didn't matter where they were from – players helped each other if they could. It was a precarious business. Tomorrow it might be you handing round the hat and standing in need of a good turn.

5

'There shall be no more cakes and ale'

The Hollander had seen better times. It had once been a grand house with a moat, but now the buttresses struggled to prevent the bulging walls from collapsing altogether. Over the years, so many storeys had been added, one overhanging another, that the whole structure seemed ready to totter and fall. The moat was reduced to a mere ditch pooled with green stagnant water, hung over by houses of easement and clogged with debris from the nearby tanner's yard. Tod's nose twitched. The place gave off a powerful stench, even in a city full of stinks.

Tod held Violetta's arm and helped her over a runnel of filthy water. She stopped outside the door.

'Thank you for walking back with us,' she said, 'but you can leave us here.' She did not want to invite Tod inside. It shamed her to be staying in such a place.

'Yes, on your way, master,' Feste said with a jerk of his head. 'Didn't you have a message to deliver?'

The clown heaved the box from his shoulder. It got heavier as the day lengthened. The box dropped with a bang and a rattle. It was the chains that added the weight, but escaping from bounds was a popular trick.

'Oh yes. I had quite forgotten.' Tod patted his pockets. The packet seemed to have migrated from one side of his breeches to the other. Feste winked at Violetta.

'Off you go, then.' Feste put an encouraging hand on his shoulder. 'Don't let us keep you.'

'Don't mind Feste,' Violetta smiled. 'He was born without manners.'

Tod took his leave and Violetta helped Feste get the box through the door. The entrance opened straight on to a long hall, ill lit with smoking tallow candles and tapers. It was cold, the stone walls sweating damp from the river. The fire was a mound of ash in the centre of a cavernous fireplace. Violetta never saw anyone clean the grate or reset it, so it choked on itself and gave off little heat. The rushes on the floor were worn and ragged, clotted into clumps, blackened with rancid fat and discarded food. They slid and squelched about underfoot and gave off a sweet, rotten smell which was sour at the same time with spilt beer and wine. Groups of men and some women sat clustered at the ends of the long tables. One man had clearly had enough; he lay face down in a puddle of beer. The girls were half dressed, the men poor and rough. They had eyed Violetta when she first arrived, calling out to her, but the leering and jeering had soon been extinguished by Feste's glare.

Nobody looked at them as they went up the rickety staircase. They carried the box between them, along the gallery to a second flight of narrow stairs. Violetta helped Feste manhandle it round the tight corner and then took the weight as he began to haul it up the stairs. They worked well together, with silent efficiency. She was back to being Feste's assistant, the Fool's Girl, and had to do her share.

Feste stopped on the landing to take a breather. She joined him on the box.

'You should not have let him go so easily,' he said.

'Who? Tod?'

'No, not him!' Feste shook his head. 'You'll have a job getting rid of that one. He'll be howling outside like a dog every night. No. I meant t'other. Master Shakespeare. He'll pack the story up in his trunk and be away. That's what men like him do.'

'Maybe, maybe not,' Violetta replied.

Their meeting with him had been no accident. The man was a player. He lived hard by. Such men can never resist a performance, so they set up in his way. They had wanted a meeting and they had got it. That was good, but Violetta did not want to rush things. She was not ready to reveal their intention. Not yet.

'It is not wise to be too eager.' She went on. 'A man like him needs to be played carefully.' She was not at all worried. Intuition told her that he would follow the story. 'He's picked up the thread. He'll be back.'

'Perhaps.' Feste frowned, head hanging down. 'Even if the poet does come back, your idea is madder than anything I could dream up. Just the *thought* of it is filling my belly with seeping black melancholy. It will never work.'

'I thought your job was to keep hope alive and spirits up.'

'Not me, madonna. I'm not that kind of fool. But just in case your intuition is wrong – which has happened before, no point in denying it –' Feste looked up at her, smiling now – 'I've thought of another way to bring him back to us.'

'What's that?' Violetta stood up, ready to heave the box up to the next floor. Maria and Sir Toby lived right at the top of the building in one of the penthouses that jutted so far out that they seemed to float suspended over the street.

'When your young man –' Feste said as he picked up his end.

'He's not my young man!' Violetta objected.

'When your young man,' Feste went on as if she hadn't spoken, 'can think with his head instead of his other parts, he will remember the business he was about, and when he does, Master Shakespeare will find that he is in want of a clown.'

◆▶◀◆

Maria was waiting for them. She must have heard them on the stairs. She held the door wide as they carried the box the last few yards and dropped it with a rattling thump.

Their lodgings were tiny. One room divided into two by a thin partitioning wall. From the bedchamber, where Sir Toby lay, came muffled noises. He had no strength left for roaring and raving. What they heard was more like the querulous whimpering of a frightened child left lonely in the dark.

They had come here a week ago, directed from the Elephant and Castle. Violetta had not known what to expect, but it wasn't the Hollander. She had been shocked to find Sir Toby and Maria living in such a poor way. There was no covering on the floor, and the walls were crumbling, wood and plaster eaten away by decay. Maria had covered the worst of it with cloths, but these were patchy and discoloured, attacked by the rot beneath. There was no real furniture except for a little three-legged stool. The table was a rough board set upon four small barrels, the chairs upturned buckets or boxes covered in sacking. Maria had tried to make the best of things, but all the proper furnishings had long since been sold to pay Sir Toby's debts.

When they first arrived, Feste had looked round with a wry smile. He had not been surprised at all. Sir Toby had always been a wastrel and a tosspot. Such men do not change. He'd pissed away what little money there was when he was able, now it went on doctors. Maria confirmed as much, but not in those words.

'You haven't changed one bit.' Maria's eyes had filled with tears when she saw the clown. 'I remember when you first came to the house, 'prentice to Old Feste. Even then you looked like a little old man!'

Feste had not known what to reply to that. Instead he'd taken her into his arms and executed a little dance, as he might have done once upon a time with the girl with the nut-brown eyes who delighted in mischief and playing tricks on her betters. The eyes were the same, but the spark in them had long since died. The lines on her face showed that life with Sir Toby had not been easy. Time had thickened her at the waist and hips and the hair escaping her cap had more grey in it than black. Maria no longer played tricks on anybody.

'Who's this with you?' She'd looked past him, squinting as if short-sighted. 'My lady? But that cannot be . . .'

Her frown returned and her fingers hastily sketched the shape of a cross.

'It is me, Maria.' Violetta had stepped forward. 'Violetta.'

'Violetta?' Maria's look, almost of fear, had

disappeared. She took the girl by the arms, the better to see her. 'For a moment I thought you were your mother. How old are you now? Fifteen? Sixteen?'

Violetta nodded.

'When she came to us, she was not much older. You are the very spit of her. Where does the time go? When I left, you were a child. You are a woman now.'

Violetta had always been told that Sir Toby was a great man in this land, that he lived in a castle, and she'd come in hope that he might be able to use his influence to help her. Any hope of that had fled as soon as she saw the Hollander, but they had stayed, having nowhere else to go. Besides, Maria had been kind to her when she was young and Toby was still the nearest thing she had left to a kinsman, if only by marriage.

'How has he been?' Violetta asked.

'Bad today,' Maria said with a shake of her head.

The door to the room where Sir Toby lay was ajar, and a sweetish smell seeped out, the cloying stench of medicines and illness. Sir Toby was on his back in a lopsided bed that was near to collapse. A small truckle lay underneath, where Maria slept. He had always been an ample man, but the great spreading mound of his belly was distended by sickness, not good living. The rest of him was wasting away. His arms lay like sticks by his sides and his legs scarcely disturbed the coverlet.

'He's not how he was,' Maria kept saying. 'His mind is apt to wander. Don't expect too much.'

Since they had arrived, his decline had been sharp. Dr Forman came to see him and dosed him with poppy. That was all that could be done for him now.

'Go into him, Feste,' Maria said. 'Your presence cheers him, brings him a little way out of his melancholy.'

Feste bowed his head. He took his flute from his pack and his little drum and went in to see the old man, even though he was bone-tired. He did this every night, but such was the slippage of the Sir Toby's mind that each time it was as if he had just arrived.

'Peace be in this house,' he began. '*Domine. Agnus Dei, qui tollis peccata mundi, parce nobis, Domine. Agnus Dei, qui tollis peccata mundi, exaudi nos, Domine. Agnus Dei, qui tollis peccata mundi, miserere nobis.*'

He stepped into the room, treading softly, intoning the words, his back slightly hunched, his eyes cast down and his hands folded at his chest as if he carried a Bible or prayer book. He did not need props or costume. The character was contained in the tone of his voice, the droop of his shoulders, the angle of his head.

Sir Toby blinked awake. His blue eyes were faded and cloudy, the whites yellow, clotted and bloodshot. His face was wasted and ravaged. His formerly florid complexion had a greyish cast, the flesh of his cheeks hanging in sagging swags. His nose was bluish purple, pitted like a strawberry, swelled out of shape.

'Who is that? Who is there?' he whispered, and reached out to push back the bed's canopy. His thin hand was a span of bone webbed with yellow skin, criss-crossed with a snaking tangle of thick, twisting veins.

'It is I, Sir Topas,' Feste murmured in the same sing-song voice. 'Don't you remember me? I'm come to visit you, my son.'

'Sir Topas! Good Sir Topas!' The sick man's face

cleared for a moment; his short, sighing laugh brought on a fit of coughing. 'Here! Come here! Feste, lad? Can it be you?' He blinked, confused again. 'Am I dreaming? Or am I already in the other place?'

'*In nomine Patris, et Filii, et Spiritus Sancti.* Aye, 'tis me.'

'You old knave.' Sir Toby reached up to hug and kiss the clown as he did every night. 'To think I never thought to set eyes on you again! Dear me! It does me good just to see you. Better than any doctor's jalap. Good jests we had, my boy, did we not? Merry times. Tell me, do you have your instruments? Pipe and tabor?'

'I do, Sir Toby.'

'I would have a tune, then. Something with life in it. And we'll sing a song. An old one: "Three Merry Men", or "The Baffled Knight", or some such. A bawdy rhyme, eh? Something to make us laugh. Here, give me your arm, help me sit up. Maria! Bring me an egg beat up in some sack. I think I can manage that. God's blood, I feel better already.' He looked past the clown to the room beyond. 'Do you bring someone with you? My eyes have grown dim of late, but my ears are sharp. I could have sworn I heard another voice, a woman's . . .'

'It's only Maria,' Feste said. 'No one else.'

He laid the old man back gently. Sir Toby's moment of lucidity was over; he was back to muttering and plucking at the covers. Feste put the flute to his mouth and played a few plaintive notes. Then he began to sing a nonsense rhyme, as might be sung to a child. Sir Toby's agitation began to subside. His ragged breathing steadied and his eyelids fluttered and closed.

Violetta was careful to keep out of the way. Her

presence upset him. When he first saw her he shrank back, whispering that he was, indeed, in Hell, and had fallen to raving, calling her 'Devil's spawn', ordering her 'Away! Away!' and saying that she was there to torment him. He had thrashed about so wildly that Feste'd had to restrain him or he would have tumbled from the bed.

Even Maria had been shocked by his reaction. 'He's likely confusing you with your mother. You do look just like her.'

That did not explain his upset, but Maria could not guess at the reason, his mind being so distempered. She'd shepherded Violetta out of the room, leaving Feste with him. While the clown played and sang to the old man, Violetta had told Maria her story.

'He's been bad today,' Maria said again. 'Sir Andrew has been here.' She spoke quietly, as if he was still there and could hear. 'I didn't mean to listen, but the walls are thin.' She paused, pressing her hand to her mouth. 'Some things it is better not to hear.'

'Sir Andrew?' Violetta asked. Maria had not mentioned him before. Until now, he had just been a name in a story.

'He hasn't been here for more than a year. You won't remember him. He left Illyria before you were born. He was there to court Lady Olivia and was not best pleased when she married another. Not that he stood any chance, but Sir Toby encouraged him, while busy spending his fortune. He was a bit of a fool then, Sir Toby and Feste making merry at his expense.' Maria gave a fleeting ghost of a smile as if recalling happier times, but then her face grew serious again.

'The Sir Andrew I knew was a drunkard and a

wastrel, but he's grown sober and serious. You'd think him a puritan, but he's just the opposite. He's stayed faithful to the Catholic Church and his zeal has grown over the years. It's dangerous to hold such beliefs here. Especially dangerous for priests or those who harbour them.' Maria kept her voice low and looked about as if spies and informers were lurking just outside the room. 'You can end up with your head on a pike, stuck up on London Bridge, set there to rot with a score of others. You can see them any day of the week, come wind, rain and sun, bristling like some monstrous pincushion, pecked about by ravens.'

She paused for a moment, and when she began again there was a slight tremor in her voice as if she had become unstrung by her own image.

'Anyway, Sir Toby has always stuck to the old religion. Too old to change his ways. Not that his faith is all that great. He judges all priests canting hypocrites, whatever their belief. He liked them better when he couldn't understand their words, that's what he says, and he'd rather pay the fines than go to church. That was as far as it went, until a few years ago when Sir Andrew turned up, keen to patch up the quarrel they'd had. I've never seen such a change in a man. He used to scoff at churchgoers, him and Toby both. Now he sees it as his mission to return England to the old religion. He came to Sir Toby saying one of his nephews was a Jesuit, expected from France, and could Sir Toby hide him? I counselled against it, not on the grounds of faith, but on the grounds of madness. Sir Toby wouldn't listen. Helping a friend, he said, although I daresay money changed hands. Sir Andrew never lacked a penny. Sir Toby's come to the aid of a fair few *nephews*, hiding them in the cellars, helping with their passage by way of the smugglers' tunnels that stretch down to the river.'

'Is that what he wanted today? For Sir Toby to help him hide somebody?'

'No,' Maria shook her head. 'Toby's long past helping anybody. He wanted to know if we'd heard any news of you and Feste.'

'What are we to him?'

'I don't know, but that's not the only thing.' Maria twisted her hands in her lap. 'He brought greetings. From one Malvolio.'

'Oh.' Violetta's heart gave an uncomfortable lurch.

'My lady's old steward. I hadn't heard that name in a long while. Not until you came here. His fortunes have changed too, so you tell me. Why do the wicked prosper, while my poor Toby . . .' Maria shook her head. 'It's a mystery to me. Sir Andrew got no sense out of him – you've seen how he is – but that just enraged him. He fell to threatening, refusing to find a priest to shrive him. Toby is this far from death –' her fingers measured less than an inch – 'and he wants a priest to hear his confession. In this town they are as rare as hen's teeth. Sir Andrew is his only hope of finding one in time. He knows he holds power over us, and he enjoys it.'

'He threatened you too?' Violetta was stricken. Maria had troubles enough. She did not want to bring more to the poor woman's door. 'How does he know we are here?'

'I don't think he does for certain.' Maria frowned. 'Not from what he said, but how many Illyrians are there in London? And you are kin to Sir Toby. Sir

Andrew was never known for his brains, but even he could reason that you are likely to fetch up here.'

'Perhaps we should leave.' Violetta looked at Maria. 'Then you would not have to lie to him, and Sir Andrew will find a priest for Sir Toby when . . . when the time comes for that.'

'What will you do?' Maria took Violetta's hands in hers. 'Where will you go? No. I have offered you my hospitality. I wish it were better, but my home is your home for as long as you stay here. We'll make shift when it comes to it.' She laughed, but there was little mirth in it. 'There's always Sir Topas. I worry for *you*.' Her grip tightened. 'Not for us. Did you see Master Shakespeare? Did you speak to him?'

'We met him,' Violetta said.

'And? Did you tell him your story?'

'Part of it,' Violetta answered. 'But there was another man in the inn, overhearing, and then Master Shakespeare had to leave.'

'Will he help you, do you think?'

'We didn't get as far as asking.' Violetta looked away from the hope and enquiry in Maria's face. Sometimes her plan seemed barren, even to her. 'But what if he denies me? What will I do?'

'We'll just have to convince him.' Maria squeezed Violetta's hands, trying to comfort her and allay her fears, just as she used to do all those years ago when she was nurse to her. 'If we can get him here, if we can talk to him, we'll tell him about Illyria, how it used to be. He won't deny you when he knows the whole story. How can he? Now, you look tired. You should go to your bed. We'll worry about Master Shakespeare in the morning.'

6

'That that is is'

Will took off his doublet, loosened the neck of his shirt and poured himself a mug of ale from the barrel he kept in the corner, ale brewed at home and brought down for him from Stratford by Will Greenaway on the weekly wagon train. He'd ended up going back with Forman after all. Now it was late and he had no work done. He lit more candles and sat at his table. The room seemed warmer by candlelight; shadows masked its emptiness. He liked this time of night. It was the time when the city stilled itself and it was possible to hear both close and distant: the calls of the wherrymen down on the river, the churning of the waterwheels at the sides of the bridge, a man's shout, a woman's laugh, cats fighting, a bear's groaning growl from the bear garden. Far away, a dog was barking; much nearer, in the street below his window, a couple were making love against the wall of the Clink.

He often wrote at night, the days being too full of other business. It seemed easier to breathe the air. The stink of the city abated and it was possible to detect the salt tang as the tide changed, or the cleaner scent of the river water that had flowed past reed and willow on its way to London. The smell reminded him of Stratford. He had been in the city for more years than he liked to think about, but he still missed his home, particularly now when the year was finally turning towards spring and the trees growing green with new leaf, particularly today. *It's home I long to be, home for a while in my own country, where the oak and the ash and the pretty willow tree, are all waiting there in my own country.* The snatch of song chided him. After Christmas the weather had made travel difficult, but he must go home soon. His father was sick, not expected to see the year out, according to Anne, and he wanted to see how the work on his new house was progressing. Anne was a strong woman and very capable, but it was not fair to leave everything to her.

Perhaps he would go when this play was done, or he might take it to work on there. Sometimes he wrote better in Stratford, away from distractions. He opened his desk box and took out what he would need, using the small sharp penknife to cut a new nib into a goose-feather quill. He had plenty to do. He looked at the sheaf of untidy pages that made up the play he was reworking, cross-hatched with overwriting, scored with crossings-out. The fair copy was piling up very slowly; his Danish prince would have to wait for his first outing, however impatiently.

Will was a part-owner in the Globe and involved in everything, sharing the management of the company with Burbage, writing the plays, acting if need be. The present piece had to come first: changes to tomorrow's performance. He pulled the play book for *As You Like It* towards him, but still he did not write anything. He sat musing, brushing the feather, trimmed down into a V shape like an arrow's fletching, against his bearded cheek.

Finally, he took out his table book. It was the place where he caught ideas, lines of verse, snippets of conversations he heard, before they had a chance to flee. He dipped the quill in the inkwell and began to write. He had to note down the story told him by the girl and Feste, had to clear it from his head before he could start anything else. There was more to be known, Forman had hinted as much, but he would start with the prelude to the girl's own story: her mother's arrival in the country. He liked disguises; he liked twins and the confusion caused by them. Most of all, he liked Feste.

He wrote quickly. Moments like this were rare; they were always accompanied by the same feeling: a certain lightness in the head, a shallowness of breath, a quickening of the blood. It was like falling in love.

He ceased writing as swiftly as he had begun. He had as much of it down as he needed. The pages of the play he was writing reproached him, but he could not work on it now. Tiredness crept through his brain like fog spreading up from the river, obscuring all detail, turning everything grey and the same. Anything he wrote would lack savour and he would only have to score it out tomorrow. His mind drifted back to the problems with the present production and he began to amend the play book, trying to cut Touchstone's part without affecting the whole play. It was tricky. Too savage and he would alter the balance of the play between the comic and the sad and sober. Besides, clowns were popular; many came just to see them. If he cut too much, that part of the audience would become restless and they were the ones most ready to express their disapproval by mewing catcalls and throwing bottles. Even so, the present fellow, Moston, was everything he hated. Their regular clown, Armin, was sick. Clowns were much in demand at the moment – they'd been lucky to get Moston – but Will couldn't bear to watch him. He'd written the part for Armin and it made him furious to hear Moston mangle the lines in ways he considered to be comical and see him set about destroying the delicate mechanism of the play with his overacting, unscripted asides to the audience, additional matter he saw fit to put in himself, while the dog he insisted on having with him wandered about pissing all over the stage. That got a laugh, but always in the wrong place.

Will worked hard and long to put all that right. He was so lost in the work that he did not hear the muffled knock at the door, then the faint whisper of paper on rough boards. His landlady knew better than to disturb him so late into the night. It was not until he had put his writing things away and closed the box that he saw the note with his name on it lying just inside the door. He recognised Burbage's hurried scrawl. What could this be? And who had delivered it? The street outside was deserted. Will opened the paper, reading quickly. The night's work had been wasted. He need not have bothered with all that rewriting. After an exchange of words, not all of them pleasant, Moston had taken himself off to the Rose.

Something had fallen, fluttering to the ground as he opened the letter. He bent to retrieve a card of the type used in games of chance, or for telling fortunes. Will stood up, brushing the card against his beard. He could have the clown he wanted. How had this come to be? Even while he was rewriting, some part of his restless, shifting mind was deciding that he needed a new man. One to whom clowning was instinctive, but who had the depth and range that Will required. One who could switch from mirth to sadness in a breath and take the audience with him. Feste would be perfect. He spoke good English and was an excellent mimic. If the man was quick to learn, as every indication showed him to be, he would con the part quickly. He would be perfect, if only they could get rid of Moston. Then this note was slipped under the door. Will's wish had been answered, so it seemed, at the very moment of wanting. Like a summoning.

Will went down to his landlady to find that the note had been delivered by a lad in a green velvet cap. Young Tod. He had searched for Will in every inn from the Falcon, Bankside, to the Mermaid on Cheapside. Giving up and wanting his bed, he had dropped the note here on his way home. Will thanked her and went back to his room. That explained much, but it did not explain the card that had fallen from the letter. It showed a man dressed in motley, strolling along with a bundle over his shoulder and a dog at his heels. *Il Matto*. The Fool. The card that cannot be beaten, but neither can it win.

❧❉❧

Will spent a restless night. He did not like puzzles, or rather he did not like ones that were not of his own devising. The card was Italian, of the exact same type he had seen passing under Feste's restless fingers. What did it mean? How did it get into a note from Burbage? *There's more to those two* . . . Forman's words came back to him.

Feste would be the new clown, but first he needed answers to questions of his own. He rose with the dawn just paling the windows. It was early, but there was no time to be wasted. He set off for the Hollander, going by way of the Globe, where the watchman let him in to the silent, deserted playhouse. He left a note for Burbage, explaining what he was about, and collected the part he needed. He took the scroll from the post where it had been set as a reminder to the now departed Moston, rolled the pages carefully and tucked them into his jerkin.

The Hollander was hardly stirring. There was no one about, other than a pair of rough-looking fellows skulking back towards the river. They watched Will knock at the door. Perhaps they were waiting for the Hollander to open. South of the river there were always men looking for drink or women, whatever time of day.

The door opened a crack and a woman peered out at him. 'What do you want? None of the girls are up.'

'I'm looking for Sir Toby and his wife Maria.' Will had his foot in before she could close the door. 'I'm told they lodge here.'

'Might do.' The woman opened the door further and looked him over. 'But it's powerful early.' She yawned, her few remaining teeth brown stumps in blackened gums. 'Who wants to know?'

She was a large woman and stood barring his way, her beefy arms folded, her small eyes squeezed to slits in her coarse, fleshy face.

'My name is Will Shakespeare. Tell Mistress Maria that I am here to talk to Violetta.'

The woman withdrew without another word, leaving

him outside. Will stood there staring at the warped boards of the old door with its rusted studs. She was gone a long time. He was beginning to wonder if she had even taken his message, or just left him outside to shiver in the damp coming up from the river, when Violetta opened the door.

'Come in, come in.' Violetta beckoned to him. 'It's cold.' She pulled a thin shawl closer round her shoulders. 'Johane shouldn't have left you standing outside.'

The big woman was collecting pots left from the night before. There was a man lying face down on one of the tables, arms stretched out. She wiped around him, wrung the cloth out on the floor and moved away.

'Don't mind her,' Violetta said. 'She barks worse than she bites.'

'I'd expect that with those teeth,' Will remarked, and Violetta laughed. She looked younger. She was just a girl. She shouldn't be living here like this. The world had treated her harshly.

'What brings you here so early?' she asked as they began to mount the stairs.

'I have a favour to ask from Master Feste. I think he knows what it might be.'

Violetta smiled as she mounted the stairs ahead of him. She'd been surprised when Johane had said who was calling, but Feste was full of tricks. Once in a while, one of them worked.

Maria was waiting for them at the top of the last flight of stairs.

'Mistress Maria? I am Will Shakespeare.'

'I know you, master,' she smiled a welcome,

smoothing her apron. 'I've seen you and your players at the playhouse. Sir Toby was a great play-goer when he was well. He loved your work especially. He swore Sir John Falstaff was him to the life!'

She rattled on, made nervous by his presence, the coincidence of his being here. She apologised for the meanness of their lodgings. 'Do forgive us, we live in a poor way now.' Sir Toby was a little better, thank you for asking. Feste's playing seemed to soothe him. He had even taken a little sustenance. 'Posset laced with sack. Dr Forman says no strong drink, but it is the only way to get it down him. Now, master, what can I get you? We have little here, but I can offer you small beer and some bread with cheese, or bacon.'

Will refused politely. He was a courteous man and did not want to offend this good woman, but he was here on other business and would not be deflected.

His eyes fixed on Feste, who had sidled into the room. 'First,' he laid the rolled scroll on the table, 'I have a proposition for you. I want to know if you can con this and con it quickly.' He took the Fool card from his pocket and set it on the table next to the script. 'I find I'm in need of a clown.'

'I don't know, master. We will have to take a look at it, won't we?' Feste came forward talking not to Will but to Little Feste, whose small, twisted face had suddenly popped up in the crook of his arm. 'We will have to see.'

'Ooh, yes. We'll have to see.' He answered himself in a cracked little voice. The puppet's head turned round, craning down at the unfurling roll of pages. 'Looks hard to me.' He peered up at his master. 'Can we do it? Can we? We will certainly have to see.'

'Enough fooling, Feste.' Violetta stared at him in warning.

'Fooling? Who's fooling?' Little Feste's head whipped round to look up at Violetta. 'Not us, it can't be.'

'I said, stop it!' Violetta's voice was sterner now.

'Very well.'

'We will help you,' Violetta said, 'if you will help us.'

Will looked at her, perplexed. 'I would help you, if it is in my power to do so. But tell me, for it puzzles me mightily, why all this?' He picked up the card again. 'Why can't you ask me plain?'

'Because I thought you might refuse us, just go on your way.'

'I'm here, am I not? While Feste cons the part, you can tell me – what do you want from me?'

Feste took the scroll and sat down cross-legged on the floor, leaning against Violetta. Maria sat opposite her, hands in her lap. She thought back, tracing her way through the crooked lanes of memory and longing to the gilded time when she was young and Illyria was the best place in the world. She looked up at Violetta. Maria would start and they would pass the story between them, backwards and forwards, as women wind wool.

7

'After the last enchantment'

MARIA

It was a golden time. Beginning with the weddings. A double celebration. The city had never seen such a thing. People poured in from everywhere. The streets were lined from well before dawn as folk took their places to see the grand procession.

The day chosen was known to be auspicious. From early the bands and companies paraded through the streets to the main square. Each guild and family represented, splendid in their livery, waving and hurling banners high into the air. Young girls came dancing after them, strewing flowers, so the couples would walk over a thick, soft carpet and sweet scents would waft up with every step they took on their way to the cathedral.

Orsin and Sebastian were crowned with flowers, their white satin suits all embroidered with gold and silver and worked with precious stones so that they glittered in the sunlight like princes from fairyland. Their brides walked beside them, arm in arm, one dark, one fair. Viola in the palest rose; my lady in the soft grey-green of oleander leaves. Their bodices were all embroidered with tiny seed pearls that I'd selected and sewn myself. Their veils were so fine that they were worked with needles as thin as hairs and single threads of silk. The delicate lawn floated before their faces like breath on a frosty day.

The cathedral was packed with guests from every neighbouring state and further, from Venice and Sicily, Tunis and Tripoli, from the Sultan's court at Constantinople, all there to celebrate this blessed day. The couples came in to fanfares of trumpets. Choirs sang as they approached the High Altar to make their vows of love and obedience before our most holy relic.

Afterwards they stood on the steps of the cathedral, smiling and blinking in the strong sunlight. The grooms kissed their brides and the people all cheered and threw their caps in the air. As the couples returned to the Duke's palace, roses rained down from every window until their shoulders were covered in petals of scarlet and white. The feasting and celebrations went on for the rest of the day and into the night. Not just in the palace, but all over the city, in each district, tables were set up in the streets, and the squares were filled with singing and dancing.

The couples were taken separately to their marriage beds, as was the custom. The men carried shoulder high, accompanied by bawdy songs and raucous laughter, wreathed in herbs known to heat the blood and sustain performance. The women wore garlands of crane's bill, lavender, lady's mantle, wheat and yarrow, to awaken their passion and increase fertility. They were led to their bridal chambers by their ladies, who were hardly quieter than the men, quite as ribald and no less excited.

Once the couples were put to bed, the celebrations continued far into the night. The next day the bridal gowns were inspected, according to ancient tradition. Guns were fired to show that the marriages had been successfully consummated. The festivities went on until all but the hardiest had sunk from exhaustion. It was a wonderful time, full of song and laughter, each detail to be salted away, to be kept in the memory. The guests departed, wishing the couples health and happiness. No one bothered much about who was absent, or stopped to think what trouble they would cause in the future.

When I think of that time, it is always summer and we're at the summer palace. Duke Orsin had it built as a wedding gift to his wife. He chose the site with such care. He loved her then. The house is on a terrace overlooking a wide, curving bay of white sand, surrounded on three sides by dense dark groves of cypress and pine. He was not the first to build there. When the workmen began to clear the ground, they found broken pillars, pieces of statues, blocks of marble. The remains of some ancient villa. The Duke sent for the very best architects, builders and craftsmen from Rome, Siena, Florence, Urbino and Ravenna, to build his own house by the sea.

The palace became a place of wonder. The Duke spared no expense. There were airy rooms with frescoed walls and mosaics set into marble floors. At the centre he made a paved courtyard shaded with orange and lemon trees, cooled by fountains. A wide terrace faced the sea, and gardens, each different from the others, descended to the shore with ruined arches and hidden secret places: little grottoes made from the fallen masonry and broken columns saved from the ancient site or dredged up from the sea.

Although Duke Orsin had built the summer palace for his new bride, he didn't spend much time there, staying in the town even in the hottest weather. He had matters of state to attend to, he said, fleets of ships coming in and going out. When he was not attending to such matters, he was in his library, overseeing the scriptorium that he had established, working with the scholars he had gathered. On the hottest days of the year he might ride out as the day cooled to evening, to eat supper, drink wine on the terrace and listen to music made by his wife and her ladies, but the summer palace became Lady Viola's domain. She loved to be by the sea and hated the heat and stench of the summer city.

Viola soon had her own court. She gathered ladies around her: young women from the city's leading families, daughters of the local nobility. Lady Olivia spent all her time there, and I with her. The days went by in idleness: singing, playing music, reciting poetry. When the day grew hot, they would swim in the sea. Any man found spying would be likely to suffer the fate of Actaeon. My Lady Olivia and Viola were as close as sisters, closer. They were always together, from when they took breakfast on the balcony overlooking the sea to when they retired at night. They lived in each other's eyes and could not bear to be separated for even a day.

When the year turned, the summer palace was shut up and Lady Viola returned to Illyria town and became the Duchessa. She charmed the court, bringing the light and laughter of summer back with her to the ducal palace. The Duke seemed lost in his admiration of her all over again, her wit and her brilliance. When she came into the room, every head turned towards her, and everyone wanted to be rewarded by the flash of her smile.

In Illyria, the winter festivities were always a time of great celebration, with feasting, dancing, plays and masques every day from Advent to Twelfth Night, but that first midwinter was especially blessed: Viola gave birth to a daughter, Olivia to a son, Stephano, born within hours of each other on the Feast of St Stephen. Outside, snow was falling. It covered the earth in a mantle as a soft and white as a christening gown.

VIOLETTA

In my earliest memories I am always at the summer palace. That was the time I was closest to my mother. She liked to walk by the shore in the early morning, and I would go with her. I would wake early, listen for her footfall and follow. It was likely to be the only time I would be alone with her that day. She would take my hand and we would cross the wide terrace and thread our way down through the gardens while the dew was still wet. As we walked, we met statues of fauns and maidens, suddenly looming out of the mist, looking secretive and furtive, as if the rising sun had surprised them in the middle of some forbidden frolic.

The garden slopes were all in shadow and the beach was pale in the dawn light, with little waves crisping along its margins, the sand cold underfoot. The sea beyond looked greyish purple, like wine spilt on pewter. Then the sun would emerge over the rim of the hills behind and touch the water, like a molten river of gold stretching out to the horizon. My mother would loose her gown and plunge in, leaving me to watch from the shore. Sometimes she would take me with her. I could swim before I could walk. Then I would take her hand and we would wander barefoot as the incoming tide sewed the sand with silver. We would pick up pebbles bright from the water, collect delicately whorled shells, fine-fingered starfish, fragile purple and green urchins. Then we would go back. She would return to Lady Olivia. I would hear them conversing in low voices and laughing while I added our finds to my collection. Stephano would come out yawning, rubbing his eyes with his fists. I would show him the things that I had collected with my mother and we would arrange them together.

Everyone said that he was as good-natured as he was handsome, with his mother's mild grey eyes and her fair hair, his short-cropped curls as shiny in the sun as a heap of gold coins. I was older by all of an hour and thought that gave me precedence. Stephano never argued. He was happy to follow my lead in the games we played. The garden was our outdoor palace, the rocks on the beach were our fleet, the forest was our terra incognita, to be explored and conquered. Through all our adventures, Stephano was my friend and my companion and we were constantly in each other's company.

He was sharp-eyed, good at finding things: tesserae from some long-crumbled mosaic floor, bits of pottery, coins scoured by the sand and worn smooth by the sea.

One day, when we were five or six years old, he found a gold ring on one of the terraces in the shape of a snake, with an eye made from a tiny red stone. He picked it up and took it to my mother and Lady Olivia, thinking one of the ladies might have lost it. No, the ladies shook their heads, it was none of theirs; it was his to keep.

'Give it to the one you love,' my mother said,

thinking that he would give it to Olivia.

He turned and gave it to me. It was ancient, I could see that. The ruby eye was bright, but the finely etched scales were hardly visible, the gold worn thin on a hand long turned to bone and dust.

'It is too big for her!' his mother said, laughing.

Stephano looked up at her, his expression grave and solemn. 'One day it won't be.' He took my hand in his. 'Then we shall be married.'

Our mothers and their ladies rocked with laughter and then clapped their hands and cried, 'Blessed be!' We were meant for each other. When we grew up, we would be married. It was our destiny.

MARIA

There were things a child could not know. With Viola spending so much time at the summer palace, rumours grew. Some whispered that the Duke had lost interest, preferring his books to his young wife, and she, in turn, had lost interest in him.

They also whispered about Lord Sebastian: that he resented his sister, that he was jealous of her. He was *Count* Sebastian, but she was Duchessa. Not only that, but he had lost his wife to her. Olivia might have married him, but there was no doubt which twin she preferred. It was as though she'd made her vows to the sister, not the brother, they said as they laughed behind their hands, but no one said such things in his hearing. He had a violent temper on him and was always ready to draw steel.

Who knows what goes on in men's minds? Who knows what causes a canker to root there and grow to bitter hatred? Lord Sebastian attracted followers, young men who found the Duke's court as dull and boring as the dusty old books in his library. Without my lady there, her palace became more like a barracks. My Toby was supposed to keep an eye on things, but you might as well have set a sot to oversee a brew house. The men spent their days hunting in the forest, or hawking in the hills. They spent their nights getting drunk. When they weren't out hunting, the Count's men swaggered around town, dressed in his black-and-white livery, causing trouble. They often clashed with the Duke's men, and over time the two groups became sworn enemies. The young men of both courts wandered the town, seeking each other out, swapping slights and insults. Fights were frequent and often bloody. What began with single fights and skirmishes ended up in pitched battles. The followers were acting out their masters' rivalry. However much Count Sebastian might crow over siring a boy, while the Duke could only manage a girl, he bitterly resented the power that Orsin held over him.

About this time, the fortunes of our country began to decline. Illyria had always been rich and prosperous, had rarely known want, but her prosperity came from the sea. There were bad trading seasons. Ships were lost: argosies failed to return, or never arrived at their destination. The Duke took each loss upon himself. It was not the money or the goods. The sailors were men from the port, or the islands off-shore, or the villages along the coast. A ship going down meant widows, fatherless children. The Duke grew thin and haggard busying himself to make sure that each family was provided for, the losses covered, and that there was enough food for his people.

Lord Sebastian was often absent abroad. It was said that he had grown bored with life in Illyria and was seeking excitement in Italy and Spain. Like his sister, he loved the sea and he loved adventure. The ills of the country began with his travels. He was seen in Venice, on the Rialto and at the Doge's palace. His friend Antonio was banned from the city, but they were seen together in different ports. Antonio was an Uskok, a pirate, with a particular hatred for the Duke, and Venice had long been Illyria's enemy.

None of this happened in the time it takes for night to turn to day. It takes months, years, from the day the ships leave port to when they return, or are never seen again. Life went on, much the same as ever . . .

VIOLETTA

. . . Until the year when I was ten years old and everything changed. At the end of each summer, the palace was closed up and we went back to the city. I saw less of Stephano during the winter, but that year he did not appear at the summer palace at all.

'Sebastian has claimed him,' Lady Olivia said. 'Made him his page. He wants to make a man of him.' She laughed, but there were tears in her eyes as she said it.

I missed him sorely, but I hid my sorrow in the way that children do. I always had Feste to teach me new tricks and laugh me out of my misery. He's no child, but he can enter into a child's world. He can be savage and kind by turns, as children are; he sees with a child's clear and pitiless eye. He spies what lies beneath surface appearances and will punish pretension and hypocrisy with merciless mockery.

He went where he wanted, but he was the Lady

Olivia's Fool, so came with her to the summer palace. He taught me to juggle and tumble, to walk a rope without falling and do magic tricks. He taught me how to whistle like a bird, hoot like an owl, how to make all manner of noises and sounds and use them for mischief and trickery.

Feste's lessons were useful to me as a currency with the boys who had been sent by their families to my father's court. In the winter months I took lessons with them. My father believed that girls should be educated like boys, and was happy to find that I had a quick mind and an aptitude for learning. I counted the boys my friends and became an honorary page. Feste had shown me the value of duplicity. I created pockets of freedom within my life as the Duke's daughter. The palace was very large. Often no one knew where I was, or who was supposed to be looking after me; by telling one person one thing and something else to another, it was easy for me to pass under everybody's notice.

My favourite among the pages was Guido, the son of an Italian duke. He was small, with a mass of curly brown hair springing out from under his blue-and-red cap. He was a handsome boy, with clear olive skin spattered with freckles, and large green eyes flecked with black. His friends called him Gatto, Italian for cat. He could usually smile and talk his way out of anything, no matter how stern the master, or how serious the scrape. He was wild and mischievous and now that Stephano had gone from my life, he was the perfect substitute. I taught him tricks, swearing him to secrecy. If Feste found out, he would be furious. A Fool does not divulge his secrets, and I was the Fool's Girl. We would outdo each other in feats of daring:

walking along the battlements and roof ridges, mounting raids deep into Count Sebastian's territory, south of the Stradun, the wide thoroughfare that divides the city. We would go there to steal peaches, shout insults, steal buckets of blue wash to daub the Duke's colours and his motto on their walls.

It was the end of August. I'd come back early from the summer palace. I'd missed Stephano. Without him there, I was expected to join the ladies. I was ten and no longer a child. I felt the adult world close in on me: sewing and poetry. I could not wait to get back to the city to be free.

When Guido suggested we went on a raid, I was more than willing. We collected a bucket of blue wash from outside a house that was being painted and set off through the twisting narrow alleys, steep flights of steps and hidden squares that make up Illyria town. We were safe enough in our territory, but more cautious after we crossed the Stradun. The alleyways often lead nowhere, or turn in on one another like a maze. It is easy to get lost in an unfamiliar district, possible to turn a sudden corner and be face to face with an enemy without any warning, avenues of escape limited, or absent.

The noise from the Stradun should have warned us, but we paid it no attention. We were right up the other end, and fights were always breaking out down by the market. Insults and name calling easily turned into scuffles and the flash of steel with stalls overturned, the fruit and vegetables used as missiles or crushed underfoot in the melee. We heard the shouts, the city guard running to sort it out, but we thought that we would be safe.

'This'll do.' Guido stopped in front of a high wall. He looked up at the expanse of cream stucco, as a painter might eye a canvas. 'I'll get started. You stand lookout.'

He dipped his brush and daubed *VV*, short for *Veritas Vincit*, my father's motto. He was just finishing the open triangle with a bar across the top, which had come to mean my father's insignia, the eagle, when I heard men coming up the steps. Not just one or two, but a lot of them. I went to look. There must have been ten, walking five abreast, blocking the steps. They were talking loud, laughing and bragging, as men do when they have been fighting. Their black-and-white tunics and hose were torn; one or two were bloody.

'Count's men, Guido! Quick!'

I was already running. I expected Guido to follow me, but when I looked back he was standing at the top of the steps, laughing, with the bucket in his hand. He'd thrown the paint all over them. I heard their roar of fury, the stamping of their boots as they took the steps two at a time to get him. He hurled the bucket for good measure and took off into a tangle of little alleys that led up to the walls. This part of the town had been abandoned, the houses tumbled in an earthquake. There were plenty of hiding places in the ruins and overgrown gardens, so I wasn't worried; besides, I had problems of my own. One of the Count's men was following me, running swiftly and gaining. He was shouting my name. He'd recognised me. That made me run even faster. I didn't stop to think how he knew me; I was in trouble enough. I hitched up my dress, but the skirts twisted and tangled round my legs. He would outrun me for sure.

He caught me at the top of the steps that led down

to the gates, where I knew I would be safe, grabbing me from behind and pulling me back. I had no weapon, but I thought I could take him. He was a page, not much bigger than me. Feste had taught me how to fight, and fight dirty. I kicked back and felt my heel connect with bone, then I jabbed him in the midriff. As he doubled over, I planned to grab him and pitch him down the steps. I caught hold of his collar, twisting so he couldn't breathe, and got ready to push and kick him on his way.

'Violetta!' He wriggled to get free of my grip. 'It's me!'

I let go of him then, looking down the long, steep flight of stone steps. He could have broken his neck. *I* could have broken his neck. It was Stephano. I hardly recognised him. I hadn't seen him for a year and more and he looked different. Older. I'd never seen him in his father's black-and-white livery before.

'We have to go after the boy who was with you,' he said.

'Guido? He can look after himself.'

'My father's men – they took a licking on the Stradun. They will be after blood.'

'There's plenty of places to hide up there,' I said. 'He'll be all right.'

'You don't understand!' He looked around. 'My father has had the buildings blocked up to keep out beggars and people living there without a permit. The alleys lead nowhere – they are just dead ends.'

We found him in a small square surrounded by tall tenements, their doors blocked with stone, their windows roughly bricked up. He was propped against a well surrounded by the Count's men, their black-and-white livery flecked with blue splashes. They were taking their time with him. His mouth was swollen. Blood glistened on his hair and ran in a thick streak down his face, dripping on to his tunic. The fun was nearly over. One of them drew his stiletto. Another was easing his sword from his scabbard. Guido was looking up at them, death in his eyes. The Cat's luck had run out. He'd used up all his lives.

Stephano started forward, dagger drawn. He would likely be thrown aside by his father's men, but he would not stand by and watch Guido butchered.

A sudden shout of command held his step. The Count's men turned, disconcerted, as the first shout was answered by another. Then came the tramp of marching feet, the sound of men approaching the square from all directions. The Count's men stepped back from their quarry. Their leader reached down, his stiletto angled for a quick thrust up into the chest, ready to gut the boy like a fish, but a loud command stayed his hand. He turned. The rest of the square was deserted. The shouting seemed to come from nowhere. The marching feet were getting closer. New orders rang out, although there was no one to be seen. The Count's men crouched, swords drawn, standing back to back, ready to strike out. The echoing shouts became too much. It was as though an invisible army of ghosts and spirits was coming for them. They turned tail and ran.

I looked about, trying to work out what had happened, and then I saw Feste, seated cross-legged on the balustrade of a balcony, wiping the tears from his eyes. When I looked again, he had gone.

I saw him. 'Here. Through here.' Feste was pushing loose bricks from a window. He beckoned to us.

We carried Guido between us, and Feste took us through the ruined house and out into a garden hard against the city wall. The garden was cultivated, with fig trees, orange trees, flowers and herbs. Broken steps led to a little door that opened directly into the wall.

We followed a winding staircase up to a long, narrow room. On one side, pointed windows opened on to the sea; on the other, they showed a jostling tide of terracotta roofs. Swallows and swifts flew in and out, swooping up to nests high in the rafters. The room was loud with their shrilling and chirruping. I looked about in wonder. There were birds perched about everywhere: some drab little sparrows, others far more exotic with bright plumage. Not all of them were real. Some were carved from wood, cloaked in feathers and painted in artful imitation of their living counterparts. The room was full of carvings: birds, animals, human figures. Puppets hung by their strings from the rafters. Saints and angels, devils and Madonnas stood grouped in corners as though whispering one to another.

Richly patterned fabrics covered the rough stone walls. A loom stood at one end, and from a corner came the sound of a spinning wheel. The spinner looked up as we stumbled into the room.

'We need your help, Mother,' Feste called.

She stilled the wheel, taking care not to break the thread, and came towards us. She was dressed like one of the wandering people, or those who came from the East: her headscarf fringed with little copper discs, the bodice of her red-and-purple dress heavy with rows of silver coins. As she walked the coins jingled together, and I had to plait my fingers behind my back to fight the temptation to cross myself. I knew her by reputation. Her name was Marijita and she was *vjestica*, a witch.

She smiled, as if she knew what I was thinking.

'Don't believe all you hear, my pretty.'

Feste called her 'mother', but there was no look of him about her. She was tall, her dark face lined, especially about the eyes, which sparked as dark and bright as those of the hoopoe that perched on her shoulder, its feathered crest erect, its orange head turned at the same angle as hers. Some whispered that her birds were so tame that they had to be the captured spirits of her enemies. She uttered a light trilling sound and the bird flew up to perch on a rafter, where it continued to stare down at us with beady black eyes.

'Like I say,' she said, looking at me, 'don't believe everything you hear.'

I began to introduce myself and her laughter chimed like the coins she wore.

'I know who you are, little Duchessa. Does your father know you are here? Your mother?' The gleam in her eye grew needle sharp. 'Do they care?' She took my chin in a firm grip. 'You look like her. Lady Viola – she's a strange one. From the sea she came, and the sea will claim her. And what about your father?' She pinched my cheeks harder. 'I don't see much of him about you.'

Bunches of herbs hung down from the beams along with other things: dried and scaly, dark and leathery, the desiccated remains of snakes and lizards, toads, frogs and bats' wings. Many came to her for charms, to ward off the evil eye, to guard against the sprites and spirits that haunt graveyards and deserted places, gather at crossroads, lurk under gateways or hover close to running water. Illyrians are a credulous people, ready to see malevolence everywhere, but she was no ordinary market charm seller or fortune-teller. My mother had never been to her, as far as I knew, but other ladies consulted her, including the Lady Olivia, who was of the country and as superstitious as any. Even my father sometimes summoned Marijita to find out which days were auspicious. My people keep the feast days and go to church on Sunday, but they are ever mindful of other forces at work around them and she was a mistress of that invisible world.

'Let me see that wound.' She examined the gash on Guido's head, gently probing with her long, thin fingers. 'Looks worse than it is. Boys have thick skulls. You, Count's boy, fetch me some water.'

Stephano filled a basin while she went to a long cupboard set against the far wall. The shelves were crammed with different-coloured bottles and pottery jars. She took what she wanted and came back to Guido. She washed his face and swabbed at his matted hair, parting it carefully to find the long, jagged cut still oozing blood on his white scalp. She dabbed the wound with sharp-smelling liquid that made him wince. Then she threaded a needle and Guido did his best not to flinch as she held the edges of the gash together and sewed it as neatly as she would sew a seam.

'There!' She stood back to admire her handiwork. 'That will heal clean and leave no scar.'

Feste leaned against a bench covered in carvings at different stages of completion. He whistled softly to himself and whittled away at a piece of wood, while above our heads the swallows whirled about like birds on a child's stick.

'Feste, stop whistling at my birds. You are confusing them.'

While she tended Guido I stood by the window, looking at a stone set on the sill: a milky white moonstone about as big as a man's fist. I found my eyes drawn to it, to the different hues of violet and blue playing across its shining surface. This was the seeing stone that she used to tell the ladies' fortunes. It was like looking up into the sky on a cloudy day. I began to see shapes there, and then something else in its depths: little dancing spots like agitated grains of sand. It was like being in that state between waking and dreaming when fancies take form. The spots began to come together and turn themselves into a fleet of tiny ships. I blinked, thinking it was a trick of the light, that an image had been captured from outside, like the pictures cast on to the wall in Father's dark chamber, his camera obscura. I looked out of the window. The ships moving across the sea below were small carracks, coastal craft, nothing like the long war galleys that I had seen in the stone.

When I looked back, the stone was opaque. I could see nothing beneath the shining surface.

'My shewstone.' Marijita held the stone cradled in her two hands. 'Before you came, I had a reading. I put the stone there for the sun to burn away any lingering darkness. You saw something.'

It was not a question and she did not need me to confirm it. She knew. Her hand went to the charm she wore round her neck, a cimaruta, an amulet, made in the shape of a branching sprig of rue and hung with tiny charms: a key, the moon and a serpent. I'd seen them before; many women wore them who held to the Old Belief. The charms represented the goddess in her triple form: the key of Hecate, the moon of Diana, the serpent of Persephone.

'Is it finished, Mother?' Feste asked. He had left off whistling and was inspecting her carvings, as though looking for something.

'Not yet,' she replied. 'You must be patient.'

She drew a cloth from the piece she had been working on, exposing it to Feste's scrutiny. I had no idea what it could be. It looked just like a lump of wood to me.

Guido had recovered enough to wander over to where a sword hung on the wall. It was a Turkish yataghan, a fine weapon, with a hilt of mother-of-pearl and verses in silver and gold laid along its slender, curving blade.

'Sharp enough for a man to shave himself,' she said, as Guido tested the blade with his thumb. 'When you have a beard to cut, perhaps it will be yours.'

She turned to where Stephano stood admiring a vest of chain mail covered in beaten silver discs which shimmered like fish scales.

'Fine work.' Her fingers fluttered over the shining surface. 'It is said to have been worn by great Saladin himself and to have been blessed by the Prophet Mohammed, may peace be upon him. It is covered with verses from the Holy Qur'an.' Although the majority worship Christ, there are those in Illyria who follow different faiths. Muslim and Jew live side by side with Christians. She made obeisance to other religions, like many in the town. 'A gift from a soldier who had no further need for it.' She plucked it up and measured it against Stephano. His fair hair had grown darker, it would be like his father's, and his face had lost a child's roundness, but he was still only halfway to a man. His chest was narrow and the yoke of the mail shirt stretched well past his shoulders; the shimmering length of it fell almost to his knees 'Too big for you yet, boy.' She threw the shirt aside and clapped her hands. 'Do not wish to grow up too soon. Go away now and be children. When it is time, you will come back.'

With that, we were dismissed. We left her and followed the walls round, down into the town. The sun had fallen below the level of the battlements, the bright blue of the sky was darkening to purple and lavender, the air was loud with the sound of birds coming home to their roosts, bats just flying out. We linked arms, jumping down the steps that led down to the Stradun. The market had righted itself. The first lamps were lit and the wide street was busy with people coming out into the cool of the evening. There was little sign of the fighting that had broken out earlier, only a few rusty stains on the white paving stones. Feste stationed himself at a corner, set his battered hat in front of him and played and sang until he had collected enough to buy us lemon drinks sweetened with sugar, honey cakes and sweetmeats from the vendors. We went out into the harbour and sat on the wall together to watch the sun go down over the water. We ate and drank and laughed until the curfew bell summoned us back inside the city walls. I remember it better than yesterday. It was the last time that I was happy.

8

'The spinsters and the knitters in the sun'

VIOLETTA

'**F**rom the sea she came, and the sea will claim her.'

Marijita was a soothsayer. That is the trouble with prophecies. Once they are made, you wait for them to come true. I could not get it out of my mind. I found myself watching my mother, listening to her conversation for any hint that she might be going on a ship, or taking a voyage, but it didn't happen like that at all.

Two years passed. It was the summer when I was twelve. We were at the summer palace when my mother disappeared. Her clothes and sandals were found on the beach, left in a neat pile as if she had gone for her early morning swim. She was never seen again. Servants and soldiers searched the coast for miles in both directions. Lookouts stared out to sea until their eyes were red and aching with tiredness, but they saw nothing but the restless waves.

My father ordered boats both large and small to take up the search, ranging far out to sea, along the coast and out to the offshore islands, in case she had been swept out by tide and current. The fishermen coming into port were questioned as to whether they had seen anything and sent straight back out again.

Day after day the search went on, but there was no sign of her, living or dead.

At last my father called off the searching. He declared a period of mourning and made arrangements for an elaborate funeral. The empty coffin was draped with her purple colours and paraded through the town on a splendid bier drawn by six matching black horses. It was buried in the family vault with full funerary rights and all due ceremony, but people were struck by the strangeness and muttered that no good would come of it. Such things fed their superstitions. The spectre of the empty coffin was to haunt the city for a long time to come.

MARIA

My lady went into the deepest mourning, deeper by far than for her father or brother. She went triple-veiled and dressed in cypress black. She gave the running of her household over to Sebastian, which is what he had always wanted, and withdrew from the world. She took to the upper rooms of the palazzo, cutting herself off. She allowed no one to see her, not even me, not even Feste. She lived like an anchoress, taking food through a small shuttered window. The only person allowed to see her was Marijita, who arrived at the dead of night and left in the early morning, speaking to no one, as if she'd taken a vow of secrecy.

Feste took it badly. He had been in my lady's household from a small child. They had played together and he had taught her all sorts of tricks: how to walk on stilts and whistle like a bird. He had been her father's Fool, then hers. He won't thank me for telling you, but he pined like a dog, sitting outside her door for weeks, for months. He climbed up to her balcony and sang and played so sweetly that the birds stopped their voices and the bees their buzzing, just to listen. All to no purpose. She would not let him see her, or even acknowledge that he was there. He worried himself to a shadow and was like to die of grief, until I told him to look to Violetta. She was motherless, her father otherwise occupied, Lady Olivia too immersed in her own sorrow to take notice of anybody else. Who would care for her now? I thought they might comfort each other. At last he took himself off to the palace. In truth, I wanted him out of the way. Lord Sebastian had never liked him, and the hatred was returned in brimming measure. Feste has a sharp mocking tongue and does not try to guard it. He was safe while my lady was there to laugh at his wit, but without her protection he was vulnerable. One word out of turn and Lord Sebastian would snuff him as quickly as he would pinch out a moth.

Once Sebastian realised that Lady Olivia's withdrawal was permanent, he was not long in destroying her household. He went abroad, and in his absence the young men who made up his retinue took over bringing everything into dissolute disarray. My lady's loyal servants and followers left one by one. They'd had enough of the insults, the violence, the drunken, vile behaviour. Months went by. My lady did nothing to intervene. Toby and I saw the year out, but when Lord Sebastian came back after the Winter Festival he seemed surprised to see us there. It was as if the disrespect and disorder had been a deliberate campaign. He had us banished. It broke my heart to leave. I would have stayed with my lady, braved any amount of humiliation and cruelty – such things mean nothing to me – but I was given no choice. I packed with a knife at my back. Armed men took Toby and me to a waiting ship and stood guard on the dock until we sailed. I cried bitterly all the way here.

VIOLETTA

I mourned her in my own way.

It was as if the sun had gone from our lives, leaving everything in shades of grey. It is possible to gradually forget its brightness and grow used to living in cold and darkness. Even in the depths of winter one is conscious of the year turning, but I knew that the light would not come back again.

That year it seemed as if Nature herself shared in our sorrow, as if Demeter mourned anew for her lost daughter, Persephone. The ground froze iron hard. Birds dropped from the trees as the wind howled from the north, scattering the ships before it and bringing freezing rain that broke the trees and shrouded everything in glass. Then the snow came, blanketing a world from which all brightness had been removed. This year there was to be no Winter Festival, no holiday, no feasting, no celebration of Our Lord's birth and the year's turning. It was as if there could be no spring.

The only ritual my father kept was the Feast of the Epiphany, the most important date in the city's calendar. Every year, in the Procession of the Magi, our most holy relic was paraded through the town and shown to the people. The canopied reliquary was carried by four cowled monks, with priests swinging silver thuribles, sending up white clouds to fill the frosty air with the sweet, musky smell of frankincense. Behind them came a great pageant led by my father on Pegaz, his grey stallion, caparisoned in scarlet and azure, with his guard following, their armour shining, then all the leading families, dressed in their finest.

It was always a great occasion, vivid with colour and the flash of gold and silver, but that year it was more like a funeral procession. The people watched in pinched silence as the sombre parade wound past them. There was no colour anywhere, the thuribles were stilled and even the burnished gold of the reliquary seemed as dull as tarnished brass.

The golden reliquary, studded with gems and cunningly wrought by the goldsmiths of Byzantium, holds one of the most sacred relics in Christendom: the gift of myrrh offered to the Infant Jesus by the magus Caspar. The precious substance is contained in a small silver-lidded cup of great antiquity, set with precious stones and still containing the myrrh used to anoint the body of Our Lord. It came to our country from Constantinople. It was being taken by ship to Venice when a great storm blew up. The ship was lost with all hands, but the relic floated to shore by miraculous means and was found by a fisherman. He took it to a holy man who built a church to contain the precious object and the town grew up around it.

The cup came home, for the people believe that Caspar, a learned prince, set out from somewhere along our coast and travelled east to Persia to become a magus. The relic was regarded with great awe by Illyrians, doubly identified with the founding of our country. The reliquary was processed round the city, taken to each canton, to be reverenced by the people living there, then returned to the cathedral to be opened at the appointed time when the gift was judged to have been given.

I was in the cathedral, sitting next to Stephano. We only ever saw each other in church now. The Lady Olivia did not attend. And neither did Sebastian. She took the sacraments in her room. He was either away or did not feel the need to go to church. His absences were noted. Some said he had sold his soul to the Devil. At my father's invitation Stephano had joined us in our pew. We sat next to each other on that day, our shoulders and elbows so close that I could feel the warmth of his body through the cloth. I set my breathing to match his. We had been kept separate, but we were growing up. Our thirteenth birthdays had just passed. In Italy, girls can be married when they are fourteen. Who knew what next year would bring? I twisted the ring on my finger and looked sideways at him. A little of the gloom of the last months lifted as he smiled and touched his hand to mine. The ring almost fitted now.

That glimmer of joy did not last. I had been thinking about us, dreaming of our future, when I heard a gasp. The reliquary stood open on the altar, but the holy vessel was no longer inside. Men hid their faces. Women cried, tore at their hair and ululated as they do when someone dies. Cries of dismay and distress spread like a wave through the congregation, spilling out into the streets.

Not knowing what else to do, the priest closed the reliquary, uttering prayers and invocations. When he opened the doors, the cup was back. It was in its usual place. Wails of horror turned to sighs of relief and fervent prayers of thanks. Some swore that the cup had been there all along, but enough people were willing to take an oath that, when the doors were first opened, the reliquary was empty. Stephano and I among them. Some saw the restoration as a miracle, but I don't see it like that. The disappearance was a warning. If it was not heeded, then the relic would be lost to us forever and Illyria with it.

❖❖❖

If only my father had taken notice of that warning, but he did not.

A bad winter was followed by a worse spring, full of storms, drenching rain and contrary winds. Argosies went out and did not return. Freebooters and pirates prowled the seas; corsairs came from the north, from the east, from as far away as Africa. But my father did not sail out with his fleet to defeat the enemy. The families of his sailors begged in the streets while he retreated to his tower.

The Lady Olivia was never seen in public either. It was as though she and Orsin were wedded at last in their despair. Marijita visited them both, a midwife to their grief.

They were both consumed by the memory of my mother. Some might say possessed. My father was more obsessed with her in death than he had ever been in life. He was hollowed out by doubts about what had happened to her. Had she taken her own life? Had it been an accident? Was she alive somewhere? Had she contrived her own death, perhaps to turn up on some other shore, as she had done here? Was she alone in this, or did somebody help her? The questions ate into his mind like maggots burrow into flesh, allowing him no peace, no rest.

At first he was certain that she must have survived to begin a new life as someone else. He sent agents to search up and down the coast, on the islands, across the sea to Italy, as far north as Venice, as far south as Greece, looking for any word, any sign, just in case she had survived. When no news came back, he turned to other means to find out what had happened to her.

He scoured the libraries and bookshops of Europe, the bazaars and souks of the East, for obscure volumes in Arabic, Hebrew and Greek. He called in mullahs and rabbis, wise men to help him with translation, but he had picked up many languages over the years and he began to work more and more alone. He was never seen in public now.

One day I was summoned to see him in his private library high up in the Tower of the Winds. He needed a sharper pair of eyes to help him with the work. I was shocked by the change in him. His black hair had developed a white streak and was receding at the temples, leaving a pronounced peak. He'd let his beard grow, trimming and twisting it to a point, and he was dressed in black, wearing a long velvet robe over his spare frame like a doctor or a scholar. Or a wizard.

He took me into his Internabibliotheca, his secret study. The air was close. The room smelt of ink and dust, candle wax and old books. He hardly seemed to notice me. I was to be as much of an instrument as the eyeglasses balanced on his nose or the pen in his hand. He set books before me and put me to work, copying words, signs and symbols into squares and triangles drawn on to parchment. Some of the signs and symbols were mathematical, others alchemical or astrological, set against words in Latin, Greek or Hebrew. When I had finished, he took the sheet from me and pored over them. He worked with a fierce intensity, as if he could compel the page to give up its meaning, his brows drawn together in a ferocious frown. He then took my workings to a separate table, adding figures to sheets already so densely covered that they were almost black.

'It is not madness that drives me,' he said. 'Whatever people say. There is a code in the words and symbols. A clavis. A key. I can use it to uncover the knowledge hidden within these texts, just as a key may unlock a casket.'

'What is inside it – the casket?' I asked.

'It is not a real casket.'

I thought about that for a while and then I asked, 'What if it contains just another key?'

'That would at least be something.' He gave me one of his rare smiles, his teeth white and even, and I could see a ghost of the handsomeness that had so captivated my mother when they first met. 'There are patterns in everything, in the whole of Nature, from the way the stars turn in the heavens to the whorl of a shell or the petals of a flower and the way leaves arrange themselves about a twig. There are forces, hidden forces. If I can discover what they are, how they operate, I will have my hands upon the levers of creation and can work them myself.'

'Creation is God's work,' I said quietly. 'Man can have no part in it.'

He followed the obsessive thread of his thought as if I had not spoken. He was searching for a way to summon my mother, to call her back from the realm of the dead, and he would use any means. I worked, my hand trembling enough to bring down his wrath. What he was doing reeked of sorcery, of necromancy. I feared for him. I feared for all of us. This was forbidden. Even a duke is not above the attentions of the Inquisition. I pictured the great doom painting that covered the walls above the altar in the cathedral; vile monsters and hideous creatures busy torturing the souls who had been consigned to Hell. What if he loosed such a legion upon the world?

I tried to reason with him, but he would not listen. I was replaced by a Dr Grimaldi from Padova in Italy. He came with a trunk of books and a square leather box which contained his magical instruments. He would work with my father now.

Many thought that my father truly had lost his senses. Guards were set at the base of the tower. Urgent envoys were ignored. Letters and messages from far and near gathered dust, their seals unbroken. My father neglected everything in order to concentrate on his secret studies. Rumour began to seep and spread through the city like a foul, low-lying miasma. The sharp stench of sulphur clung to the area around the tower, along with something putrid, like seaweed left by the tide to rot in the sun. There was talk of spirits walking. Parts of the battlements went unguarded. The Tower of the Winds became known as the Wizard's Tower, and citizens passing under its shadow crossed themselves thrice.

'Dead is dead,' Feste said, his thin face twisting in

distaste. 'Best to let her rest. The dead are not supposed to come back; there is probably a reason for that.'

My father was not the only one searching. One evening I was told that Marijita was waiting for me in the Evening Gallery: a long, light room painted with arcadian frescoes and panels decorated with plants and flowers, so detailed and lifelike they might be growing. It was one of my mother's favourite rooms. The gallery faces west and gives on to the Garden of the Box Trees. The garden was still well kept, the paths raked and free of weeds, but the plants were wilting for lack of water, their leaves dusty and drooping. I found Marijita staring through the central glass doors, sealed now against the scent from the orange and lemon trees, the bushes of lavender, rosemary and sweet-smelling myrtle.

'No one walks there any more,' she said. 'Ah, well . . .'

Her sigh was full of regret for times past and fear for times to come. Things begun must be finished. My presence was needed. That was all she would say.

She threw a scarf over her head as we left the palace and we hurried through the dark streets. A full moon was rising, casting the town in a cold bluish light. We crossed the Stradun and skirted an old church. We were going towards Lady Olivia's palazzo. We took a long flight of wide steps, each one worn in the centre, the stone gleaming, polished to marble by the passage of many feet.

The palazzo stood on its own, the grandest house in a street of fine mansions. Wide balconies jutted out in the Venetian manner, each one carved with the family coat of arms. The lower windows were barred and shuttered, the huge front door closed for the night. We rang the bell and the doors were opened by Lady Francesca, one of Lady Olivia's attendants. I knew her. She had once served my mother. She was originally from Italy and wore her fair hair pulled back from a high forehead in the fashion of her native court.

I could hear laughter, the rumble of male voices coming from the main part of the house. It was now Lord Sebastian's domain. Lady Francesca took us away from there, up a side staircase that led to Lady Olivia's private apartments. I had not been there since my mother's disappearance. The rooms were dimly lit, furnished with white lilies, the mirrors covered as if for a funeral. The only spot of colour was a small, jewel-bright portrait of my mother, her eyes like dark sapphires, her pale pink cheek as translucent as alabaster. She was looking over her shoulder, her rosy lips slightly parted, caught between smiling and laughing as she swaggered in her scarlet-and-blue page's apparel, a feathered cap upon her head.

The painting stood on a table, flanked by candles. It was cased in a small folding frame, like a portable Madonna, and I stopped to gaze, as if at a shrine.

'That is how I first saw her. I had the portrait painted from other likenesses and from my memory of that time.'

I started as the voice came from the shadows. The Lady Olivia must have been there all the while.

'I'm sorry.' I curtsied. 'I did not see you there.'

She waved a gloved hand as if it were no matter. She was dressed all in black, her face obscured by the triple layering of veils.

'Come with me,' she said.

As she turned, I caught the shine of her large, lustrous eyes and the livid sheen of her pale skin. We followed the rustling silk of her skirts up another flight of stairs and then another, up to the roof. Lady Olivia's house was tall. From the top, it was possible to see over the city walls to the sea. We walked on to a wide terrace, planted with trees and flowers, bleached of colour in the moonlight, their fragrance strong.

'Come, child,' she said, beckoning me on. 'Don't be afraid. There is something I want you to see.'

The terrace was set out with a silver bowl on a tripod. Lady Francesca melted into the background as Marijita stepped forward. She took a stone from a soft leather pouch that she wore at her waist. This was the shewstone, the seeing stone that I had found on the sill in her room in the walls. She held up her arms, holding the stone up to the moon's brightness.

Lady Olivia had been engaging in the same rites as my father but with more success. I felt my mother there. I sensed her nearness, like a cold breath. I would have turned and bolted, but the Lady Olivia had hold of my arm, her gloved hand tightening like a vice.

'Oh, no,' she whispered. 'It seems that your presence is needed.'

I was propelled forward towards the place where the silver bowl stood. It was filled with water. The moon floated like a bone counter on the black surface. Stars showed around it like a scatter of diamond dust.

'She will come to you,' she whispered.

Marijita lowered the stone into the water, rippling the stillness, and went to the very edge of the terrace.

She raised her arms and began the Summoning: '*Hear us, Great Hecate, Triple-faced Goddess, Mighty One, Queen of the Night, Goddess of the Pathways, Lady of the Crossroads. Hear our prayer and answer . . .*'

'Look! Look closer!'

Lady Olivia's hissing command came to my ear as Marijita's voice rose and fell. I clutched on to the sides of the bowl and gazed into the water past the reflected moon and caught the blue-white glimmer of the moonstone in the silver depths. As I looked and looked, moon and stone joined together and I saw something lighter than a moth's wing moving across the surface. As I stared on, the form seemed to free itself and come floating up towards me. The water became agitated. Ripples moved in circles out to the edge of the bowl and back again until the whole surface began to bubble and roil, as if the water was coming to the boil, although the silver under my hand remained cool.

I started back, fearing that the thing would spring up into my face. Beside me, the Lady Olivia stood transfixed, her veils moving in and out with the rapidity of her breath. I looked up. The shape of a woman was coming towards us. She moved between earth and heaven, between air and water, following the broad silver path made by the moonlight across the glittering black surface of the sea. Swathed in a shining mist, her outline as yet indistinct, with each step she gained solidity. I remembered what Feste had said. Dead is dead. My mother would never walk in life again. I would never hear her voice soften in affection, or be held in her embrace, or feel her kiss, soft as a butterfly's wing on my cheek. This was not her. This was a spirit, maybe sent by the Evil One to beguile us.

I shrank away, but Lady Olivia did not share my doubts.

'Viola!' she called, and started forward as if to meet her. Marijita held her from the brink and spoke in warning.

'You may speak to her, but she may not answer. Do not on any account touch her, or she will take you with her to the realm of the dead.'

'But that's what I want! Don't you see?'

She tore the veils from her face. It was if she was dead already. Her beauty had gone, eaten away by grief. The skull showed clear beneath skin as pale and dry as parchment. Only her eyes were alive, blazing out from their bony orbits, full of hunger and longing.

She gazed at the approaching figure as one long starved might look at a feast. She stepped past me. Divining what she was about to do, I put out my hand to stop her.

Suddenly Marijita was by my side.

'Let her go,' she whispered. 'The dead are hungry for the living. She will take you too.'

Her hand held on to me as, between one blink and another, Lady Olivia stepped out, arms stretched towards the spectre. For a moment she seemed to walk on the air and the couple floated together, arms around each other; then one of them disappeared, as insubstantial as a bubble, while the other plummeted to earth, being made of more corporeal stuff.

There was no cry; she made no sound as she fell. I found myself listening for the muffled thud of impact, but there was nothing. Then came shouts of alarm and the sound of running feet.

In front of me, the tripod started to shake, the sides of the bowl began to quiver, the surface of the water shiver and quake. There was a deep rumbling roar which seemed to come from the depths of Hades. The whole building was moving. The shouts from below turned to screams. I struggled to keep my footing. The house shook like a toy in a giant's hand. All around us tiles were falling, chimneys toppling. Bells began tolling, wild and spasmodic, shaken to life in the church towers.

The shaking stopped as suddenly as it had started, and there was a moment of still silence, before the air was filled with a distant, different kind of roar. I looked out to see land where all had been water. Boats lay stranded, rocks and weed gleamed in the moonlight. The sea had been sucked away, and now it was coming back to shore. We threw ourselves down as the great wave broke against the walls, drenching us with water, tossing boats up on to roofs, flinging weed to hang from balconies and fish to lie on terraces, flopping and gasping.

It was put out that the Lady Olivia had fallen, frightened by the earthquake, or had been pitched from her balcony by the force of it. But many refused to believe it. Those first on the scene insisted that she fell before the earth began to shake. Many suspected that she had taken her own life, and that her sin had made the earth to quake. Others suspected darker forces and pointed to my father's tower, second and third finger curled tight to the palm, forefinger and little finger extended like horns in the sign to ward off the evil eye.

Lady Olivia was to be buried alongside her ancestors in the family vault beneath the cathedral, but many kept to their houses; those who dared turned their backs as the funeral procession passed them. Lord Sebastian was there, dressed in deepest sable, with every show of sorrow, although he stood to gain everything. He led the mourners, although he would not allow Stephano to attend, punishing him for something that he had done. Sebastian was growing in his cruelty. He was chief among the pall-bearers, helping to carry his wife's coffin down into the vaults. The stone steps were still strewn with flowers from my mother's funeral. The pall-bearers crushed the dried and withered blossoms under their boots. As they emerged, even the attending priests were white-faced and shaking. The vaults' heavy sealing stone was quickly lowered, thudding back with such speed that it all but trapped the robe of the last to leave. The priests stood in a cluster, praying with great fervour, swinging incense and sprinkling holy water. After the ceremony, the great processional cross was moved from its normal place close to the altar and positioned above the entrance to the vault. It might have been a settling of the earth following the recent quake, but some of those who had gone under the ground swore that they had heard a great sigh, as if two lovers had been reunited, at the moment Lady Olivia's coffin slid on to its stone resting place.

Lord Sebastian left on a sea voyage soon after the funeral. When he came back, he did not come alone.

9

FESTE

I can read and listen at the same time, can't I? He's listened to you two long enough. It's my turn to tell.

Don't put your trust in your betters, master. That's the lesson here. Don't put your trust in those set to rule over you. Illyria was a fair town, but it's not any more. Illyria was a prosperous country; now it's laid to waste, its people wandering the high roads. The truth of it is, the Duke and my lady between them had succeeded in pulling our world down about our ears.

To glimpse invasion in a magic stone is not to live through it. The attack came with no warning. Lord Sebastian and his fleet made up of all our enemies arrived out of the bright blue morning. You have been threatened here, master, have you not? By a mighty Armada sailing up the Channel, but you had time to prepare yourselves, and the gods smiled on you, giving you the luck and the strength to fight them off. We had neither. When the walls were breached, my first thought was for Marijita, how would she fare in her chamber high up there? But my duty was to Violetta.

When I got to Marijita, it was too late. We found her with her throat cut. The wound fresh, gaping like a second mouth. Her eyes were empty, her face like dirty parchment, her lifeblood pooled around her like her spreading skirts.

A length of white wool hung in the frame of her loom. She had been weaving her own shroud. The shuttle was carved from a man's thigh bone, the warp weighted with skulls filled with sand. She must have finished just as they broke in on her. The last thread was cut, but the stool by the loom had been overturned and there was blood on the scissors that she held in her hand. I had a feeling it was not hers. She had something else. I bent down. A folly stick, bound to her bosom the way working women tie their babies to them with a shawl. I lifted it away from her. It was stained across the head with her blood, like a baby new-birthed. I looked at the face and saw the likeness. She had been making it a long time, looking for the right burl of wood. Olive. Hard to carve with that little knife she had, but smooth as silk to the touch. It hefted heavy, as newborns are wont to do. A little Feste. He was mine now. I stuck him in my belt.

This happened quicker than the time it takes to tell it. I picked up a sound, faint and stealthy. We were not alone. I motioned Violetta to keep out of the way and quiet. I took out my knife and my little friend from where I'd stowed him. As good as any cudgel.

Someone was creeping along the wall from Marijita's balcony. I could hear the shallow whistle of his breath. I waited until I saw the flash of a sword and sprang forward. If Violetta had not called out, he would have been gutted and his brains all over the floor.

'Stephano!'

The boy started back in surprise. 'What are you

doing here?' he asked as he lowered his sword.

'Violetta must get out of the city,' I said. 'We came to Marijita. We came . . .' Who knows why we came? 'What are *you* doing here, more to the point?'

'I had a sudden feeling that I must come, to see if she was all right. If she was safe . . .'

'She is neither.' I turned on him. 'Thanks to your father.'

'I know . . .' The boy stood, head bent, taking the shame on himself. 'I surprised them, a gang of Venetians,' he said, a shake in his voice. 'Marijita was dead, and the birds, but they had hardly got started. Do you think there would have been anything left? If . . .' He reached up to wipe his face with his sleeve. 'If you don't believe me, you'll find what's left of them underneath the balcony. They won't be coming back again. It's a long way down to the rocks.'

And whose fault is it that they were here in the first place? I wanted to say, but held my tongue. There was no point in blaming the boy for his father's pride and ambition. Fathers are as like to heed their children as they are to listen to Fools. *Her* father was just as bad, neglecting his dukedom for dreams fed by a charlatan. Who suffers for it when the world turns mad?

I left the two wronged children to comfort each other and went back to Marijita. She was the nearest thing that I'd ever had to a mother. I rubbed my eyes with the heel of my hand. I had business to do before I left this place.

Violetta helped me lay her out. Stephano cut the shroud from the frame with his sword. We placed her upon it and I covered her eyes with coins for the ferryman. Before we wrapped her, I lifted the cimaruta from her neck and gave it to Violetta.

'This is for you. She would want you to have it, to keep you from harm.' I looked at Stephano. 'Where is the shirt she promised you?'

We found it folded neatly, the yataghan on top of it.

'It is almost as though she was expecting us,' Stephano said.

'Almost.' I held the shirt out to him. 'You had better put it on.'

There was scuffling and shouting coming from below. It was time to go. I'd left the boy, Guido, on guard at the foot of the stairs. It sounded as though he was no longer alone down there. I took the Turkish sword, then kicked wood shavings and threads together and threw Marijita's little oil lamp on to the pile.

Guido was holding his own, but the Count's men were forming a line to fight him. I joined in at his side, wielding the yataghan. The sword was his, but I'd blood it for him. I thought we were going to have a tussle, but as soon as the men saw Stephano they put up their weapons. The captain of the guard, tall and young, twenty or so, bowed low, calling Stephano 'my lord'. Very polite, but his offer to escort us to the Count's headquarters was not one that we'd be refusing. His men formed a guard around us. They were ten to our three fighting men. None of us would risk Violetta. We had no choice but to go with them.

My Lady Olivia's beautiful palazzo had turned fortress. The windows were covered in metal sheets. The fancy bronze gates that gave on to the street had been taken down to be melted into cannon, replaced by wooden doors as thick as a tree. The captain banged with the heel of his sword and there was a lot of throwing back of bolts and removing of barricades. Eventually, the doors creaked open and in we went.

The courtyard garden was trampled dust dotted with piles of manure. The ante-rooms, once so delicately perfumed, stank of men and horses. We were taken through to the Hall of the Horses. In Lady Olivia's day it had been the Hall of the Muses, a place for conversation and recitals. Muses dancing with Apollo and playing on the flute and lyre had all been painted over. Replaced by great snorting warhorses, hunting scenes and prick-eared, big-bollocked mastiffs. The room was full of men going about the business of conquering, standing about in huddles talking or hunched over maps, with messengers moving to and fro and boys and women serving wine. Lord Sebastian stood at a table, leaning over a plan of the city, using a Turkish dagger as a pointer. The room went still as we came towards him, but only a lift of an eyebrow showed that he knew we were there. He was going to ignore us for as long as it suited his purpose. It left me time to taste how much I hated him, like bile in my mouth. Eventually he looked up. His eyes are darker than his sister's and without her depth or sparkle, opaque and lustreless, like lapis. His lip curled, as if he did not like what he was seeing. He left his map and came towards us.

He had been considered good-looking – my lady thought so anyway – but he would never get back the bloom he had when she first saw him. The weakness that had been there all along was beginning to show; his cheeks were broken-veined and florid from too many nights drinking with his men, the youthful pout was gone from his mouth and the lips were thin and the colour of half-cooked liver, compressed into a line that pulled down at one side. His dark curls were greying and arranged carefully to hide what he was lacking. That jade Francesca was standing near, simpering and fawning, offering a wine cup to him. She had taken my lady's place in his bed. Now she stood at his side, as bold as you please, the double-dealing Venetian whore.

Stephano spoke first, trying to soften his father's wrath. He only made it a thousand times worse. The young are fools enough to put us poor clowns out of a job.

'Father,' he started, 'I beg you . . .'

He made a good start, I grant you. Son begging a father. They all like that.

'I beseech you . . .'

Beseeching? Even better.

'Have mercy . . .'

This is where it began to go wrong. Sebastian never had mercy on anyone.

'. . . on the people of this city . . .'

Sebastian's face began to colour. As if that was likely to happen. Considering the slights against him, all the times he had been ignored.

'Stop the sacking or you will have nothing left, no people to rule.'

There was truth in that. Sebastian relaxed a bit, or at least the blood stopped beating in his temple quite so hard.

'That is what I am trying to do. As you would know, if you had not run off to hide like a cowardly child.'

The young captain who had escorted us smirked. That was unfair. Stephano was as battered, besmirched and battle weary as any there.

'I did my share,' Stephano said, but his father wasn't listening.

'Ran off to see *her*, I'll warrant!' He pointed at Violetta. 'I know what's been going on between you. Paddling palms in church. My own son consorting with the enemy. I should banish you as a coward and a traitor. You are no son of mine.'

'Disown me if you like,' Stephano said. 'Banish me – I'd welcome it. I only have one thing to ask of you.' The boy linked hands with Violetta. She smiled and nodded, encouraging him, as though they might have made this up together, stupid children that they were. 'I ask only that, whatever our fate, we share it together. We will go away, far from here. We will never return. I give my word.'

That was a big mistake. Whatever they wanted, Sebastian would do the opposite, just because they wanted it. Surely the boy knew that? I wished I could have collected his words as they spilled and stuffed them back into his mouth.

Sebastian did not explode with rage. He spent a long time, as if considering, but that vein was pulsing in his temple again and the knuckles were white on his clenching fist.

'Your word? What is that worth? I have plans for her, and of one thing you can be very sure: you will never see her again. Her fate is decided. She is to be sold into slavery. I already have a buyer.'

'Father!' Stephano stepped towards him. 'You can't do that! She's a duke's daughter and your own niece, your sister's child!'

He looked around, as if others would support him in his pleading, but they'd all turned away.

Lord Sebastian continued as if his son had not spoken.

'You will go into the service of Sale Reis, the Barbary corsair.' He indicated the man standing by his side. 'He can do with you what he likes: galley slave or catamite. It is of no concern to me. I do not know from whose loins you sprang, but you are no son of mine.'

Stephano didn't lack for bravery. He leaped forward to defend his mother's name, grabbing the Turkish dagger from the table. He had it at his father's throat, the needle point pricking through the skin. Sebastian swallowed, bright blood trickling past his Adam's apple. The boy should have jammed the knife right in and ripped through his windpipe, but he couldn't do it, and then Sale Reis had the knife.

'To kill a father is a grievous sin in any man's religion,' the corsair said. 'You do not want such a crime on your conscience.'

He was a big man, the dagger looked like a toy in his hand, but he had struck quicker than a snake to force Stephano's hand down. He smiled, his gapped teeth white against his swarthy skin, his glossy beard touched with henna. He wore a white turban and was swathed in robes in the manner of his people. He put the dagger back down on to the table. In case there was any more trouble, he rested his hand lightly on the short curved sword stuck into his sash.

Sebastian ordered the guards to seize his son, but Sale Reis put up his hand.

'He is mine now. I've lost many fine men. I need all I can get. What about the other one?' He nodded towards Guido. 'What's your name, boy?'

'Guido Ad Romano, of Pavia.' The boy spoke up with courage and dignity.

'He will be hanged.' Sebastian turned to the guards. 'Take him away!'

'You can't do that!' Stephano shouted. 'He's a nobleman's son.'

'I can do what I like.' Sebastian's lips stretched into a smile. He dabbed at the blood on his neck with a kerchief. One victim was better than none.

'I will take him too, if I may. As I said, I have lost many men in your service.' Sale Reis bowed slightly, as if in deference, but it was clear that Sebastian was in his debt.

'Very well. Take them.' Sebastian looked cheated, then he saw Violetta.

'Your father, the Tyrant Duke, is dead,' he said to her, his tone as curt and dismissive as if she were a kitchen maid. 'He was killed in the fighting, which is unfortunate. I'd have had him blinded and hung outside his own tower for all to see, left there to starve to death. I could take your life as forfeit for his, but I have been prevailed upon to be merciful. You are sold into slavery. Meet your new master.'

A man stepped out from the shadows. It was sixteen years since I had last seen him, but I would have known him anywhere. He's got spindle sticks for legs and walks as if someone's stuck a stave up his arse. Age had not improved his beauty. His goose-green eyes, once popping out of his head, were now sunk into little hammocks of flesh. His long upper lip curled back to show teeth a deeper shade of yellow and even more bucked than I remembered. His long face had grown pendulous and wattled; his hair seemed to have migrated from his head to eyebrows, ears and nostrils. I hardly had time to look at his face. I could not keep my eyes away from the great crucifix that hung at his chest. He had become a priest – by the size of the cross, and the blackness of his robes, a Jesuit at least. He had found his true vocation. I almost put up two fingers in benediction. He moved with stately dignity, as befitted his station, and I smothered a smile. Monsignor Malvolio. And it got better. The Lady Francesca, whom everyone took for Sebastian's whore, was hanging on his arm, simpering up at him, her pale blue eyes bulging with fawning admiration.

In the old days, what a gift for fooling it would have been. These were not the old days, and this was no time to laugh, but sometimes solemnity only worsens the thing, just as a man on the gallows might notice a bubble of snot in the nose of the hangman, or a gob of egg on his chin. The desire grows until it can no longer be controlled. Every time I looked at him, I could see Sir Toby and Maria. I squeezed my eyes shut and bit my cheek; I tried to think of other things. He was speaking now. Below his long nose, his upper lip quivered like the tip of an oliphant's trunk. I couldn't listen. Soon the tears were leaking and I was shaking. The laughter backed up until I could hold it no longer; I had to let it out or my bladder would give way. Sometimes laughter spreads like a contagion, with no man knowing quite why he is joining in. So it was now. My laughter spread through the hall like a quick-running fire, until all were roaring, except for Sebastian and Malvolio.

'What ails you, man?' Malvolio was shouting at me through the din. 'Have you lost your wits?'

'Aye, I fear so, master. I'm a Fool!'

The laughter redoubled even though, as jokes go, it was in every way feeble. After laughing at nothing, men will find anything funny.

'Feste! You always were a barren rascal,' Malvolio snarled. 'Amusing nobody but yourself!'

Robbed of speech, I gestured round at the laughter.

'You never made *me* laugh!'

'Quite so, my master,' I said, wiping the tears from my eyes. 'Even the God of Laughter could not do that.'

'Enough of this roar!' Sebastian shouted through the noise, hammering on the table. 'You!' He pointed at me. 'We'll see how funny you can be when you are chained to an oar night and day. Get them out of here!'

The laughter died in my throat as Malvolio put out his long white hand to claim Violetta.

My lady was not his only prize. Venetian sailors and Uskok pirates were bringing in booty to be tallied and portioned. It looked like they were taking all the wealth of Illyria, and Sebastian did nothing to stop them. This was their share. Their help had come at a price. These were godless men. They handled crucifixes, gold crosses, jewelled Bibles and precious icons as if they were sticks of furniture. A Venetian captain came in bearing the most precious relic of all, the Cup of the Magi. This was not added to the other plunder from the cathedral. He brought it straight to Malvolio, who took it into his charge.

IO

'This fellow is wise enough to play the fool'

Violetta stood up and began pacing the small room. Recounting the story had made her restless, agitated, reminding her of how far they were from their purpose.

'That's the reason we are here. Feste and I escaped from our different captivities and we have been following this man, Malvolio, ever since. He is here and he has our precious relic in his possession. He stole it from us.' She turned to Will. 'You must understand. The relic *is* Illyria. The country grew from the city, and the relic was the reason for our city's foundation. Since my father is dead, I am the rightful ruler. I have vowed to return it, for without it our country does not exist.'

'But what do you want from me?' Will frowned, puzzled. 'You set yourself up in my way. You engage me in conversation. You tell me your story. Then there is this.' He picked up the Fool card from the table. 'You insinuate it into a note telling me that we are in want of a clown . . .'

Time was running on. He needed to get back to the playhouse, with or without Feste. He felt the stirrings of annoyance. He was beginning to wish he had never set eyes on them. He did not like to be picked out in this way, selected and targeted like one of the marks that they tricked at cards.

'You talked to us, master,' Feste said. 'Not t'other way about. If you don't want me to help you . . .' He threw the scroll he had been studying down on the table.

'Hush, Feste.' Violetta glared at him. 'There is no point in pretending any longer.' She turned to Will. 'We did deliberately put ourselves in your way. If we could get you to stop and watch, then we would have a chance to engage you, tell you our story, and you might be willing to help us.'

'But how, mistress?' Will's frown deepened. 'You still have not told me.'

'We have been watching Malvolio,' she said, her expression intense. 'We know he stays in the house of the Venetian Ambassador, north of the river. Near the Strand. We thought, *I* thought, that your company might perform there, and if they did, we could come with you. Then, when the audience was occupied with the play, we could steal the relic back.'

The words came out all in a rush. Violetta looked at him, her blue eyes anxious, searching for his reaction. Will stared back. Of all the things he thought she might say, he had not been expecting that. He would have laughed, if the girl had not been in such dead earnest. Such a thing was impossible. His company had to be invited to perform. They could not just set up in a great house as if it were an inn yard. An instant refusal sprang to his mouth, but he bit it back. She was young and very beautiful, but she had used no feminine guile to win him to this. Quite opposite. She believed in her cause, the rightness of it. Her belief that others would see it came from her youth, but also her station. Despite the darns in her sleeves and the ragged hem of her faded blue dress, she was a duchess. Will could not meet her expectant eyes. The clown's face was already twisting into a cynical smile. He knew that Will would refuse. Likely knew that such a thing was not in his power, but Feste had protected her, kept the truth away from her, lest it crush the little hope that she had left. He looked from Feste to where Maria sat, hunched up on her little stool, the only real stick of furniture in the room. Bright hope was fading in her eyes too; her face was falling back into its tired, sad lines as she looked to the room where her man lay dying.

'You are very silent, sir,' Violetta said at last.

'I'm thinking.' Will looked up at her.

'And what are you thinking?'

He sighed. 'That what you suggest is beyond my power.'

He had thought to be angry with them for presuming too far, for trying to trap him into helping them. Now that anger was fast turning to pity. Violetta saw it in his deep brown eyes that took in so much and gave so little away. She fought hard to hide her disappointment from him. She would not plead and she would not beg. Pride was all she had left. She would give it up for no man. Everything else had been taken from her. If he would not help them, so be it. They would find another way. But whatever happened, they would fulfil their part of the bargain. It was a matter of honour.

'Very well.' Violetta tried to smile and smooth her features. 'I think Feste has the part now, Master Shakespeare. It is time we went to the playhouse.'

She led the way down the stairs. Will followed. He

recognised all she had tried to hide. Her mask of affected indifference was as thin and brittle as glass. He might have been wishing that he had never set eyes on her, but at that moment she won his heart.

Richard Burbage, actor and theatre owner, was standing in shirtsleeves shouting directions up at the stage.

'No, not there! To the right! That's left!'

Someone dropped something, which fell from the height of the theatre and landed in the pit, puffing up dust and scattering nutshells. Three storeys up, the hammering and sawing stopped momentarily as the carpenters looked over to see if the fallen mallet had hit anybody or done any damage. Then it started up again. In the theatre, there was always something that needed doing: thatch replacing, holes patching, benches repairing, loose planks hammering back into place. Everyone shouted over the noise, adding to the din. The only time it was really quiet was in performance.

'I've found a new clown.'

Will brought Feste forward for inspection. Richard Burbage owned a lion's share of the theatre and felt losses keenly as pennies falling from his own pocket. If audiences were disappointed, they went elsewhere. Competition was sharp, with two theatres within throwing distance, not to mention the bear garden.

'Good, that's good, Will.' He wrinkled his high forehead and pushed a hand through his thinning sandy hair. 'Because until two minutes past, I thought you'd have to do it.' He looked at his playmaker and laughed. 'You may be many things, but a clown isn't one of them.' He turned his bright brown eyes to Feste. 'Is he any good? Will I have seen him in anything? His face looks familiar, but I don't recall from where. Who have you worked for, fellow? What company? Does he talk?'

'He hasn't worked here.' Will spoke for Feste. 'He's a stranger. I found him performing in the street over by St Mary Overie.'

'*That's* where I've seen him. Juggling with chairs and such?' Feste nodded. Burbage turned from him to Will. 'Are you out of your wits? We'll have the Revels Office down on us in a trice. Now, I've got a performance to stage.' He was already walking away.

'He's good!' Will followed after him. 'He can do it. I swear it!'

'How can he?' Burbage turned back with an exaggerated sigh. 'He can't have had time to learn it properly. Anyway, he's a foreigner! I'm not even sure it's legal. And who's this?' His eyes fell on Violetta. 'What's she doing here? A playhouse before performance is no place for a woman. Get them out of here!'

'Wait, Richard. He's good, I promise! What's the harm?'

Feste left the two men arguing and pulled himself up on the stage. He was small, thin as a starved hound, but very strong. He scampered about, reciting snatches of the play in different voices, peopling the stage with Rosalind and her cousin Celia; Touchstone himself, the banished Duke and his court, using Burbage's jaded, world-weary tone for the melancholy Jaques. Actors emerged from the tiring house to watch, led by Tod with a long blonde wig in his hand, his face already whitened for Rosalind. They stood about the margins and watched the little man leaping from place to place on the stage. When he finished with a curtsy, they let up a roar, clapping and stamping and shouting for more. Burbage joined in, wiping tears from his eyes.

'He's hired!' Burbage could already hear the money pouring in. 'I've never laughed so much at one of your plays or seen one acted so lively. What's his name?'

'Feste.'

'Well, Mister Feste,' Burbage said as the clown jumped down from the stage, 'let me shake you by the hand and welcome you into the company. Someone take Mister Feste and put him in Touchstone's motley. No foreign tricks, mind,' he said to Feste. 'No tumbling or that kind of carry-on. Just stick to the play.'

Will took Violetta up to one of the small side galleries reserved for wealthy patrons.

'I'll make sure it's roped off,' he said. 'You can watch the performance in peace from here. The crowd too. They are sometimes more interesting than what is happening onstage.'

He left her then, promising to be back when the performance began. The trumpets rang out above her and the place started to fill up with people. First a few, standing about in groups in the pit, dotted along the benches in the circling galleries, then more and more poured in until there were no spaces left. The ground was a solid mass of heads. All the galleries were filled.

Will returned just as the crowd was beginning to quieten. He did not speak, other than to utter a cursory greeting, but sat hunched forward, gnawing at his thumbnail, watching the audience. Violetta was waiting with as much anticipation as anyone. She welcomed any diversion from her own thoughts as they turned and twisted, meeting dead end after dead end. Something will turn up. That's what Feste always said. Just put one foot after another. But what if it did not? She was glad to turn away from it all, if only for a little while, and lose herself in the world of the play.

The crowd was taking a time to settle. There was a disturbance in the upper galleries. People turned to stare as two young men, richly dressed in the Italian style, made their way late to their seats. They were sitting directly opposite Violetta.

Violetta sat forward, her attention momentarily drawn away from the jutting stage. There was something familiar about the men, but she was too far away to see their faces. They both wore beards and their hats shaded their eyes. Her gaze lingered on them for a moment. Could it be? Her heart beat harder and she half rose from her seat but then sank back, dismissing the possibility. This had happened before. On crowded streets, busy docks, in marketplaces, she'd thought to catch a glimpse of him, but had always been disappointed. Fancy supplies the face we want to see.

The actors took to the stage and Violetta watched the opening scene, but every now and then her eyes strayed to the strangers in the upper gallery. When Feste came on to the stage, the smaller of the two young men nudged the other. He pointed and they both stared down, caught by more than the clown's words. The taller man looked up, his eyes searching the galleries, going through them row by row, studying each face carefully. His gaze stopped when he came to Violetta.

Will leaned forward, the girl's presence forgotten for the moment, his lips moving silently as other men spoke his words to the world. He always felt the same mixture of dread and desire when the actors took to the stage. The play became a greater and a lesser thing. It no longer belonged to him, but to the actors and the audience. He had no power, no control over what would happen.

Equally, he knew almost straight away whether it was going to go well or ill. There was an air of expectancy. All talk ceased. Vendors were ignored. People were too busy with the play to concern themselves with nuts and fruit, bottles of beer. This was going to be a good performance. He knew as soon as Feste walked on to the stage. He seemed to know how Will wanted this played. His wit and energy spread to the others like quick running fire, spilling from the stage so the groundlings stopped thinking about the ache in their legs or the rain beginning to fall and the people up in the galleries stopped signalling to friends or flirting with the ladies present. They ceased to notice the need of a cushion, or the lack of a back to the benches, or the hardness of the seats, because they were no longer in the theatre at all; they were in the Forest of Arden.

The performance was fast, funny to the last. Even Will found himself laughing. Something that almost never happened. He left the box when Tod began his Epilogue, knowing that they would call for him. He was standing at the side of the stage when the final word was spoken. There was a moment of silence when the audience seemed to wake from a dream they had all been sharing. After that came the roar, a wave of applause that rose from all sides and crashed on to the stage. The actors looked at each other and smiled. They took hands and bowed. The crowd shouted for the clown and they shouted for Rosalind and Celia, they shouted for the Duke, they shouted for Will and then they shouted for the clown again. The actors took bow after bow, the greasepaint running down their grinning faces, while the crowd roared and cheered, whistled and stamped. Then the jigs began. Will joined in, grasping his actors' sweating hands, as the crowd danced about the yard to the sound of fiddle, sackbut, flute and recorder. Feste pranced like an imp, playing on a short bone flute, keeping time on a tabor.

◆━◆━◆

Violetta did not see them take their final bows. Just as the play was ending, one of the young men in the opposite gallery had signalled across to her. They met in the passage that ran along the back of the galleries. Violetta looked from one to the other, studying their faces, measuring the changes. Stephano smiled, his teeth showing white against the fine growth of his beard, and Guido laughed, shaking back his long curly hair. She embraced them both, holding them to her. They were taller than her now and she could feel hard muscle under the velvet of their doublets. Guido stepped back but Stephano could not let her go. He pushed away a wing of hair in order to see her face better, as if to be sure that it was really her. He tucked the stray lock behind her ear and his fingers travelled to her cheek, tracing the line of her jaw, dropping to the whiteness of her throat, as if he needed to touch her skin, find it warm, feel the beating of her blood. Then he tipped her face up to his and he kissed her. Violetta's heart shifted inside her. The applause from the crowd rose up and roared around them, bouncing from side to side and all about, but in that moment they were utterly alone.

She linked arms with the two of them, just as she had done in Illyria, as they went down the stairs and out of the Globe.

◆▶◎◀◆

Will returned to Violetta in a high good humour, but the gallery was empty. She was no longer there. He glanced into the pit, thinking she might have gone down there to wait for Feste. The clown was still on stage, jumping about, but there was no sign of the girl. Will shouldered his way down the stairs and out into the open, thinking to find her among those streaming out of the playhouse, but he was quickly recognised and captured by the crowd: shaking hands, being clapped on the back while he nodded his thanks at the praise showering down on him. He thought he caught a glimpse of her, arm in arm with two young men going towards the river, but the press was too great to chase after her and he had other claims on his time.

He went back into the playhouse wondering who the young men might be. He didn't know she *had* any friends here, apart from Maria and Sir Toby. But what did he know about this girl? She kept much of herself hidden, like those ice islands said to float in northern seas. If the girl had chosen to make off with mysterious young men, then so be it. He went to collect the script. There were changes he wanted to make. What she wanted from him was impossible. His imagination was great, none greater. He could make cities, whole countries; people those with kings and princes, nobles and commoners. He could make the past live again, could create worlds that had never been, but he had been unable to think of one single way in which he could help this girl.

He began to wish again that he had never crossed paths with them. It was not fair to lay this thing upon him. People had an exaggerated idea of what he could do in the world. He was a player, no more than that. His influence was confined to the wooden walls of the Globe. Any power outside of that was as counterfeit as actors' finery.

He could do nothing. That should be an end, and yet, even if he got his wish and never saw her again, he knew that he would not be able to stop thinking about her, gnawing at her problem as he gnawed his nails. She was young, younger than his own Susannah. Not that his daughter was likely to stir out of Stratford, but if she did . . . Life was precarious: death, disease, loss of fortune could tip the most ordered existence into chaos. Who knew what disaster could yet occur to force her to leave her home, to live among strangers? If that were to happen, he'd like to think that there were those who would offer what help they could give.

He went in search of the clown.

II

'Is it a world to hide virtues in?'

Violetta looked from Stephano to Guido as they armed her down to the river. They had both changed, beyond the first growing of beards, wearing earrings and being much burnt by the sun. She was hard put to find in their faces the boys that she had known.

'How did you know I was here?' she asked.

'We didn't,' Stephano said. 'It was an accident. We came here to see the play. Then we saw Feste. At first we couldn't believe it was him – how could it be? But Guido was sure. He's never wrong about things like that. If Feste was here, you wouldn't be far.'

'How could you know that we would be together?'

'Feste would never leave you,' Guido said. 'After Lady Olivia died, he gave you his service. When you were taken, he swore to us that he would find you. So you were either near, or . . .'

'Or dead?'

Stephano shook his head. 'I would not allow myself to think on that.'

'He found me in Venice,' Violetta said. 'I've been with him ever since. But I did not expect to see you again. Not for . . . not for a very long time. I did not expect, or ever dare hope . . .' She held on more tightly to Stephano's arm, still hardly believing that he was here in flesh and blood, seeking to change the subject before her feelings overwhelmed her. 'How do you come to be here? In London.'

'We could ask the same thing of you!' Stephano laughed at how impossible it was for them to be here, together, under grey London skies with the brown waters of the river flowing past. 'We are here in the service of Signore Mazzolini, the Venetian Ambassador.'

'Venice!' Violetta stopped, disengaging herself from their linked arms. 'So that's why you are dressed like such fine Italian gentlemen.'

Stephano looked down at her shabby blue dress, the old velvet cloak rippled and patched where the nap had gone thin. His handsome features clouded. Shame and guilt began to corrode his joy at meeting her again, etching into it like acid.

Violetta stared at him. 'Venice is our enemy. You saw what they did to our city.'

'We are kept men.' Stephano looked away from her. It got worse, not better. 'Kept by Malvolio. He came upon us in Tunis and bought us from Sale Reis because it amused him to do so. He then gave us to the Venetian Ambassador, who was on his way to England. His Excellency has been kind to me. He did not like to see me treated that way. My father is Duke of Illyria now, and Illyria is allied with Venice, so he made me a kind of envoy. I sailed with him to England. Malvolio went to see his Jesuit brothers in Spain. He came on another ship. He is here now.'

'You are an envoy for your father! He is a usurper! So you are reconciled with him?' Violetta stood, arms folded. Had he come to find her just to let her know that she'd been betrayed again, and this time by one she'd thought had really loved her?

'No, I am not reconciled. The opposite, if anything. But my father approved it. It amused him to see me as some kind of pet, like a dog or an ape, kept on a golden chain by Venice. To refuse would bring shame on Illyria, he said, I had to go with them. It was my duty. Malvolio took care to let me know that he held you captive in Venice and you would suffer if I ran away. All the time I was in an agony of fear for you, but what could I do?'

'Malvolio is subtle and cruel.' Violetta's anger dissolved as she watched the distress move across Stephano's face. He was as helpless as her. 'He takes care to learn the secret levers of guilt and fear, the better to inflict pain and torture.'

Stephano shook his head. He refused to be comforted.

'I should have acted then,' he said at last. 'I should have saved you when Malvolio and my father stood deciding your fate between them, gloating over it. I should have done something. To allow such a thing to happen and do nothing –'

'What could you do?' Violetta put her fingers gently on his lips to stop his words. 'You were just a boy.'

Stephano shook his head. 'I was old enough.'

'We were little more than children. What can children do in the face of men's might and malice? We could do nothing then.'

Stephano hailed a wherry to take her back to the Hollander. He helped her into the boat and the two boys sat opposite her, close and easy with each other. They had belonged to different houses in Illyria, brought up to be enemies, but they had become friends there and they were friends now. This was the way to defeat evil and tyranny. Violetta thought. Illyria's future, if her poor country *had* a future, relied on amity, not enmity.

'There is something else,' Stephano said, he looked away, hardly knowing how to tell her. Best to say it straight out. 'Malvolio has stolen the Holy Relic, the Magi's Cup, Illyria's greatest treasure. We all saw him take it. We thought it was destined for San Marco in Venice, or for Rome, but he has it here. He carries it about with him as if it were his own property.'

'I know,' Violetta said. 'Feste and I have followed him. That's why we are here.'

The two boys looked at each other. That was not what they had expected to hear.

Violetta began to tell them about Master Shakespeare, her plan to get it back.

'It will not work,' Guido said. 'Malvolio has taken over one wing of the Ambassador's residence as his own. It has a separate entrance from the rest of the house. He has a private chapel there. That's where he keeps the relic. It's in a strong box that needs four men to lift it, and the lock on it would defy even Feste. Besides that, he has Jesuits about him. Young warrior priests who see it as their duty to die for their faith. You'd never get near it.'

'What about you . . . ?' Violetta began.

Guido shook his head. 'We wouldn't either. There might be another way. We will think on it. See how things lie.'

'Or else we could just leave.' Stephano had been staring out at the passing craft, boats large and small going up and down the river. 'Direct the wherryman to take us to Greenwich, take ship from there. Go anywhere. To France. To Italy. To Guido's father's court in Pavia.' He looked at Violetta. 'At least we would be together.'

'No.' Violetta stared down at the water. 'I will not go without the relic and I can't go without Feste.'

'We could get him from the Globe. He's likely not left yet . . .'

Violetta shook her head. They both knew what he wanted was impossible.

'Malvolio keeps things close and secret.' Guido looked across at Violetta. 'As does His Excellency. There is a reception tonight. Afterwards there will be a private meeting – certain lords and gentlemen invited to His Excellency's cabinet. We'll see what we can find out.'

They were approaching the Paris Garden Stairs. Stephano jumped out to help her up to the dock.

'When will I see you again?' Violetta asked. To find him against all odds, only to lose him so soon, was a cruelty. She was half minded to go back to his plan, to return to the boat and direct the wherrymen down the river.

'I'll find you. Don't worry. If not at the place you stay, then at the playhouse. We are often there. His Excellency enjoys it hugely. I will see you again. Soon.' He took her in his arms and smiled down at her. 'Nothing can come between us – now that we have found each other.'

He kissed her and Violetta felt her emotions tip and tilt. When they settled, the world was different. She realised that her feelings were no longer those of a child for her playfellow, no matter how fond they had been of one another, or the swooning fancies of a young girl. What she felt now were the altogether more powerful stirrings of a woman for the man she would marry. It was their destiny to be together.

Stephano ordered the wherrymen to take them across to the Temple Stairs, and Violetta turned away from the river, wishing, once again, that he had taken her with him. But that could not be. They could not run away together into some unknown future. That was not their destiny. Sebastian was now calling himself Duke of Illyria and Stephano was his son. She was no one. But the time would come. Meanwhile, he could help her. With Guido. They could do it together. They came and went as they pleased. Stephano had the ear of the Venetian Ambassador, was highly placed in his court. They would find a way to regain the relic. Together they would return it to its rightful place and Illyria would be a sovereign state again. She would marry Stephano and they would rule as lord and lady. All would be restored.

Violetta let her hopes grow, just a little. She would no longer need help from Master Shakespeare, but Feste would still act the clown's part in the play. Illyrians kept their promises. Besides, that is what Feste wanted and she would not deny him. The stage at the Globe was better than a street corner.

She wondered where Feste was now. Getting drunk with the rest of the cast. He deserved it. They had fulfilled their side of a one-sided bargain, she thought as she walked up by the side of the Falcon inn. Feste could get as drunk as he liked.

'Can't leave you, can I?' Suddenly Feste was there beside her. 'There's me, thinking you're safe in the gallery, and what's the next thing I know? You're rowing down the river with a pair of handsome young blades, as bold as you like.'

Violetta stopped in astonishment. It was as if she had conjured him.

'Don't look so surprised. I know everything, madonna.' Feste tapped his nose. 'I saw them coming in. Made enough disturbance. There was gossip backstage about their party. The Venetian Ambassador. Actors always know who's in of any consequence. Guido and Stephano, I thought. Not many in London wear a yataghan sword. When I have time to look up at the end, they are nowhere to be seen. Neither are you. Master Shakespeare says he's seen you with two young fellows, walking down to the river. So that's where I go.'

Violetta laughed. Feste's face creased into a smile.

'Haven't seen you laughing for a while,' he said. 'Are you going to tell me about your young lordling? He seems to have landed on his feet.'

'He's in the service of the Ambassador. Malvolio found him and . . .' She stopped. Feste wasn't listening. He was looking past her, over to the Hollander. 'What is it?'

'Hold on.' Feste took her arm. 'Hold up. Something's wrong. Look there!' Feste pulled her down behind a crumbling wall that enclosed what had once been an orchard. A few fruit trees, just coming into leaf and flower, struggled out of a tangled mass of bramble and briar. 'To talk of the devil is to conjure him. And look who's with him? I haven't seen him for many a year.'

Two men were coming along the road from the Hollander, going towards the river. They were both dressed in black. One tall, and so thin that his scrawny shanks hardly filled his hose. His knees showed like knots in string. The other man was bulkier, with a black cloak wrapped about him and carrying a portmanteau. He walked with a stiff-legged gait that they both knew. It was Malvolio.

'The other is Sir Andrew Agnew,' Feste whispered. 'I'd know those legs anywhere.' He motioned for her to keep down. 'I'm going to take a little look.'

He swung himself into a tall pear tree and climbed, hardly stirring the branches, as nimble as a cat.

The two men seemed safely on their way to the river when Sir Andrew turned back. He sniffed the air, as if he could smell their presence. His pale eyes narrowed and his wide nostrils flared; his thin lips drew back, twitching his wispy grey mustachios, his little bristly beard jutting as he looked from one place to another like some bony-browed hound.

The branches above Violetta quivered slightly. A single petal of pear blossom drifted down, landing like a snowflake on her hand. The covering was sparse. The leaves were not fully out yet. Violetta prayed that Sir Andrew wouldn't look up.

Sir Andrew whistled. Two men joined him, clubs swinging from their wrists. They both wore loose trousers and greasy sleeveless jerkins. One wore a close-fitting leather cap.

'In there.' Sir Andrew indicated with a flick of a bony finger, pointing to the garden where Violetta was hiding.

She wriggled deeper into the brambles as the men began thrashing about in the undergrowth. She found a narrow tunnel that reeked of fox and lay still as a vixen as a club landed one side of her, then the other. The blows were hard enough to smash her skull.

Eventually the brambles got the better of them.

'There's nothing there, master! They're at the

playhouse, like I told you!'

'The play ended a good hour ago.' Sir Andrew's high-pitched voice was very near, as though he was peering over the wall. 'I thought I saw them, coming up from the river . . .'

He had sharp eyes. Violetta cowered in her den, thinking that he would send the men back again, but eventually she heard their footsteps walk away, fading towards the river. When she was sure that they had gone, she crawled out from her hiding place to find Feste waiting for her.

'You look a sight!' he said.

Her dress was torn; she was covered in scratches. He picked a shrivelled leaf from her hair.

'How did they not see you?' she asked as she tried to tidy herself.

'They didn't look up,' he said simply. 'People rarely do. Leave the preening till later.' He took her arm. 'We'd better see what's happened at the Hollander.'

◆►◄◄◆

Maria was sitting on an upturned bucket. Her little stool was smashed to splinters. It looked as though the beasts from the bear garden had been let loose on the place: boxes overturned, their contents emptied, paper and books ripped up, Maria's few things strewn about the room, torn and defiled. They did not need to ask who had done it.

Violetta pushed the door to Toby's room. She did not have to ask about him either. She knew he was dead before she even entered the room. She could tell by Maria's stricken face.

He lay covered, his chin bound up with a strip of

cloth. His head had sunk to one side; already the blood was draining down, staining his cheek the colour of claret. Feste opened one of the old man's eyes, the white was red and bloodshot. He lifted the covers. His hands were gripped like claws.

Feste stood for the moment at the foot of the bed, head bowed. He made the sign of benediction with two fingers and went out.

Maria looked up at him, 'He didn't die natural. He was smothered.' Her hand fluttered to her mouth. 'I've seen it before in infants and children, not so very different.'

'Why kill a dying man?' Violetta asked.

Maria shook her head. 'Because they could. Who knows why?'

Feste sat next to Maria and took her hand in his. 'Tell us what happened.'

'Sir Andrew came with a priest for Toby. I said, "No need, master, I think he's rallying." I didn't want them anywhere near him. He just ignored me and barged straight in here. The one he had with him was all muffled up in a long black cloak. I didn't know who he was at first. He was different from the usual, more richly dressed. His cloak was good thick wool, his hose silk. They are usually young, plainly dressed, with a look about them as though their eyes are not on this world but the next. He put down his bag and undid his cloak. "Don't you know me, Maria?" he said. There was a smile on his face – you know that ghastly smile of his? And his eyes were all gloat. He'd waited a long time for this. He sent me out for Toby to make his peace with God. For him to send him to the Devil, more like. I had no choice but to go. When I came back, Toby was dead. His eyes red and bulging;

his mouth gaping like a fish. He died fighting. No matter how near death we might be, we struggle to prevent our last breath from being taken from us. They didn't absolve him!' Her hand went to her mouth again. 'He died with his sins still upon him . . .'

'Hush now!' Feste put his arm round her as she began to sob into his shoulder. 'God himself will forgive him. There's not overmuch laughter in Heaven, I'll warrant. His presence will be a welcome addition. Toby was a good man.'

'They know you are here,' Maria said when she had stopped crying. 'They questioned me and threatened, said there was no point in denying it, they'd had men watching. After they'd finished –' her eyes strayed to the room where Toby lay dead – 'they brought in a pair of ruffians who tore the place apart. I don't know what they were looking for. There's nothing here, is there?' She twisted her handkerchief round and round between her hands. 'We have to get you away. If they can kill my Toby . . .' She looked at Violetta as if seeing her for the first time since they came in, noticing her torn dress, the scratches on her. 'Oh, my Lord, what's happened to you?'

'It's nothing, Maria. I fell into some brambles trying to avoid a cart, that's all.'

There was a knock at the door.

'That'll be Doctor Forman,' Maria stood up, smoothing her apron. 'I sent Johane to fetch him. I didn't know what else to do.'

The doctor went in to Sir Toby.

When he came out his face was grave. 'That's no natural death,' he said.

'Should tell the constable,' Johane's deep voice

rumbled.

'The constable already knows – of the death. Not the cause of it.' Forman sighed. 'It has been reported as plague. There have been other deaths, I believe?'

The drunk stretched out on the table had not got up again.

'Plague? First I've heard of it.' Johane sniffed. 'That 'un died o' drink and being poor.'

'No matter. The constable is on his way here now. He is about to shut this house.' He turned to Maria, Feste and Violetta. 'You must leave or you will be shut up in here for forty days.'

'But where will we go?' Maria's eyes were frantic. 'What shall we do? What will happen to Toby? He'll be wanting a Christian burial, not to be tipped in a pit. That's what they do, don't they, if they think it's plague?'

Forman tugged at the sides of his long cap, something he did when he was thinking. He was a doctor, and whatever his faults and sins, and they were many, he did not believe that anyone had the right to take a man's life from him, even at the last. And who had reported this as plague? Toby was his patient; this was his parish. No doubt money had changed hands, influence brought to bear. He did not like that either. He made up his mind quickly. Aside from all those considerations, the girl was pretty, the clown amusing and Mistress Maria might need comforting, once she got over her grief.

'We must get Sir Toby out of here,' he said. 'Get some men,' he ordered Johane. 'Take him to my house in Lambeth.' He turned to Maria and Violetta. 'You can stay with me, and you, Feste. Gather your things together. There can be no delay. We must remove immediately.'

12

'God give them wisdom that have it'

The next day Will arrived at the Globe to find the place in an uproar. Half the cast for the afternoon's performance were missing, and those who had managed to drag themselves in had thick heads from the night before. Tempers were short, and Burbage, ever of a choleric disposition, was nearing apoplexy.

The cast assembled as the morning progressed and by the approach of noon they were all there. Except Feste.

'No clown, then?' Burbage growled, his temper seething like some foul brew. 'I blame you for this, Shakespeare, I really do. What were you thinking, hiring someone off the street? Bringing the wretch here, like some performing cur, when you know nothing about him. I could have *told* you this would happen. And they'll be baying for him this afternoon. If he doesn't show, they'll tear the playhouse down. Well, I'm not going crawling to Moston at the Rose. I'd rather they ripped the place up by the root. You'd better pray he turns up, Shakespeare, because they can start with you . . .'

Will was seated at a rickety table making last-minute changes and did not bother to look up from his script. Like most actors, Burbage was all blow and he relished a good row. He could carry on in a similar vein for hours. It was his way of warming his voice for the afternoon's performance; he was probably sneaking a look round now, assessing how well he was going down. The clown would turn up any minute. Will had no doubt.

As the time ticked on past noon, even Will felt the sweat prick his armpits. He was cutting it close now.

He slid out from behind his table.

'I'll go in search of him,' he said as he gathered up the sheaf of papers to be posted.

'You'd better find him,' Burbage shouted after him, 'or neither of you need bother coming back!'

◆➤❈◄◆

The Hollander was shut up. Boards crudely nailed over the door and the downstairs windows. There was a black cross daubed on the lintel and a watchman stationed outside. Will stepped back from the building.

'What's happened here?' he asked the watchman.

'Plague.'

'Plague?' Will frowned. 'I didn't know there was plague south of the river.'

'Might be smallpox,' the watchman said after some thought. 'Someone dead of summat nasty. That's all I know. Should have closed this place a long time ago.'

'Where are the people who were staying here?'

'Still inside.' The man looked up at the building. 'Supposed to be. I ain't seen no sign of 'em, but be that as it may –' he slanted his pike – 'while I'm here, nobody goes in or out.'

He stood square in front of the door. He was not about to let Will into the building or tell him any more. There was nobody around to ask. The few other buildings were little more than hovels and looked as derelict as the Hollander in the bleak morning light. The rutted road led out to fields and countryside or up to the river. It was as if they had all disappeared into thin air. What had become of them? What would become of them now? Forman might know something. If there had been sickness, he would surely have been informed. He could even know what had happened to them. Will would seek him out, but there was no time for that now. He would have to go back without the clown. What was he going to tell Burbage?

Will looked up to the sun over the river. It was well past noon now. He had to get back. He went up to the Paris Garden Stairs and walked to the playhouse along the Thames. Usually he liked being by the water; he liked to see the traffic of different craft moving up and down the busy river and to watch the wherrymen and hear their talk. They had the foulest mouths in England and the inventiveness of their insults spilled into a prurient poetry, a thing to be admired.

Today he had no time to linger and see what was being unloaded at Molestrand Dock, or listen to the wherrymen waiting at Falcon Stairs. He hurried along to Bankside with scarcely a glance at the milky brown flow of the great river. In his mind he was already at the Globe, being buffeted by the full force of Burbage's fury for returning without the clown. His mouth moved as he muttered Touchstone's opening lines. The play had to go on, and Burbage would punish him by making him play the part.

He arrived pale and sweating, the flag flapping

above him, the trumpets already sounding. He forced his way though the crush of playgoers clustered round the entrance and ducked into the playhouse. He looked around warily, but nothing seemed particularly amiss; the place was in no more of an uproar than usual.

'Ah, there you are!'

Will braced himself as Burbage came bustling out of the tiring room, already in the Duke's costume.

'Where have you been? Did you find him? What took you so long?' Will opened his mouth to speak and then closed it. Burbage always asked too many questions and never waited for an answer. 'Well, no matter. Your fellow is out of a job. Armin's back. Came in just after you left. News that another was about to take his place stopped his bowels.'

He would not have to play the part after all. Robert Armin, their usual clown, was there in his motley, chatting to one of the orange sellers. The little man waved his folly stick at Will and winked as he bit into the orange he had begged from the girl. He might be small, but he had a way with women.

Will's delight was short-lived. The doors were opening, the crowd streaming in; the afternoon's performance would soon begin. Burbage had to go off to finish getting ready for his part, but just before he did he reached into his doublet and took out a letter.

'This came for you.' He hefted it in his hand. 'Looks official.'

Will took it from him, relief replaced by sudden foreboding. He stared at his name written in secretary hand, felt the quality of the paper. He turned it over carefully, as if it might explode. It was closed with a blob of black wax, marked with a very big seal. Burbage looked over his shoulder, curious to know what such a missive might contain, while Will eased a knife blade under the wax and opened the folds.

It was worse than he could have imagined. Will swallowed. The paper shook slightly as he conned more slowly, disbelieving his first quick reading. His eyes rested on the signature. The letter was from Secretary Cecil: Sir Robert invited him to an audience at his earliest convenience.

At the sight of that name, even Burbage paled.

'God's blood, Will! What could he want with you?' The actor's sonorous voice was soft now, the enquiry tinged with fear.

Will shrugged. He had no idea.

'What have we done now?' Burbage tugged at his beard. 'I hope to God he's not going to shut us down. From frying pan to fire, eh? You'd better get over there and find out what this is about. Now, I've got a part to play.'

Burbage went back to the tiring room. Will waited for the crowd to thin to latecomers and slipped out of the theatre. He made his way back to the river at Bankside to find a wherryman who would take him over the river to Whitehall.

❦

Will had been here before and had marvelled at the portraits and paintings, the rich tapestries and strange objects collected from everywhere, but this time he had no eyes for the wonders afforded by the great Palace of Whitehall. He stated his business and was conducted through a series of galleries, past portraits of kings and queens, noble lords and great statesmen. Among these, he recognised Lord Burghley, Sir Robert Cecil's father and Secretary before him. The son had taken over his office on his death and since the fall of the Earl of Essex had become the most powerful man in the land.

Will broke out sweating. He did not like to be close to great men. They were akin to the gods of old, liable to scorch any who came within their compass. What could Sir Robert want with him? Among his many other duties, the Secretary was responsible for keeping the Queen's Realm safe from conspiracy and those who would harm Her Majesty. His spies and intelligencers were everywhere; city and country swarmed with his agents and pursuivants, hunting down Catholic priests and nosing out recusants. It did not do to be involved on either side.

Will took care not to fall under any suspicion. He tried to keep out of the way of the law, going to church as often as was necessary and combing contention out of his plays. This was not always possible, but he did his best not to invite trouble. He did not want to end up like Kit Marlowe, stabbed through the eye in some room in Deptford. Kit had been reckless in written word and spoken – some of his plays were still under prohibition – but that was not what had brought his life to an end. Kit had been on some secret service for Her Majesty and had been murdered by one of his fellow spies, his death very likely ordered by the man Will was about to see.

They were nearing the Privy Council Chamber and the Queen's private quarters; beyond lay the Privy Chamber and the Presence Chamber. The Queen was not in residence, and she had taken her court and Council with her, but the corridors were still thick with those who had business with the Secretary or one of the other Officers of State. Will was taken through the knots of anxious men, the sweat beading on his own brow and prickling his beard.

The servant led him away from the more public areas, down a stone corridor. He was passed on to a dark-robed clerk, who in turn conducted him into an antechamber, where he was told to wait. The windows were too high to see outside, so he paced about until he was called. A bell tinkled and the clerk motioned him forward.

'Secretary Cecil will see you now.'

Will followed the clerk into a wood-panelled room. He straightened his jerkin and hoped his cuffs were clean. Secretary Cecil sat behind a wide desk piled high with bundles of papers. The clerk withdrew and Cecil did not look up from writing notes on the pages he was reading. Will thought it best to wait to be noticed.

The Secretary's delicate hands were heavy with jewelled rings. He wore a finely worked cambric ruff about his neck and a rich, fur-lined robe pulled about him as if he felt the cold. The robe bunched at the left shoulder, which was higher than the other, showing that he was hunchbacked. Some thought this the sign of an ill nature, the mark of the Devil. Will did not think that, but he was uncomfortably aware of the comparisons he had made between a twisted back and a twisted character in his play about the crookback Richard III.

'Ah, Master Shakespeare.' Sir Robert rose, hitching

the robe on his left shoulder, as if conscious of Will's scrutiny. 'Thank you for coming to see me.'

'My lord.' Will bowed very low and said nothing more, judging it prudent to wait and see what Sir Robert Cecil might want with him.

The Queen's Secretary was near dwarfish in stature, his head big on his narrow, uneven shoulders. It was easy to see why the Queen called him 'my imp' and 'my pygmy', but though he was small in size, an aura of power hung about him as close as his fur-lined mantle. Only a queen would dare to take such liberties. He was a man in his middle years, the grey beginning to streak the tawny brown of his formal, square-cut beard and to show where his reddish hair swept back from his high forehead. The excessive work and strain of his high office showed in the tight set of his mouth and the tiny creases of tiredness that had formed like webs round his large grey-green eyes. His forehead was heavily lined, and blue veins snaked beneath the papery, oat-pale skin at his temples. His gaze was calm, thoughtful, slightly amused, his eyes like windows into a subtle mind that retained much and missed nothing.

'How do you do?' he asked.

'Well, my lord,' Will replied. 'And you?'

'Well enough.' He subsided into his seat, as if standing too long was uncomfortable for him. Will remained standing. 'I expect you want to know why you have been summoned.'

Will nodded.

'Very well, I will not preamble.' Cecil steepled his slender fingers. A diamond sparked fire and the large ruby on his right hand gleamed like a heavy drop of blood. 'It has come to my notice that you have recently made the acquaintance of a dangerous pair of strangers.'

This was not what Will had been expecting. He searched his mind briefly and found the strangers there. How did Cecil know about them? What did it matter? He was rumoured to know everything. Perhaps what they said was true.

'Yes, my lord,' he answered. 'And then again, no.'

'I am aware of your work,' Cecil sighed, 'your skill at smithing words. I have seen many of your plays. You are quite a favourite of Her Majesty's and I hope to see more.' He leaned forward, knotting his fingers more tightly together. 'But do not riddle with me, sirrah. It is not long since one of your company was here making full and grovelling apology for that disgraceful performance by *your* company of *your* play Richard II the very day before the Earl of Essex's ill-starred rebellion.' His voice became quieter as the threat in it grew. 'Did you think us such fools that we would not note that the play's meat contains the deposition of a king?'

Shakespeare opened his mouth to defend his company. They had been *told* to put on the performance. Actors do not argue with lords and earls. But he judged it best to keep silent. This would not be a good time to speak. He kept his eyes fixed on Saxton's map of the counties of England and Wales that hung above the fireplace, trying to make out Warwickshire. It looked like Old Whittington, the Shottery shepherd, with craggy brows, a big hook of a nose, his chin tucked into his chest against the wind.

'You are the Lord Chamberlain's Men, are you not?'

Cecil demanded to know. Will assumed he did not require an answer. 'One word from me, Master Shakespeare, and his patronage is withdrawn. Another to the Master of the Revels, and you lose your licence. Your company are reduced to strolling players, subject to arrest at the first squeak of a performance. I can have you closed down. I can have *all* of you closed down. I can invoke the Bills of Mortality. There is always plague somewhere in the city, or 'prentices marching and making a riot. I do not even need *that* as an excuse.' He leaned forward, chin resting on his interlaced fingers. 'I can have the playhouses plucked down around your very ears.'

Will knew all this to be true and was mindful of the need to tread carefully. Cecil was setting out the rules of play, making sure Will knew he held all the high cards. In his mind he saw the Fool: the card that can neither lose nor win.

'Forgive me, my lord,' he said. 'I am aware what you can do to us, to me, to my company. I merely meant by my answer that, yes, these two strangers are of my acquaintance, but I cannot see how a girl and a Fool could be a danger or be of any interest to you.'

'Strangers are always of interest.' Cecil leaned back against the red leather padding of his chair. 'And I did not say that these two were of danger to us necessarily. But they may well be *seen* to be a danger by others and therefore a danger to themselves. I do not want foreign quarrels and broils brought to our shores. We have enough of our own. I want to know exactly what they are doing here. I have to decide whether they are innocent and in need of protection, or if they are here for a more sinister purpose. I could take them in and put them to the rack,' he added with a casual wave of his small jewelled hand, 'but that is not how I do things and, besides, information received that way is often poor quality.'

'I'll find out what I can.'

Will bowed low. In his mind he saw Violetta and Feste tortured and broken. He could not risk that. He would keep what he knew to himself for a while yet. Just in case something he said led Cecil to change his mind about employing the rack.

'Good man.' Cecil was already sifting at the papers before him. 'Report here to me tomorrow at three in the afternoon.'

'But that is when . . .' the play begins, Will was going to say, but did not finish the sentence. Cecil knew that. It was best not to argue with the highest in the land. 'Very well, my lord.'

'If you fulfil this task to my satisfaction, then your company will be allowed to continue. You might even find greater honours bestowed upon you. Who knows?' Cecil did not look up. 'You will be serving Her Majesty in this. I'm sure that the Lord Chamberlain's Men can do without you for one performance.'

He reached for the bell on his desk. Will was dismissed.

'I'll do everything in my power, my lord,' Will bowed again as he left Cecil's presence. *But first I have to find out where they are.*

Will boarded a wherry at Whitehall Stairs. Simon Forman might well know where they were, and the doctor also knew about Cecil's world of intelligencers and spies. It was a sphere that Will had taken care to avoid, especially after what happened to Kit Marlowe. There was no avoiding it now, and Simon was his only hope. Forman had a shrewd mind; his knowledge was wide, as was his social acquaintance. He had known Marlowe well. They had glided in and out of many different circles. They had mixed with dukes and earls as members of the atheistic cabal who had clustered round Raleigh and Northumberland, the Wizard Earl. The group had pursued the esoteric arts; there had been whispers of worse than atheism, if worse there could be. Will had never cared to know too much about the dark and arcane secrets they discussed. He could not afford to be so dainty now. The girl had hinted at such, when she talked about her father and that Dr Grimaldi. He had to know in which directions this thing ran. He needed Forman's knowledge, but the doctor was unlikely to be at his house at this time of day. Will directed the wherrymen to take him to Billingsgate.

13

'The melancholy god protect thee'

Forman was in his consulting room dispensing physic and advice. A veiled woman left as Will entered. Wealthy, judging by her gloves and her clothes, perhaps even titled.

'Came to me with pains in her head, pains in her stomach, but what she really wants to know is whether her husband is being unfaithful,' Forman remarked. 'They come with one thing, but want to know something other. The secret is to know what they are really about.' He fixed Will with his hot brown eyes. 'So what brings you here?'

'I went to the Hollander today, to fetch Feste the clown, and found the place shut down. I need to find him and the girl. It's an urgent matter. Do you know where they are?'

'I do. They are safe at my house in Lambeth. Sir Toby's in the ice house. Funeral's tomorrow.'

'The old man's dead?'

'Yes. Yesterday. Bad business, Shakespeare. He didn't die naturally.'

'Murdered? But why kill a dying man? To ease his passing?'

'It happens –' Forman shrugged – 'but not, I think, in this case. I saw it in his forecast. That's the odd thing . . .'

'Then why?'

'An act of malice. Pure and simple. I have it from the girl.'

'Malice?' Will stared at him. 'It must run deep to do that.' He frowned. This was worsening by the minute. He heard Cecil's quiet voice again: *I do not want foreign quarrels and broils brought to our shores . . .*

'I have a feeling it does.' Simon sat forward in his chair, chin resting on his folded hands. 'Those two bring their quarrels with them. Why do you need them so urgently? I heard Armin's back, so it can't be the need of a clown.'

'No, it's something else. I have just come from Whitehall, from an interview with Robert Cecil.'

'Cecil, eh? You are moving in high circles,' Forman pulled at the flaps of his doctor's cap. 'I treat his niece, you know. Lady Norris –'

'It wasn't a social visit,' Will said, cutting short Forman's name-dropping. He described his recent interview with Sir Robert: the Secretary's interest in Violetta and Feste. He wandered the room while he talked, absently examining the various instruments, medical and astrological, that were lying about, noticing the patterns on the painted pottery vessels ranged along the shelves. 'How could he know?' Will turned back from the cabinets to face Forman. 'What can he want with them, Simon? What could his interest possibly be?'

Forman did not answer straight away. His already furrowed forehead set into even more of a frown as he squinted at the charts before him on the desk.

'Riche could have told him. He's one of Cecil's spies. And those two are not exactly unknown. I told you about Doctor Grimaldi. In certain circles, Illyria has gained a notoriety. They say the Duke, her father, overreached himself. Dabbled too deeply in the dark arts. Unleashed forces he couldn't control. Could be to do with that.'

'I don't think it has to do with anything supernatural.' Will picked up an astrolabe, turning it round in his hands. 'It has to do with the collapse of the state. That's why the girl's here. Everything stems from it.'

'Leave that alone.' Forman reached across the desk to take the instrument off him. 'It is very delicate and carefully adjusted to the exact date and time of birth of my next client. And don't touch that!'

Will was now toying with a tiny agate pestle and mortar instead.

'Why not? It is exquisite.' He held it up, admiring the way the light struck through the semi-translucent green-and-red stone.

'Because I use it for grinding poison. Don't lick your fingers. Sit down. Stop roaming about.'

Will set the little pestle and mortar back in its place and sat down opposite Forman.

'Now, back to the matter in hand.' Simon leaned forward and picked up the compass he used for measuring charts. 'Perhaps Cecil doesn't know any more than we do. Perhaps he just *suspects*. What happens in one place in the world can have unseen effects elsewhere.' He began describing circles. 'Cecil collects information from every country and every city. He has intelligencers everywhere.' Forman looked up at Will and gave a wheezing laugh. 'It looks like he's just recruited you.' He thought for a moment, his face serious again. 'Perhaps it is not what those two *know*, as such, which makes them of interest to him.

It might be –'

'Who they are.' Will finished his sentence for him.

'Precisely.' Forman smiled. 'She's not just anyone, is she? She's a duke's daughter. Never mind what's happened to her. There could be reasons we are not privy to that make her important.'

There could be. There could well be. Will had been right to come to Forman.

'But why choose me?'

'You already know them.' Forman spread his hands. 'You have their trust. She's a fetching young thing.' His reddish brown eyes gleamed. 'Who would not want to help her?'

'She's also very young,' Will said. He did not want the conversation going down that track. 'I must see her. I have to talk to her.' He stood up. 'Tell her to come to the Anchor this evening. I'll be there after the play.'

'Wait.' Forman put up his hand. 'If I help you, I want something in return.'

Will frowned. This was unexpected.

'I have some money,' he said. 'I can pay you, if that is what you mean.'

'It is not what I mean.' Forman walked the compass across his desk.

'What then?'

'You must allow me to cast your chart.'

Will hesitated. 'I've told you before, I have no interest in astrology. I do not want to know what the stars hold for me.'

Forman smiled. 'That is my condition.'

'Oh, very well.' Will sighed his impatience. 'I cannot think why. I come from the country. I am a poet and an actor – one of many. What can the future hold for me that could possibly be of interest or note?'

'Who knows?' Forman's smile widened. 'That is the point, surely? Anyway, that is my condition.'

Seek not to know . . . Will's knowledge of the dark arts was not inconsiderable. For a while he had shared a house with a Master Wilhelm Koenig, late of Prague and Bingen, an old alchemist who had been impressed by the young poet's quickness of mind and had offered to take him on as 'prentice. Will had declined the offer, once he'd found out from the old man all that he wanted to know. To Will, this book magic, that so fascinated Master Wilhelm, Forman, Dee and the others, was dry stuff compared to the wild magic he knew from home: like a dusty old cabinet, sprung at the joints, compared to living willow.

'Come on, man,' Forman prompted. 'What harm can it do?'

'None, I suppose.'

'Splendid!' Forman gave him a gap-toothed grin. 'I will send a messenger to Lambeth right away. First, a few questions.' He pulled a scroll of paper to him and dipped the nib of his pen. 'When were you born?'

'You are not going to do it now?'

'No. I'll take a note or two, that's all. When were you born?'

'April.'

'What day in April?'

'That's the difficulty – I'm not certain.'

'Not certain?' Forman put down his quill. 'How so?'

'I was born betwixt one day and the next, so nobody could quite decide which was right.'

'A chime child! Born within the sound of midnight's bells.'

'It could have been one side or t'other,' Will protested. 'It was a hard labour. No one was paying that much attention.'

'That's by the by.' Forman waved aside his objections and picked up his pen again. 'A chime child is special. Able to see ghosts and fairies. Can you see them, I wonder.' He looked at Will, his eyes full of questions. 'Which days?'

'Twenty-second and twenty-third.'

'But that was yesterday!'

'Or the day before.'

'What year?'

'1564.'

'Place?'

'Stratford-on-Avon.' Will sighed. 'You know that!'

'People lie. You'd be surprised.' Forman put down his pen and dusted sand over his notes. 'Thank you, Will. That is all I need to know.'

❧❧❧

'You wanted to see me, Master Shakespeare.' She appeared at dusk, just as the setting sun was colouring the Thames, turning the water to blood. She had the clown with her.

'Aye.' Will had taken a private room in the inn so they might talk without being overheard. 'Would you like something to eat? Drink?'

She shook her head.

'Thank you, sir.' Feste helped himself to wine. 'I'll have a little something.'

'Simon Forman has told me what happened at the Hollander, and about Sir Toby.'

'Yes, the doctor has been kind,' she said. 'I do not

know what we would have done without him.'

'He's a good man.'

Violetta looked at him. 'You did not ask me here to talk about Doctor Forman.'

'No . . .'

Will cleared his throat and took a drink as he wondered where to start. She seemed to have changed in the short while since he last saw her. She looked older, and even more lovely: her skin as pale as ivory; her dark hair glossy as a raven's wing. He shook his head slightly and looked away from her enquiring violet eyes.

Something about him has changed, she thought. Something has happened to make him afraid.

'You have come to the attention of someone very powerful,' he said quietly. 'It appears that you are of interest to him. You could even be in some danger.'

Violetta laughed. The clown did too.

'We know that, master,' he said. 'Someone wants us dead. Same villains who killed Sir Toby.'

'Malvolio knows we are here,' Violetta said. 'He'd have killed us yesterday, if he could.'

'And you are not afraid?' Will frowned. Their laughter might show a genuine lack of concern, or could be brittle bravado, a kind of recklessness. Either one could be dangerous now.

'Of him? No.' Violetta gazed out of the window, her eyes following the motion of some craft across the brightened water. 'Hatred is not the same as fear.' She looked back at him. 'I see a change in you. What's happened?'

'This afternoon I was summoned to appear before Sir Robert Cecil,' Will said. 'Lord Secretary Cecil, the

Queen's First Minister. He is the man I was talking about, not your Malvolio. He is the most powerful man in the land. He can have us all imprisoned, tortured, tried for treason, hanged and quartered. At the very least, he can close the theatres. He can do anything he likes. You might not be afraid –' he looked at her, his brown eyes no longer mild – 'but I am.'

'I didn't want to bring trouble upon you.' Violetta looked stricken.

Will sighed. 'It seems you already have.'

'We'll go.' She stood up. 'We'll leave you. You will never see us again.'

'Leaving will not help matters. Where would you go? Into what danger?'

Will tried to curb his impatience. Despite his anger, he did care about her, and it had nothing to do with her beauty, whatever Forman might think. Will was a father, more absent than present. This girl was of an age with his daughters. They were safe in Stratford, and he prayed they stayed that way, while she was alone and set about with dangers that grew with every day. If he didn't help her, who would? He had to do what he could. He'd been willing to act out of genuine concern, but since Cecil's intervention he really had no choice.

'It appears that we are now in this together,' he said after a while. 'If I am to help you, if we are to help each other, I must know everything so I can consider what to do.'

'Very well.' Violetta sat down again. 'I will tell you the rest of my story, Master Shakespeare. I will tell it to the point that brings us to here.'

14

'I'll be revenged on the whole pack of you!'

VIOLETTA

I was taken from Illyria, loaded like a slave on to a galley that flew the winged lion of Venice. The galley rode the waves in the outer harbour. Broken spars and bloated corpses, wreckage left from the recent sea battle, rolled in the waves. Smoke from my city brought the bitter, choking stench of defeat on the freshening wind. I didn't want to look, but I couldn't help gazing up at the broken towers, the breached and blackened walls. As I did so, a woman reached for the amulet that I wore round my neck and tore it from me. I thought she would rob me, but all she said was, 'They will take that from you, madonna. Keep it safe. Hide it in your clothes.'

I thought that I would be herded below with the others, but I was taken aft and locked into a small cabin. The galley rose and fell, the banks of long oars clicking together. Malvolio kept the captain waiting. I heard him complaining that we were missing the tide. Eventually he arrived, along with Lady Francesca and crates of baggage. He likes to keep people waiting. He likes to make them think that he's an important man.

The oars fell into the water and the ship began to move, slowly at first, then faster, rocking and bucking as we hit open water. I watched from my tiny porthole as the ship left the harbour. This was the last of Illyria.

I did not know if I would ever see my homeland again.

At first we hugged the coast. Waves crashed against the rocks at the base of the great cliffs that reared above us. Then the cliffs gave way to steep hillsides patched with forest trees and marked with the black strokes of single cypresses. In between them lay little squares of green, scraps of cultivation. The tang of burning came on the salty wind. The destruction had spread out from the city into the country around. Plumes of smoke rose from the scattered villages and homesteads and drifted down towards the sea, and I wondered who would be left to tend the fields and man the fishing boats pulled up in the little bays.

The ship began to steer away from the coast and out through the offshore islands. The channels here are treacherous with strong, contrary currents and full of hidden rocks and reefs. Depths were sounded and directions shouted. The voice issuing the commands had a local accent. The pilot was native to Illyria. I turned away as the islands slid slowly by, turned ghostly by the shrouding mist of evening. How many had been in the pay of Venice? I thought on how deeply we had been betrayed.

❖❖❖

On the evening of the second day I was summoned from my tiny berth and emerged on to the deck. We were out of sight of land. The sleek vessel hissed through the oily swell, propelled by a light wind that ruffled the long red pennants flying fore and aft and filled the slanting lanteen sails. I was taken to a much larger cabin, spacious and luxuriously appointed. From the rolled navigational charts and various instruments lying about, I assumed that this belonged to the captain, but it seemed that he had been forced to vacate his quarters to make way for another, who sat waiting for me, a chessboard in front of him, the pieces carved from red and white gold, the board made from black onyx and marble. I recognised the set as belonging to my father.

He smiled, showing large teeth, the long yellow canines gleaming like fangs, and waved a hand, inviting me to sit opposite him.

'What else have you stolen from us?' I asked.

'You should treat me more civilly,' he answered, careful not to let his smile slip.

'Why should I be civil to a thief and a villain?' I asked.

'Your fate is in my hands.'

'I do not care what you do to me.'

The light from the swinging lamp shone on the black silk of his cassock and glinted off the large silver cross that he wore on his chest. Malvolio might have risen to greatness, but I knew him as Lady Olivia's steward. He left her service before I was born, but I had been brought up on tales of his pomposity, his pride, his preening self-love, as bottomless as it was baseless. All this had made him the butt of Feste and the other servants. Why should I respect such a one? He had left the court spraying impotent curses, swearing revenge. They had laughed and then forgotten him. Now here he was: the instrument of our nemesis. His smile said that he had waited a long time for this. Time had brought him what he wanted. He had betrayed us, connived with our enemies who had destroyed my city, killed my father and despoiled our household. He beckoned and another stepped forward out of the shadows.

'You know my companion, the Lady Francesca?'

'Lady,' I said, barely nodding in her direction as she took her place to the side, from where she sat watching us with her colourless, pale-lashed eyes. Whether she was there because she wanted to return to her home city, or because she had cast aside one lover for another, I neither knew nor cared. I stared back at her until she lowered her eyes and commenced stitching at an embroidery frame she had on her lap.

'Do you play?' he asked, indicating the board in front of him.

'Yes.' I nodded. 'But I do not see the point of it.' I stared him in the eye and kept my hands still in my lap. I despised him and was determined to show no fear. 'You have already won.'

'Nevertheless,' he said, pushing one of his pawns forward, 'indulge me. You have nothing better to do.'

I had been taught to play by my father. I frowned, studying the board. Perhaps it would help to pass the time. However uncongenial the company, I did not want to go back to the cramped confines of my cabin. What he said was true: I had nothing better to do. I pushed my pawn forward to counter his move.

⟡

So it began. We played each day, while Lady Francesca sat, never speaking, working on her embroidery. He was good, but I was better, being more daring and impetuous. He was cunning and clever, but less inclined to take risks. I won more games than he did, not that it mattered. We were playing for more than the pieces on the board, but whatever the outcome, I had already lost. The games were a refined kind of cruelty. Sometimes he would let me win deliberately, just to watch and savour my elation, knowing it would soon be dashed.

He toyed with me, as a cat might play with a mouse, and just in the way he conducted the games, so our conversations were likewise barbed, laden with hooks buried in some innocent-seeming remark.

'You have the better of me this time,' he said, when I had beaten him fair and square. 'You have your mother's looks, but your father's brain, I see. I hardly knew her, but she struck me as being a spirited young woman. Witty. Educated. Accomplished. I saw that straight away, for all she was disguised as a man. You are very like her. You should do well in Venice . . .'

The Lady Francesca smiled and nodded her agreement, as if to confirm that this was not a compliment, either to me or my mother. It was a warning. One of the possible fates he had in store for me was that of a courtesan, the mistress of a rich man. He owned me, as he never ceased to remind me, and would dispose of me in the best way he saw fit. He had thought to sell me off as a scullion, relishing the idea of a duke's daughter working in a kitchen, but could see now that would not do. I was too fine for that, he would muse aloud to Lady Francesca as she worked her needle in and drew it out again. How I longed to stab it into her linen-white skin and see the blood bead red like the rosebuds she was stitching. Why throw a diamond away for the price of glass paste? He would say such things to tease and torture me. I tried not to show it. I strove hard to show them nothing, but to be spoken of like that, as though I was a commodity or an animal to be bought and sold, ate into my very soul. His eyes would take on an oily sheen as I stumbled in my game and my concentration wandered to what fate had in store for me, my mood corrupted to self-pity.

'Checkmate, I think.' He would smile and knock over my king. 'That is enough for today.'

With that, I would be taken back to my cabin.

'It does not have to be this way, you know,' he said one day as he set the pieces out for yet another game. 'All you have to do is tell me the whereabouts of the shewstone. Shall we begin? Your move, I think.'

I tried not to react, even though the pawn trembled in my hand.

'Oh, yes, I know all about it. I sent some men to search for it, but they were surprised. Then, when I sent again, I was told her house was fired. When you were brought in, I questioned your guard closely. You were taken at her door, along with that rat Feste and Sebastian's traitor of a son.'

'I don't know what you are talking about.' I swallowed the insults and pushed my next piece forward.

'I think you do. The shewstone belonging to the witch Marijita. Lady Francesca had been to consult her the day before the fleet landed in Illyria. She had it then.' His eyes slid sideways to where Francesca sat smiling as she stabbed the needle in and pulled the thread through. 'A thing like that is not destroyed by fire. I've had men sift through every inch of ash in what is left of her hovel and there is no sign of it. I am losing patience! She tells me that you have the skill to use it. She's seen you, girl! You cannot deny that!'

I studied the board and said nothing. I thought only of Marijita foreseeing her own death, weaving her shroud.

'Such a thing is highly prized, and someone with the skill to use it even more so. Tell me where it is, show me its uses, and I'll set you free.'

As if that was likely. I shook my head. 'I do not know,' I said. 'I don't have it. I have only what I stand up in, as you can see. Lord Sebastian made sure of that.'

'You know where it is though, or at least who has it.' He looked at me, his eyes as hard as onyx. 'That wretch Feste.'

'I thought he was in captivity. If he has it, you will find it. He can't run far chained to an oar.'

'I thought so too, but he escaped. I should have had him hanged from the balcony of his beloved mistress's palazzo. Too late now. Still, I dare say he will come after you, like some faithful mangy mongrel hound. Then I'll have him, the stone and you.'

The news of Feste's escape was a glimpse of happiness, but I took care to hide it. I would show him nothing. Besides, his mind was following its own track.

'I never forget a slight to me and I have a long memory. Feste did me great injury. He destroyed my reputation, my life, all for a cheap jest. When I find him, he will suffer mightily, but that will be as nothing to the punishment he will receive hereafter. May he roast in Hell for all eternity.' He spoke the curse like a blessing. 'And others with him. That sot Sir Toby and his trull Maria. I swore to be revenged on everyone who was there.' He was silent for a moment, brooding on the past. 'Your father, your mother, Lady Olivia . . .' He marked them off on his fingers. 'You and that whelp Stephano. Unto the second generation, and further.'

I could make no answer. His malice silenced me.

'Only God can judge,' I said eventually.

'But I do God's work!' He stared at me as though I was an imbecile. 'Don't you see? I was accused of madness and dragged to the dark room, cruelly used and taunted by that devil Feste. He came to me in the guise of a priest, offering comfort and solace, all the while tormenting me further. I suffered, as Our Lord suffered. Then I saw a most holy vision. It appeared to float before me, a glowing light in the darkness, that most sacred of vessels presented as a gift to the Holy Infant. I was delivered from my tormentors, my soul was soothed by that holy resin, just as it was used to anoint the broken body of Our Lord. I left that dark place and rose again, just as He did, knowing that my purpose in life would be to punish those who had sinned against me and bring all men back to God's Holy Church.'

Lady Francesca dropped her eyes as he ranted and listened with every show of piety, like a corrupted nun. At length he sat back, passing a hand over his mouth to wipe away the spittle that had collected at the corners.

He was talking about the relic of the Magi, the precious vessel kept in the cathedral.

'It is here.'

He went to a large iron strongbox that the sailors had struggled and sweated to bring on board. He opened the gold reliquary and lifted out the little silver cup.

There had been a storm brewing. Now lightning flashed and thunder crashed, but the sea remained calm, the lamp hanging from the roof was hardly moving. The ancient silver shone and the precious stones glinted. Outside the cabin, the ship was alight with a strange blue fire that ran everywhere but consumed nothing. The sailors were crossing themselves, shouting, 'God save us, *corpus sancti*!' and calling to each other that these were spirit candles: St Peter's Fire.

'One of the most holy relics in Christendom.' When Malvolio spoke, he was as awed as the sailors.

I had seen him receive it, but did not think that he would dare take it from Illyria. Lord Sebastian was weak and despicable to allow such a thing. To think that he was now ruler of Illyria! I swore to myself in that cabin, before the holy vessel, that I would take it back.

'What is the point of it languishing in some poor church in some obscure country,' he said, as if he could hear my thoughts, 'when it can be put to such good work elsewhere? It belongs to the world.' As he spoke, his eyes glittered with fresh intensity. 'The world is full of godless men. Heretics abound. I have been chosen to root them out. The Cup of the Magi will be taken to wherever the godless reign. Heretics will be put to the Question. They will be put to the flames.'

For such a marvellous thing to be used for such a dreadful purpose, to justify torture, to feed the bonfires of persecution, it was hideous. I knocked over my own king. He had won the game.

'That is a powerful story,' Will said when Violetta had finished. 'You *believe* in this thing?'

Vials of the Holy Blood, shards of the True Cross, the chains of St Peter, the bones of saints: these things were no longer venerated in England. They belonged to a past age. The pilgrimages had stopped long before Will was born, the shrines torn down, the rich reliquaries plundered, the relics cast aside as dross. Churches had been turned into places for plain and sober worship, the statues had been smashed, the rood screens taken down, the doom paintings whitewashed.

'Of course I believe in it!' Violetta looked at him as though he was mad. 'Illyria will not prosper until it is returned to its rightful place in the cathedral. My father and mother are both dead. I am the Duchessa, so it is my duty to find it and return it to my country. I swore a holy vow before it. That is why I am here. Malvolio has brought it to your country for a fell purpose. You are heretics, ruled over by a heretical monarch. In his mind, it is logical. He has brought it here to rally the faithful, to overturn your Queen.'

That was treason. No wonder Cecil was interested. Will gave up a silent prayer of thanks that he had taken a private room.

'What about you?' he asked Feste. 'Do you believe in the power of this thing?'

'Not me, master.' Feste shook his head. 'It's just a piece of tin. I believe in this.' He tapped his temple. 'And this.' He grabbed his groin. 'The rest is nothing.'

'So why do you help her?'

'I hate Malvolio,' the clown said simply. 'Besides . . .'

He stopped and his face grew dark and brooding. 'What is it to you, poet?' he snarled. 'You would not understand!'

Feste was devoted to his young mistress. Whatever he said, it was obvious that his heart overrode his reason, or his other parts.

Will looked out. Night was coming on. Little lights were beginning to show from the opposite bank, trembling across the water. The bend in the Thames prevented him from seeing Whitehall, but soon the lights would be blazing out from the great palace, rippling like a great golden carpet across the black expanse of the river. He thought of Cecil, working away in his room where the high windows looked out on to nothing, setting traps to catch the wary and unwary alike. But Will had been trapped long before his encounter with Cecil. He had been caught from the first moment that he had stopped to watch Feste performing. Lured by their tale, hooked by the tantalising prospect that they had more to tell.

'What's your story, master?' he asked the clown.

FESTE

In the world there is a land, and in the land there is a town, and in the town there is a wall, and in the wall there is a door, and through the door the babies go, posted at the dead time of night, put there by deflowered maidens, merry widows, sober goodwives, drunken whores, the women of the town and countryside around. In the morning the nuns find sometimes one, sometimes two, sometimes more, squirming all together like puppies in a litter. That's how I started, master. Plucked out of the hopper. Never knew who my parents were, never knew my ma. Brought up by the Poor Sisters. That's where I met Marijita. She was Sister Mary, then, of course: Sister Mary Magdalena. She looked after the children. We called her 'little mother', but not loud enough so the other nuns would hear. When she wasn't tending us, she worked in the pharmacy, brought us treats: honey drops and liquorice.

I'd have stayed there, passed on to the Brother House to work in the fields or in the kitchens when I was old enough, if Old Feste hadn't come walking past one day. He saw me through the open door, doing tricks and tumbling. I could always make the other children laugh. The nuns too. Well, some of them, one or two. Old Feste was looking for a likely lad to make 'prentice, so he took me off with him. He was clown to the old Count, Lady Olivia's father. I didn't have a name, not one that I owned to, and he was the nearest thing I'd ever had to a father, so I called myself Feste after him. He was a good old man, a kind master and a great clown. He taught me all he knew and over the years I've added more to the store.

Old Feste had grown stiff and stout but he taught me the trick of it. I was small and thin. Escaping became one of my specialities. It still is. No ropes, no chains can hold me. When I was taken, I was left on the dock with the others who were destined to be galley slaves. No one bothered to guard us. We were trussed like ducks. Who would want to stand on a cold dock watching a bunch of prisoners, when there was drink and women there for the taking? First I freed myself, then the others. They came back to find a pile of ropes. Those guards are probably pulling on oars for their carelessness. I hope so, anyway.

I left the town and followed the coast north. I'd seen my lady put aboard a Venetian galley and I'd seen Malvolio winched on to the selfsame one. I knew where they were bound. I hate Venice. It's a stinking, rotten city, full of supercilious pricks, forever wearing masks to cover the pox sores on their faces. I picked up a carrack at Pula that was taking a cargo of timber across to the Serene City.

When I arrived, I set out to find where Malvolio lived. A palazzo on the Grand Canal. He'd done well for himself. There was a grand gondola with a covered *felze* moored at the steps to ship his fat carcass about. I kept watch. *He* was not much in evidence, but there were plenty of messengers coming and going. I tracked them to the Palazzo Mazzolini. That was a busy place. Tradesmen going away with orders, delivering clothes, fabrics, paintings, furnishings. I found the place where the messengers stopped off to refresh themselves, going to and fro being thirsty work. I'd invite them to share a bottle, have a quick game of cards. I'd have the letters read, sealed back up and replaced in their pouches before they were back from the jakes. Signore Mazzolini had a new posting as Ambassador to England, and Malvolio was to be a member of his entourage. Before long, I knew which ship from what port, who they would be visiting, how long the journey would take. Malvolio was always a one for detail. I even had the address of the Ambassador's house in London.

When I wasn't getting acquainted with Malvolio's business, I was looking for Violetta. There was no sign of her at the palazzo, so I kept watch on the churches, especially La Maddalena in Cannaregio. It didn't take much thinking to work out the fate Malvolio would likely have in store for my lady. He is as greedy as he is vicious. He hoards up slights and grudges like some usurer, waiting to pay back with interest. He would not forget the insult Viola paid to him. He would take great delight in turning her daughter into a courtesan and selling her off to some rich man.

Whores are on their knees in church nearly as often as nuns. Not many people know that. They go to plead to La Maddalena to intercede on their behalf, as they might well do, standing in dire need of God's taking pity on them and sparing their spotted souls. I took up my place with the beggars at the door. I had to fight for my position. The girls are generous with their alms. They came in a steady stream until the candles inside were blazing like a forest on fire. I took up my station every day, and sure enough, before the week was out, along they came. It grieved me sore. I could tell by the way they had dressed her hair, by the clothes she wore, that my lady was well on the way to becoming a courtesan.

They were keeping her in a house in the Cannaregio. The woman's name was Alessandra Stambellino. It was her task to turn my lady into a *cortigiana onesta*, the highest class of courtesan. Signora Stambellino must have been fine in her time, but was too old now to practise the trade and had set herself up training others instead. I went to the ghetto to get myself some suitable clothes, hired myself a gondola and began paying court. I sang to her, I played to her, I laughed my way into her bed and I laughed her out of the keys to the house. She was a game old bird, I can tell you. Hadn't been . . .

'The short of it is,' Violetta cut in, motioning Feste to be quiet. She would take over the story now. Feste could be rather too robust and rude in his speaking, adding salt where none was needed. She did not want Master Shakespeare thinking that she had been corrupted even in the slightest by La Stambellino, or by keeping company with a clown. 'The short of it is,' she went on, 'Feste got me away and we joined a group of roving players. They worked the northern Italian states, across to France. We left them in Genoa and took ship to England, using the money we had earned to pay our passage. It took many months for us to get from Venice to England. Malvolio and the Venetian Ambassador had an easier and swifter journey. We arrived to find that they were already in residence.'

'How do you know that Malvolio has brought this thing you seek?'

'Oh, we know,' Feste said. 'Not all the letters leaving the palazzo were to the Venetian. Some were for his Jesuit brothers in Santa Maria del Rosario on the Fondamenta delle Zattere, alongside the Giudecca Canal. The Jesuits are intent on bringing your country back to the Church. They see it as a holy mission.' He looked up at Will. 'Perhaps that is what interests your man of power.'

'Oh, that is certain.' Will sighed. The trap had just yawned wider, but at least he would have something to tell Cecil tomorrow.

'I thought the stone would show us the way,' Violetta said, 'tell us what to do.'

'The stone?' Will asked.

'The shewstone.'

'You have it?'

'Yes. Would you like to see it?'

Will nodded. He'd never seen one before.

'Show him, Feste.'

The clown took out his folly stick. He twisted the puppet's little jester's cap and the whole of the top of the head lifted off. Dr Dee's stone was said to be made from a piece of black rock, shiny as glass, smoothed and polished on one side to make a dark mirror. This was nothing like that. It was oval in shape, pale and translucent, packed about with layers of soft natural wool.

Violetta gently removed it from its casing. The stone lay in her hands, a pale greenish duck's-egg shade of blue. The surface was clouded, but the stone was translucent, filling her palms with light.

She held the stone up to the window. It picked up colour from the last rays of the sun and immediately became transparent. Will looked through and saw the bridge in reversed image, bathed in orange and red with the piers in the sky, towers and roofs in the river. She held it in her cupped hand.

'Look into it now. What can you see?'

The surface had turned milky again. All Will could see was a patch of reflected light from the window.

'Nothing,' he said.

'That's the trouble.' She looked at him. Her eyes held tears. 'Neither can I.' Her fingers went to the amulet that she wore round her neck, telling the charms like beads on a rosary. 'Last night I came near to complete despair. I had caused trouble for Toby and

Maria, bringing death and danger to their house like uninvited guests. I went to where Feste was sleeping. I took out the stone. I wanted to ask what we should do. Was this the right place to be? Should we stay, or no? But the stone gave me no answers. It was as blank as it is now.' She looked out of the window at the dark clouds of evening. 'Marijita's magic doesn't work under these grey skies. We will have to shift for ourselves.

'When we first met you,' she went on, 'I had an idea that you could help us. A scheme so foolish that I blush to think of it. You couldn't do what I wanted, but you listened to our story and that was help of a kind. Then you needed Feste to be your clown.' She looked at him. 'Now we need each other. Our lives have become twisted together.'

She smiled. In his mind Will saw two strands of yarn: one drab and one bright.

15

'My shroud of white, stuck all with yew'

Sir Toby was being buried in St Mary's, Lambeth. The party left from Forman's house. The coffin, draped in black, was carried by six pall-bearers, Maria, Violetta and Feste following along as chief mourners. Will and Forman fell in behind them. There were no others. If Sir Toby had any friends, they had melted away. A few people stopped to watch as they passed by, the men snatching off their caps as a mark of respect.

Sir Toby had been a big man. It was with some relief that the sweating pall-bearers laid the coffin on the wooden hearse, ready to be taken into the church. Violetta stepped forward and set down the posy that she had gathered in Forman's garden: rosemary, fennel and rue. The funeral party formed up to follow the hearse down the aisle.

Will and Forman joined the mourners scattered through the pews. Most of them seemed to be creditors, come to see that he was really dead.

'When do you next see our crookback friend?' Forman whispered as they bowed their heads.

'Three this afternoon. I go directly from here.' Will glanced up at Violetta's slim black form kneeling in the first pew. 'The girl has a shewstone,' he added quietly. 'Did you know?'

'I did not. She's been keeping that well hid. A

shewstone? Has she really?' Forman whistled softly through the gap in his teeth. 'You'd better keep quiet about that when you see Cecil.'

'Why?' Will asked, disconcerted to find yet another unsuspected snare in his path. 'What interest could he have?'

'It is an intelligencer's dream,' Forman whispered. 'They love them. Or the idea of them, I should say. That is why Cecil, and Walsingham before him, took such an interest in the good Doctor Dee and his Mister Kelley. Except the man was a charlatan, with Dee his dupe. If this girl has such a thing, and has the skill to use it, the possibilities are infinite.'

'She says it doesn't work here,' Will whispered back.

'They don't know that!' Forman hissed. 'Best they don't find out.'

The minister's voice rose and they fell silent.

'*I am the resurrection and the life, saith the Lord; he that believeth in me, though he were dead, yet shall he live; and whosoever liveth and believeth in me shall never die.*'

The words from the Book of Common Prayer, plain and simple, pure as rain dropping about them, bowed every man's head and turned his thoughts to his own mortality.

The minister found it hard to describe Sir Toby as a spotless and God-fearing man, but he was generous in his eulogy. He took as his text a sinner come back to the fold, and there was truth in that. For all his faults, Sir Toby had been a merry fellow, kind and generous. There were worse things to be.

'*We are mortal, formed of the earth, and unto earth*

shall we return. For so thou didst ordain when thou createdst me, saying, "Dust thou art, and unto dust shalt thou return."'

The service over, Sir Toby began his last journey to the burying ground. Will did not follow. It was nearing the time for his appointment with Cecil. As they left the church, the bell began to sound. The minister was holding out his hand. Forman was paying for it to be tolled. He reached into his wallet for the fee and found the chart that he had prepared for Will. He'd forgotten he had it on him until that moment.

'Will!' Forman called after him. 'Your chart!'

The poet had other things on his mind and was already on his way to the Horseferry. Forman tucked the scroll back into his wallet. There was to be a funeral feast later at the Three Compasses. He would give it to him there.

❖

Will presented himself at the Palace of Whitehall and was shown into Cecil's private office. To his relief, the Secretary seemed pleased. He walked up and down as Will told him the girl's story, his gait a trifle ungainly, keeling to the right as though the twist in his spine threw his body off balance.

'Tell me, Master Shakespeare, do you believe these things have power?'

'Relics, you mean?' Will shook his head quickly. 'Oh, no. Well, that is . . .' He paused, wondering what exactly to say. Cecil's questions were as easily sprung as a poacher's gin. To hold such a belief would amount to idolatry, but to express the opposite, to believe in nothing, could be accounted just as dangerous.

'It is a matter of belief,' he said at last. 'The girl believes that this thing will restore her country. Others believe something else entirely.'

'Yes!' Cecil looked pleased. 'That's it exactly. It doesn't matter if this thing was really presented to the Christ Child or knocked up with a dozen others in a workshop in Constantinople. It's the belief that matters. And many do believe in such things. Here. In this country. A surprisingly large number. A *dangerously* large number. More than you would think. We have information that the papists are gathering these things together, collecting them from inside this country and abroad. They were not destroyed in the Dissolution. Not all of them. Most of the shrines were empty. The relics spirited away to papist houses, private chapels. The papists are hoping to use them to rally the faithful and bring back the Old Religion. They plot to overthrow our sovereign Queen Elizabeth and put a Catholic impostor on the throne. There are plenty of candidates. Europe crawls with pretenders.'

Will bowed his head. He still paled to hear such talk. From anyone else, in any other place, it would be treason. Enough to get a man hanged and quartered.

'There is a plot, and I thank you for the part that you have played so far in uncovering it. This Jesuit Malvolio is at the heart of this conspiracy. He is the prime mover, the engine of it. He is set to travel England, showing this relic off to the remaining Faithful as one of the most holy in Christendom, brought with the Pope's blessing, all that kind of thing.'

'If that is the case, why do you not have Malvolio arrested?'

'I could do that.' Cecil gave a sigh, as if disappointed by the quality of the question. 'But why trap one wasp in a bottle when you can scotch the whole nest? No, we will let him run. We will wait until all the papists are gathered in one place together. Then we will take them.' Cecil looked towards the map that hung on the wall behind him. 'We have an idea that it is likely to be here.' He picked up a rule, like a schoolmaster. 'Your own county of Warwickshire. A veritable nest of recusancy, with Catholics everywhere, barely bothering to hide their faith. Malvolio has been in close touch with one of them, a Sir Andrew Agnew. He has estates there. Do you know him?'

'Of him,' Will said. 'How do you know all this?'

'I don't have to explain to you how I have gained this knowledge.' This time the sigh was louder, more pronounced. 'But I will. These are state secrets.' He stared at Will, his heavy-lidded eyes sombre and calculating. 'Breathe a word of what you learn here and you will hang for treason. I know all Malvolio intends. I have it on the very best authority. I have it from the Venetian Ambassador.' Cecil put his hand on a large globe that stood next to his desk. He spun it round until it showed the crooked boot of Italy. 'Here is Venice.' He tapped the place with the rule. 'And here –' he drew the pointer diagonally across the blue expanse of the Adriatic Sea until it rested on a minuscule nub of land – 'here is Illyria. It is a small country. Tiny. But by no means insignificant. Look at its position. The Illyrians are seafarers, traders. They have a deep, safe harbour. Their fortified city would not have fallen if it had not been betrayed from within. They are well placed to control the shipping lanes going up and down to Venice. The Venetians had no love for the old Duke, the girl's father – too independent for their liking, that's why they got rid of him – but it appears that they like their new Duke, Sebastian, even less. Illyria has become a nest of pirates and a great threat to their trade. Venice is a trading nation, as are we. We don't like pirates. They are looking to replace him, and who better than the usurped Duke's daughter married to the present Duke's son? Such an alliance would be perfect for their purposes. The girl is in London.' Cecil revolved the globe with a flick of the wrist. When it turned to England, he stopped the spin. 'She was seen boarding a ship in Genoa. I was asked to look out for her. They have the boy safe in their hands, but not her. Now I have intelligence that she's here in London, first from Riche, now from you.'

So he had become one of Cecil's intelligencers, just as Forman had said.

'It is a simple exchange.' Cecil explained. 'I help the Ambassador find and secure the girl. He keeps me informed about Malvolio and this papist plot: what they intend, the plotters' whereabouts, and so on. The Ambassador is not involved, of course. What we do with the information is up to us.'

Simple? Will raised an eyebrow. There was nothing simple about it.

'The whole thing could come unstuck if Malvolio finds out Venice's intentions,' Cecil went on. 'He is in the pay of this Duke Sebastian, among his other crimes. He might arrange for the girl to be killed, and that would spoil everything.'

'I think he might already know,' Will said quietly.

'Hmm.' Cecil frowned. 'How did that happen? The Ambassador should have been more careful. That's the trouble with the Italians. Can't keep secrets.'

'I don't think that he found out through the Ambassador,' Will said, 'but by other means.'

'That's good. I would not like to think his court so unsafe.' Cecil stopped to consider. 'Too bad that he knows, however he found out. You'll have to keep her safe. I'll help you with that. Who better?' Cecil was warming to the thought. 'She trusts you, and you can keep an eye on her. I am appointing you to act as her guardian, so you'd better make sure no harm comes to her.'

'Why don't you take her into your custody?' Will asked. That seemed to him a much better idea. How was he supposed to keep her safe?

'I could do that, of course, but any hint of my involvement may well abort the conspiracy. And that is what concerns me, not Venice's control of the Adriatic Sea. I have to stay well hid. Now, I think she will be safer out of London. You can take her . . .'

'But I can't leave London!' Will protested. 'I am needed here. It is our busiest time!'

'You can. And you will,' Cecil snapped. He did not like to be interrupted. His eyes turned cold as the Thames on a winter's day. 'I have something here that might make it easier. A writ to close the theatres.'

He waved an order, complete with scrawled signatures and a big red seal. Will stared at the document as Cecil laid it on the table. He had it all worked out.

He really was a remarkable man. In between all the affairs of state he kept in his head, all the other calls on his time, he had been busy thinking up a scheme that would affect the lives and livelihood of hundreds of people. Not just Will's company, but all the others in London. What would they do? And if this ever got out – the theatres closed on his account? Will began to sweat at the thought of it. What would he do? How would he live? He would not be able to work. He would not be able to write.

'You can always write poetry,' Cecil supplied. He had been watching him, tracking his thoughts, as a hawk might watch a blundering vole.

'It's not the same,' Will said. He studied the seal, seeing but not seeing the way the wax had been pressed into petals so it lay like a gillyflower with the royal coat of arms at the heart of it. His eyes travelled to the globe, still showing the islands of Britain where Cecil's finger had stopped it. He then looked up at the map of England on the wall above the fireplace and found his own county of Warwickshire. He began to have an idea. It came to him complete, all of a piece. That was what made him different from other men.

Will rested the span of his hand on the writ and turned it around with a twist of his wrist.

'I have a proposal for you,' he said.

Will paced up and down as he explained his scheme. Cecil stayed behind his desk, stilled with concentration. Will had his full attention. As he listened, his green eyes brightened. Every now and then he nodded his approval. His expression lost its severity and he began to smile. When Will had finished, Cecil laughed at the elegance of the thing, his laugh surprisingly rich and deep. The clerks in the outer office looked up, startled. Their master's laughter was a sound they seldom heard.

'That is a rare plan! You are a clever fellow,' he said, smiling broadly now, his grave face almost merry. 'None cleverer. I was right to put trust in you.'

The interview over, one of the dark-robed clerks was summoned to conduct Will from the room, while another glided past him, bringing papers for the Secretary's attention. Cecil frowned down, his mind already turned to the document set for him to sign.

Will heard the scratch of the pen, the scatter of sand across paper. He thought himself forgotten, but just as he was leaving Secretary Cecil looked up.

'I'm writing an order to keep the girl safe. Lambeth, you say? Staying with Forman?' Will nodded. Cecil handed the note to a clerk. 'I will see you at noon tomorrow, Master Shakespeare, at my new house on the Strand.'

Will stood on the Whitehall Stairs, waiting for a wherry to take him across to Bankside. He had to get to the Globe. He might just catch the last part. They were changing the play today: *The Merry Wives of Windsor*. A fitting epitaph for Sir Toby. He would say nothing about the playhouses being closed. The Master of Revels would let them know soon enough, and it must be as much of a shock to him as to everybody else. No one must know that he had any part in this, or his withdrawal to the country would be permanent.

16

'For such as I am all true lovers are'

'He was an old scamp and a scoundrel, but I'm going to miss him. Pickled pigs' feet was one of his favourites.'

Maria had hardly cried since the funeral. She stood for a moment, thinking on their life together, then wiped away the first trickle of a tear with a corner of her apron. Sir Toby had put money by for a feast. He'd wanted a good send-off and she was determined to honour him as best she could.

Inn servants were bringing in food: trotters and brawn, veal and mutton, pies, pastries, cakes and tarts.

'Is there enough, do you think?' Maria kept asking, as more things came through the door.

'More than enough.' Violetta looked on, arms folded. 'Why should a funeral be the cause of celebration? I've never understood that.'

'It's custom,' Maria said, as if that explained everything. 'Should happen straightway after the ceremony, but I thought it best to hold it later, when the day's work is done.'

The funeral party had broken up early. Master Shakespeare had gone to his important appointment, Dr Forman to his consulting rooms, and Feste had taken himself off to the Globe. They were changing the play, so he wouldn't be performing, but he went anyway, already besotted with the place. Violetta would have liked to have gone with him, thinking that Stephano might be there, since his master liked the plays so much, but her duty was to Maria. She didn't want to leave her on her own. She was beginning to regret her decision now. Time was moving excessively slowly and the innkeeper's wife was happy to keep Maria company. She had piled extra wood on the fire in case Maria felt the cold, so the room was sweltering. Once the table was arranged to their satisfaction, the two women would pull the settle up close to the fire, ready to spend the rest of the afternoon knitting and swapping recipes for pickling brine.

'I think the table lacks something,' Violetta said to them. 'Flowers. That's it.'

'You don't put flowers on a funeral table.' Maria's nose wrinkled disapproval. 'It's not a wedding!'

'Sir Toby loved flowers – you said so yourself. He'd like it. I'm going to get some from Doctor Forman's garden.'

Before they could stop her, she was out of the door and away.

She knew the way to the river and from there to the theatre. It would be quicker to take a wherry, but she did not want to waste money on that. Besides, it was not far to walk. Maria did not want her to go out for fear of the men who had been watching the Hollander, but they would find the place shut up and guarded. How would they know she'd gone? Anyway, they were unlikely to take her in the broad light of day. Violetta was tired of being confined for no reason except her own safety; she could look after herself.

She turned right at the top of the Lambeth Road and followed the curving bank of the Thames. There was the high wall of the Bishop's palace on one side, and the river on the other. There was no one about. No inns or houses, docks or warehouses, like in Southwark. From what she could see, the way ahead was riverbank and empty marshland. Her confident step faltered. Perhaps she would take the wherry after all.

She turned back, towards Horseferry. There was a man standing by the jetty. She thought she recognised him from the Hollander: bare arms, sleeveless jerkin, leather cap. She turned back, but another one had emerged from a side road and was bearing down on her fast. She was caught between the two of them with no means of escape.

She set off at a run, hoping to dodge past Leather Cap, but he caught her. He held her close. She could smell his rotten onion breath, see the scabs bedded in the straggling growth of his beard. The other one was behind her now. She heard the creak of his jerkin, felt a sharp point jab into her side.

'Not a word, mistress,' he whispered. 'Not a sound. You'll come along with us, nice and peaceful.' The two men fell in one each side of her. 'We'll go arming along, as friendly as you please.'

They held her fast, arms pinned to her sides, and marched her towards the Horseferry.

'Don't shout and don't draw attention.' The shorter one pushed her towards a boat, moored and waiting. 'Or it will be the worse for you.'

'One peep,' the other one leered down at her, 'and we'll go back for your little friend.'

They were almost at the end of the jetty when they heard a shout.

'Hey! That's my boat!'

Violetta turned to see a gentleman running towards them, sword drawn.

The taller of her two captors swore and let go of her to reach for the heavy club that he wore at his belt. He swung the weapon but it spun out of his hand, falling with a thud and rolling into the river as a thin rapier blade lashed towards him, slashing through the tendons of his wrist. The man let out a thin scream and clamped his other hand to the wound, trying to staunch the blood that streamed through his fingers and dripped on to the deck. The smaller one faltered as the swordsman came towards him. His grip on Violetta slackened. She spun out of his grasp and used one of the holds Feste had shown her to throw him off balance. His knees buckled and she pitched him forward off the edge of the jetty. He fell into the river with a great splash.

'Bleed to death in the river!' Her rescuer kicked his friend in after him. 'Horses don't like the smell of blood.' The man put his sword up and bowed to her. 'George Price, at your service. I've been sent by Secretary Cecil to keep an eye on you. I'm one of his Linksmen; he calls us that because we watch and keep people safe.'

'I didn't know I was going to be so protected,' she said.

Things were moving swiftly. She sensed powerful forces moving in closer. She had become used to being ordinary. There was freedom in anonymity. She felt as though she had stepped from one sphere into another. To be given a guard, as if she was an important person again, made her feel both safer and more threatened.

'Why would you?' He smiled, interpreting her doubt as a request for reassurance. 'The order only came through an hour ago. My master acts fast when he has a mind to it. And I'm not seen until I'm needed. I could watch you for days and you'd never know I was there. Concealment is part of my job.'

He had been fast and agile in the fight, but Price was older than he looked at first sight. His greying hair was cropped short, like a soldier's, and a scar, an old sword cut, showed in a livid seam down one side of his face. His skin was dark and weathered, as if he'd spent time in the sun; the corners of his light brown eyes set into deep crinkles when he smiled. He reminded her of the sea captains who came to see her father: honest, brave men who sailed his argosies across the world. He was not very tall, but there was no spare flesh on him and the ease with which he moved and stood suggested hidden strength. He was dressed like a gentleman, in dark doublet and hose, with a short cloak slung over one shoulder to keep his sword arm free.

Violetta put her misgivings away. Whatever the reasons for his being there, he was a useful fellow to have walking at her side.

'You are not from these parts, are you?' His tone was light. He was using gentle conversation like a horse-master with a high-mettled animal, to gain her trust.

'No, I'm from Illyria,' Violetta answered, with no expectation that he would know anything about her country or where it was in the world.

'I've been there!' He smiled, his eyes narrowing as if he could see the town before him. 'On the Adriatic coast, with white walls and a wide thoroughfare running through the middle, polished to marble by so many feet walking upon it. Ruled by a duke. Now what's his name?' He frowned, trying to recall it.

'Duke Orsin,' Violetta supplied.

'Yes, that's him! A good man, fair to his people. A fine town, as I recall.'

'It isn't any more,' Violetta replied. 'The Duke was my father. He's dead, the town destroyed.'

'I'm sad to hear that.'

Violetta thought he would want to know more, but George Price had been well schooled by his master. It was not his place to question those he was set to watch. Instead he began to tell her about himself, his life as a mercenary soldier in Italy, and then as a mariner, guarding ships sailing from the port of Brindisi. Violetta was glad of his company and drew some small comfort from talking to someone who knew something of her homeland. She saw no reason to go back to the inn, now that she had this man to guard her. She sent word so Maria would not worry, and asked him to take her to the playhouse.

❦

Maria had been concerned that no one would come to the feast she had prepared. Then they all arrived at once from the playhouse, bringing the coldness of the day into the warmth of the room. Violetta was with them, on the arm of a young man. All her worry over how Violetta had disappeared and the scolding she'd had ready died on her lips when she saw who he was. Violetta had been thinking to surprise her, but Maria knew him immediately. It was like a miracle to her. She had not seen Lord Stephano since he was just a boy, and here he was a man, and the image of Lady Olivia. And Guido with him. Maria remembered him as a naughty little boy stealing peaches, and now here he was, all grown-up. It made her heart glad to have men from Illyria here to honour Toby. And to see Violetta smiling, to see the way she and Stephano looked at each other. It was a dash of happiness at a time of sadness, a splash of colour against the funeral black of the day.

Will saw it too, and was happy for them. Let them enjoy the moment. The dark clouds were already gathering. Feste was less pleased. He watched the lovers with surly disgust and set himself to getting drunk.

The room was far more crowded than the church had been, with people intent on toasting Sir Toby and wishing him well, whether in Heaven or in Hell.

Stephano steered Violetta through the throng. He found a settle well away from the food and the barrels.

'We have news,' he said. 'We are leaving tomorrow. His Excellency the Ambassador has been invited by various gentlemen to visit different parts of the country. Malvolio is going too, of course.'

'There's more to it than that.' Guido sat down beside them. 'Malvolio is taking the relic. It is already packed in a crate ready for travelling. These visits are so that His Excellency can become acquainted with the country, the leading families, but Malvolio's using this progress for his own ends. He has been meeting with certain gentlemen separately. He's very close with one he knew from the old days in Illyria.'

'Sir Andrew Agnew,' Violetta supplied.

'You know about him?'

Violetta nodded.

'Well,' Guido went on, 'there is some kind of plot afoot. His Excellency knows it, of course, and he is careful to distance himself. I think he is using it to trap Malvolio in some way, or he may have some other purpose. We have to be careful. Lady Francesca serves Christiana, the Ambassador's daughter,' Guido said. 'She and Malvolio are like that.' He plaited his fingers. 'She reports everything straight back to him.'

Stephano had been silent. 'Perhaps we need not worry about this any more,' he said.

'What do you mean?'

'I mean, we could be married.' He took Violetta's hands in his. 'We could go to His Excellency. Be restored to Illyria . . .'

'How? How could that be possible?'

'His Excellency told me today – Venice is no longer happy with my father's rule. The pirate Antonio has too much power. They are raiding together, attacking convoys, taking galleys, demanding ransoms. They want to replace him . . . with us.'

Violetta's smile spread wide. 'Why, that is great news –'

'Tell her all of it,' Guido said.

'They want to keep the relic,' he said. 'In San Marco.'

'What?' Violetta stared at him. 'Oh, no! I will not go back without it. I have vowed to return it to our own cathedral, where it belongs, not in San Marco with all the other relics that the Venetians have plundered. It's like a robbers' cave in there, with the arm of St Ivan and the foot of St Trifone and I don't know what else.'

'That is the price of their help, and we'll not regain Illyria without them. Tell her, Guido.'

Stephano turned to his friend, hoping that he would

help persuade her, but Guido was not so sure. He was Stephano's friend, but his loyalty was to Violetta. He had sworn fealty to her father. With the Duke dead, he was her man now.

'We do what Violetta says. The other way is too easy.' Guido frowned. 'We cannot wholly trust the Ambassador. Venetians are never straightforward. Their motives are opaque and changeable, as opalescent as their own lagoon.'

'There are other factors involved.' Violetta said, grateful to Guido for siding with her. 'I have an obligation to Master Shakespeare. He has offered to help me, and I cannot turn my back on him now. Someone powerful has taken an interest in this. I would not see Master Shakespeare suffer or come to harm because of me. I've seen what the powerful do when their plans are thwarted. They will crush him like a shell.'

'What does that matter?' Stephano looked at her, exasperated.

'It matters to me.' Violetta glared back.

Stephano threw his hands up and walked off.

'Go after him, Guido,' Violetta said. 'You understand. I have to go through with this. Make him see sense.'

Guido nodded and followed him. Immediately Feste hopped up on the settle, taking his place.

'What's the matter?' he asked. 'Lovers' tiff?'

Violetta was sniffing back tears. 'Don't you start!'

'Look at him. Flashing his money about, buying barrels of sack for the company, trying to be every man's friend . . .'

Violetta didn't rise to that, or any of his other

comments. She ignored him, sunk in her own misery. Feste hopped off the settle. Time to liven things up.

'Very good of you, young sir,' he said, lurching over to Stephano. 'And what coinage might that be? Venetian ducats, by any chance?' He held out his hand. 'If it's their money you've got, how about sharing it around?'

'Of course!' Stephano shook out coins from his purse.

'Thank you. Very kind.' Feste pocketed the money. 'Now let's have a dance,' he shouted over the growing hubbub. 'Clear the tables. Let's have a jig. Sir Toby was a great one for a jig. And a round, masters, he loved a round.'

He jumped up on to a table and began to sing, conducting those around him. Bit by bit, the rest joined in, playing anything that came to hand, rattling spoons and bones together, beating out time on pans. Once the round was established, he jumped down and caught hold of Maria, dancing her about the floor.

'Like old times, eh, mistress? Merry times they were. Do you remember? When we were all together. When we were young.'

Maria begged him to stop, pleading she was quite out of breath. She wiped away tears, whether of mirth or sorrow it was hard to tell.

'I'm sorry, love. Let us not quarrel.'

Violetta looked from where Feste and Maria were dancing. Stephano had come back to her.

'I wanted us to be together,' he said as he sat down next to her and took her hand. 'Forgive my eagerness. I had not thought of what it would mean. I do not want us to be the clients of Venice. I'll do whatever –'

'I've been looking for you.' Feste came staggering

towards them, waving his empty tankard at Stephano. 'Sack's gone. You have plenty of money, young master. Your purse fairly bulges with Venetian gold. Another barrel for me and my good friends here.' He waved his arm in a vague way, indicating the company, and nearly overbalanced.

Stephano put out a hand to steady him.

'Perhaps you have had enough, my friend,' he said.

'Who says?' Feste stood swaying. 'Who are *you* to say?' He squinted up at Stephano. 'Who says you are my friend?' He shrugged him away. 'Whose friend are you, anyway?'

'I meant no offence.' Stephano put up his hands to placate the clown, unsure if what he said was serious or in jest. 'I just meant . . .'

He did not want any further quarrels. He went off to buy more wine.

'What did you mean?' Feste shouted after him. 'What did you mean, exactly?'

'That is enough!' Violetta grabbed Feste by the arm. 'What do *you* mean?' she whispered furiously as she dragged him down next to her on the settle. 'Being rude and discourteous to Lord Stephano. Begging off him. I saw you. We do not do that to friends.'

'He's no lord here, and he's no lord to me. No friend, neither.'

'He is my friend.' Violetta glared at the clown. 'What is the matter with you?'

'How do you know?' Feste suddenly sounded remarkably sober.

'How do I know what?'

'How do you know this isn't a trick to make us trust him? Mighty convenient, his turning up at the playhouse yesterday.'

'There is no art in it. He was just there,' Violetta said. 'The same could be said of me. Or you.'

'You've changed your tune. Hardly a minute ago you were sitting here weeping.'

'I was not weeping!'

'Not far off it.'

'We had an argument, that's all.'

'Care to tell me about it?'

'I might. When you're sober.' Violetta turned on him. 'What's wrong with you, Feste?'

'I just don't trust him.'

'You don't trust anybody!'

'Not true, although I trust very few. I trust you. Even though you are young and the young are apt to be betrayed by their hearts, and other parts.' Stephano was now talking to Will Shakespeare, but all the while glancing towards Violetta. He could not keep his eyes off her. 'I do not want to quarrel with you, over this or anything else. What's left, if we fall out? If he be true, then he will show his metal. If he be false –' Feste shrugged – 'there's no helping us. And who's that man over there?' His eyes narrowed to slits. 'The one dressed in black who holds himself like a sword for hire. He's been watching you all the time.'

'His name's George Price. He's been sent by Secretary Cecil to look after me.'

'Tell him to go away. 'S not necessary. 'S my job.' Feste set off muttering, 'Tell him myself.'

Halfway across the room his knees gave way. He began walking as if he was sinking into the floor. George Price caught him by the arms and hauled him to a corner where he could sleep it off.

Will had remarkably good hearing and the equally useful ability to talk and listen at the same time. He went over to Violetta.

'It seems your clown has doubts about Stephano,' he said to Violetta.

'Feste can be wise when he's sober,' she said, 'but he is a fool when he's drunk. He's just jealous.'

'I wonder if we might talk.' Will beckoned for Stephano to join them.

He told them of his meeting with Cecil and what he proposed to do. Violetta looked at Stephano. They could not betray Master Shakespeare now. After Will had finished telling them what was in his mind, she took Stephano's hand and they slipped away together. The quarrel had been patched, but they had more to say to each other now. Violetta would be leaving London, the day after tomorrow at the latest. Stephano would be leaving tomorrow. They would each be facing their own separate dangers and might not see each other for a good while. If Will's plan succeeded, they would be returned to their country, Lord and Lady of Illyria. If it failed . . .

It was best not to think on that. Will's scheme was still growing, forming and changing in his mind. He was not about to tell the whole of it to anyone, any more than he would share the workings of a play, because he never quite knew what was going to happen. Even then, when the work was finished, each actor conned his own lines, so the entire thing existed only inside Will's head until it was revealed in performance. Only he knew how each part was put with another, how they all fitted to make the whole. So it would be with this enterprise. He had his cast assembled, in his head, at least. Will felt a chill of excitement running through him. The risks were great. It was impossible to know if he could bring it about. Even if he had everything in place, the cast was likely to be unpredictable. Lives and liberty depended on this, and life is not a play.

'Penny for them.'

He turned to find Simon Forman by his side.

'Not worth a groat.' Will smiled, accepting the cup of wine Forman offered him.

'I've done your chart.' Forman held out a rolled-up scroll.

'Oh.' Will took the scroll tied with black ribbon, but he did not open it. 'Thank you.'

'It makes interesting reading.'

'I'll look at it later,' Will tucked it into his jerkin. 'My thanks again.' He drank off his wine. 'I must go.'

Forman would have liked to discuss the chart with him, but Will was already moving away. The doctor watched him making an easy progress, saying farewell to one and then another, thanking Mistress Maria. He was a thoroughly pleasant fellow, nothing unusual about him, nothing to make him stand out from the ordinary. But the chart said otherwise. Forman had checked and checked again, not quite believing what he was seeing. He had done charts for the lowest to the highest, from innkeepers' wives to peers of the realm and Her Majesty's ministers, but he'd never seen one like it before. He wondered what Will would make of it.

Someone called his name. He turned to see one of his patients approaching, so he did not see Will toss the scroll into the fire.

17

'Thought is free'

By the morning, the news was out that the theatres were to be closed. The Globe was in a roar.

'They talk of plague, restless apprentices,' Burbage fumed, 'but I've not heard of either. There's always plague somewhere, and the young are ever restless. If they want disturbance, they'll get it when this becomes common knowledge. If you ask me, it's neither reason.' He paced up and down in front of the stage. 'It's those Puritans among the City Fathers putting pressure on the Privy Council. They would close us down for ever if they had their way.' He turned to Will. 'It will happen one day, mark me. Not in our lifetimes, maybe, but it will happen. They would kill all joy and amusement; have us on our knees night and day.'

Will voiced his outrage as loudly as the others. Closing the theatres meant lost revenue, which hurt him too, although sometimes he welcomed a hiatus. The appetite for plays was never satisfied and often left him exhausted, his wellspring of ideas reduced to a trickle. This time he had other reasons, but he was careful to keep them well hidden.

He waited until Burbage had run through his stock of dramatic postures, from head-clutching despair, to hair-pulling frustration, then fist-clenching rage, snarling and roaring to match the bears in the garden. Only when he had finished did Will suggest that he might take a group on tour. The very idea brought on another bout of snarling. Burbage hated touring, declaring he had done enough of that in his youth, traipsing behind a cart, covered in mud or choking on dust. He wasn't about to start again now. He did not like leaving London, or the comforts of home. Unlike most actors, he was notoriously uxorious, enjoying the company of his wife in a house that swarmed with children.

'I did not say *you*,' Will pointed out, 'but *I*. Perhaps north. Up to Stratford. I have been thinking of paying a visit. Kill two birds with the one stone.'

'Hmm.' Burbage left off his railing. 'Not a bad idea. At least we'd have some money coming in.' He rubbed his chin. 'Not a bad idea at all. You can't take my best men,' he warned, 'in case we open again.'

'I wasn't thinking of doing so.' Will smiled. 'Just a small company, mostly 'prentices and men who live in the shadow of others. We can double parts, triple if need be. We will need a few props and costumes, but it might be worth it. We could do well.'

'That you could, that you could. Might as well put the trappings to work as let them lie idle. Men too. High Wycombe, Oxford, Banbury . . .' He began counting off towns on his fingers. 'Not less than twenty shillings in a small place, forty in a larger. I'll dust off the cart, pack it with the things you need. Axles need greasing. Hasn't been used for a long time. You collect your company together. And be sure to keep strict charge,' he added as an afterthought. 'Don't let them get into fights!'

Will left Tod to get the word around to those he wanted to take with him. He had a meeting to attend.

The new house that Cecil was having built on the Strand was a vast mansion facing on to the river. It was not quite finished. Cutters worked on blocks of pale stone, and the facade was still covered in a framework of wooden poles.

'I hear that you are now a man of property, Shakespeare,' Cecil said, rolling up the plans that he had been studying.

'Why, yes.' Will tried not to sound surprised at how much Cecil knew about him. 'I have bought a new house in Stratford, although it is little more than a hovel compared with this and has needed much work doing to it.'

'Houses are a grievous expense. They eat money.' Cecil looked up, his eyes hooded. He had a way of making the most innocent utterance sound like a threat. 'You must be anxious to see how it goes.'

'It should be done by now.'

'In my experience, the work is never done. One job begets another. There always seems to be some other thing to do.' Cecil glanced about as all around men scurried, wheeling barrows, carrying hods, shinning up and down ladders. His presence acted like a stick in an ant heap, stirring the workmen into frantic activity. 'I find I must visit often or nothing is accomplished.'

'My wife, Anne, oversees the work.'

'The good Mistress Anne, quite so. She must miss you when you are in London.'

Will assented.

'Another sound reason to return to Stratford. We must keep our intention well hid, as I've said to you before. I've closed the theatres, so you are free to tour.'

Will nodded again. 'I've just come from the Globe. They are preparing the cart.'

'When do you intend to depart?'

'We go tomorrow. We'll join up with the carrier Will Greenaway. He leaves from the Bell Inn on Carter Lane.' It was best to travel in company as a safeguard against thieves and rogues on the road.

'Very wise. You've met my man George Price?' Cecil did not wait for an answer. 'He and some of his men will be joining you, to keep an eye on things. Now, it is my understanding that the party of interest, this Sir Andrew, the Jesuit Malvolio and the Venetian Ambassador, will also be travelling shortly.'

'They are set to take a circuitous route north, visiting various houses.' Will told him what he had gleaned from Stephano.

'Dispensing Mass and sedition.' Cecil frowned. 'Visiting houses sympathetic to their cause.'

'Indeed.' Will agreed. 'No doubt.'

'How did you find this out? By means of the shew-stone?'

So he did know. The news jarred him, but Will fought hard not to show it.

'Oh, yes.' Cecil nodded rapidly, as if he'd guessed Will's surprise. 'I know about that.'

'How?'

'You do not deny such a thing exists?'

Will shook his head. What was the point of it? His

face darkened. It must be Forman. He was a fool to ever have trusted him.

'Not your friend Forman,' Cecil said, guessing that thought too. Will wondered why he wanted the stone. 'I have it from another source. The Ambassador may or may not know of its existence, but someone at his court certainly does. Some woman who serves his daughter went to see a City soothsayer. During the consultation, she boasted of a stone of rare power that would soon be in her hands.'

'No.' Will thought to take the conversation back to Cecil's earlier question. 'That is not how I know about their plans. I have a spy in their camp.'

'Do you now?' Cecil's face showed something like admiration. 'Very enterprising. More than I've managed to establish. His Excellency is a source of information, when it suits him, but he is hardly likely to supply day-to-day intelligence.' He gave Will a thin smile. 'Well done!'

'He tells me that they should arrive at Sir Andrew's estate something short of midsummer. They will wait there for others to join them from other parts of England. Once they are in residence, my spy is set to do me another service.'

'Who is your spy?' Cecil asked. 'The boy Stephano?'

Will nodded. 'I think he will prove useful and I believe that he can be trusted.'

'I don't doubt it. We have the girl. Now, what of this stone?' Cecil asked, suddenly eager. 'Have you seen it yourself?'

'I have,' Will answered warily.

He reminded himself to go carefully. To Cecil, people were pieces on a gaming board, to be moved here, moved there, knocked over, discarded. He had reminded Stephano to be just as careful. His Excellency the Venetian Ambassador was likely to play the same way.

'I would dearly love to see it.' Cecil's eyes grew dark and took on a sudden gleam, like lead new cut.

'Things like that are seldom to be trusted,' Will said. 'It could be nothing more than a conjuring trick.'

Secretary Cecil did not like to be contradicted. His look sharpened to steel.

Will was aware of the danger, but he would protect Violetta. He would not deliver her and the stone into Cecil's hands. Who knew what he would or would not do to get the secret from her? To be able to see from a distance, without the need for any physical presence – it was a sorcery sought by all in Cecil's world.

'What I mean is . . .'

Will paused while he drew the right words together. He had to find ways of placating this man of power, while diminishing any offence offered to him and drawing his attention away from Violetta.

'What do you mean, Master Shakespeare?' The Secretary's tone was ominous, his brows knitted further together. His grey eyes were dull now, as heavy with threat as the sky before a storm breaks. Then the clouds dispersed. 'But there will be time for that afterwards. Let us deal with this other matter first. When *that* is successfully concluded, you can bring her and this shewstone to me. If she has it, I want to see it. It is your duty as Her Majesty's loyal subject. I want to see this girl before His Excellency takes her into his protection.'

Shakespeare nodded, though he had no intention of ever keeping his promise. To do so could condemn

Violetta to the Tower, kept captive for ever, never to return to her native Illyria, like some princess in a fireside tale.

'I am Her Majesty's loyal subject,' Will said firmly. 'I will do all I can to prevent this plot from succeeding. I do not want to see her kingdom torn apart and bonfires set up in every marketplace.'

'I know, I know. You are right to admonish me. The stone is a distraction from our main purpose. Succeed in this, and I will see to it that Her Majesty learns of your loyalty. She is a great admirer of your work. She greatly enjoyed the play at New Year. I'm sure she will want your company to appear before her when that time comes round again.'

'We are honoured by her interest.' Will bowed low. 'I will make sure that I have a new entertainment to offer.'

'We will always be in need of entertainment.'

Neither would dare to utter it, but they both knew that, given her age and frailty, the Queen might not be there next year. Will's company could be playing to a different court. Cecil looked about; his nimble, restless mind was already moving on to other things. 'This affair must be kept most secret. Tell me, Master Shakespeare, do you like gardens?'

'I do, sir,' Will replied, wondering at this new turn in their conversation. 'So does my wife. We plan to plant one at my new house.'

'So do I.' Cecil gave a rare smile of real pleasure. 'We will be planting here.' He waved towards an unpromising area of trodden grey mud and churned yellow clay that ran down to the Thames. 'John Gerard will supervise the work. You know him?'

'I know his *History of Plants*.'

'Quite so. An excellent work. He has devised wonderful gardens at Theobalds, my country place, and Burghley House. I wish him to do the same here. He has collected many rare and interesting specimens. From time to time I will have seeds and slips sent to you from our nurseries with advice as to how they should be treated.'

'That is most kind, sir.' Will bowed.

'Not at all. We can learn from plants: which is wholesome, which is poison and which pernicious weed. Which should be kept and nurtured, which plucked out. I will let you know how things are growing here. You, in turn, can tell me how things are in your garden.'

18

There lies your way

The yard of the Bell Inn was full of snorting horses and patient ponies tethered together. Men patrolled up and down the line checking packs, testing straps, tightening girths. One of them was George Price. He looked up from the hoof he was examining and gave Violetta a fleeting smile. He was no longer dressed as a gentleman, but wore homespun and a hooded coat like the rest of the carriers. The actors' cart stood at the centre of the yard, its high side panels brightly painted, piled high with trunks, cloak bags and hampers, folded scene cloths and assorted props. Tod was having trouble backing the horses between the shafts, so Feste ran over to help him. Master Shakespeare was talking to a square-set man with a thatch of dark hair and beetling brows. He was wearing a hooded sheepskin, but from the way he stood and the orders he was giving, he was in charge. He was Will Greenaway, the Stratford carrier, impatient to be on the road.

Violetta was keen to be moving too. She looked from one part of the yard to another, eager to be gone. When Will had explained his idea to her and Stephano, she had felt her spirit rising. Hope and excitement had flared inside her at the boldness of the plan. It was also risky, dangerous, full of pitfalls, it might not even work at all, but it was better than doing nothing.

After the wake was over, she'd gone to Maria to tell her that they would be leaving.

'I'm coming with you,' Maria declared. 'There's nothing for me here.'

They had left Simon Forman's house early that morning just as the sun was rising and the Thames beginning to colour with the pink light of dawn.

Will had made no objection to Maria coming with them. In fact, he had welcomed her. She was a good needlewoman and could help with the costumes and in the tiring room. Everyone had to make themselves useful when they took to the road. She rode with Violetta, up on the wagon, with Tod driving. Feste was already asleep on top of the trunks, curled up on a bed that he had made for himself on the painted cloths used for scenery. Greenaway leased horses to Will and any of the company who wished to ride. The rest of them took turns on the wagon or walking behind.

They left the City at Newgate and went up Houlburne in the direction of the village of St Giles-in-the-Fields. From here they would take the Uxbridge Road past the hanging tree at Tyburn and on to St Mary at the Bourne. Here they would cross the stream at Westbourne and follow the road westward. They went at a plodding pace. The packhorses were heavily laden for their homeward journey.

'Greenaway brings cheeses, lambskins, woollen garments and knitted hose down from Stratford. And he takes back goods impossible to come by in Stratford, like sugar loaves and spices, cloth for the mercers, notions for the haberdashers, amber for the apothecaries, tobacco, paper, books from the printers by St Paul's . . .'

Tod was a fund of information, but Violetta did not mind his chatter. It passed the time and he was a pleasant companion.

'What do you carry in your own pack, master?' Tod called down when Will rode close up to them.

He smiled up at them. 'Oh, this and that,' he said.

His pack was full of gifts that he had been collecting for Anne and his daughters. He liked to bring them things that caught his eye or were hard to come by outside London: nutmegs for the kitchen, sugar, raisins, pepper, candied ginger, sticks of cinnamon, fragrant blades of mace. He had bought Spanish steel knitting needles, a rainbow mix of silk yarns and ribbons, a card of silver buttons, the French lawn handkerchiefs that Anne liked to embroider and pretty glass beads from an Italian pedlar. A necklace for Anne, bracelets for the girls. And seeds. He'd got them from a man who travelled to Amsterdam.

The sun was warm. They were soon leaving behind the brown pall that hung over the city. Violetta had got used to the reek of it: a mix of smoking fires, clotted kennels and rotting middens. Now the stink was thinning to nothing, replaced by the scent of May blossom and flowers.

Will rode forward to catch up with Will Greenaway. He needed to talk to him about where they would be staying each night.

'If we make good time,' Tod said, 'we could get to High Wycombe. It's a good-sized town. We can set up in the yard of the White Lion. First night we'll play *As You Like It*, because it's fresh in our minds. We haven't talked about any other plays yet. I'm hoping he'll decide to do *Romeo and Juliet*.'

'*Romeo y Julieta?*' Violetta said. 'I know it. There is a story by Matteo Bandello.'

'It was my first play with the company. I played Juliet.'

Violetta laughed. She could not get used to the idea of a young man like Tod playing a girl. He was so strong sitting next to her, legs planted apart, his hands big and square holding the reins, the muscles moving in his tanned forearms.

'Oh Romeo, Romeo!'

He spoke the words with love and longing, completing the speech in a voice that made her laugh harder, it was so exactly like her own.

'Why does a man play the woman's part?'

Feste had woken up and her question had him snorting. They both ignored him.

'That is how it has always been.' Tod shrugged. 'It is against the law for women to act on stage, so men or boys have to take their parts.'

'I find it strange,' she said. 'Unnatural. It is not the same in other countries.'

'Did you really travel with a band of players?'

Violetta nodded.

'And acted with them?' Tod shook his head as if such a thing was beyond his imagining.

'Oh, yes. Many times.'

'She's good too,' Feste interrupted from behind them. 'Better than you, I'll warrant.'

Tod smiled. 'I don't doubt it! I do my best, but I yearn to play the man.'

'Glad to hear it, master!' Feste laughed so loud Violetta bid him be quiet. He was in a mood to make mischief. Sometimes she preferred it when he was quiet and melancholy. When he was in this kind of temper, he would use his wit to mock and twist anything that was said.

◆─▶米◀─◆

They were nearing High Wycombe. Greenaway, the carrier, sent back a message to say that they would be stopping for the night. When they reached the outskirts, Will asked Feste to lead the way. The clown hopped down from the cart, put on his jester's hat, slung his drum at his hip, took out his pipe and began to play. He walked in front of the players' wagon; its painted sides and cover announced that they were a travelling company. Such visits were rare, so their arrival attracted an excited crowd.

They were to set up at the White Lion, the inn used by the carriers. The landlord assured Will that they still had the boards to make the stage, kept from the days of the travelling players. Will walked into the yard. It was good and wide, with galleries on three sides. It would do perfectly.

Violetta watched as the place was transformed. The boards were found, dusted down and placed on hogshead barrels. The stage was positioned at the end gallery. The chamber behind would be used as a tiring room, a painted curtain hung across to conceal the actors and serve as a backdrop. There were different cloths, depicting day, night, forest, town or wherever most of the action took place. The actors entered and left the tiring room by way of a window with a bench laid as a step up to the stage. The audience would be ranged around the galleries or standing in the yard, depending on how much they had paid.

Will brought his principal actors together to discuss that night's performance, while others in the company cried their arrival round the town. Feste went with them, playing on his pipe and tabor, while his companions capered and danced to the market square, where those with the skill put on displays of tricks and tumbling that would be expected by this country crowd. Violetta went along to give out handbills and cry up the time and place of performance. She watched the tricks with an appraising eye, tutting over any clumsiness, privately thinking she could do better. The crowd were easily satisfied. She listened to their groans, their quick intakes of breath, and regretted the old life she appeared to have forfeited. When it was over, she envied the performers' smothered looks of delight at the loud whistles and shouts, the applause they attracted.

Once she had given out her bills, she went back to the inn with Feste. Will was with Tod and the other actors, rehearsing. He beckoned to Feste, who vaulted up on to the rough stage. Violetta watched them pace about, getting used to the space, making sure no one was likely to take a step backwards and tumble off the boards. Will held a book in which he was ever scribbling, scoring things through, crossing things out. They were soon too busy to notice her. She wandered away from the stage, wondering what to do.

Maria was in the tiring room. She had unpacked the trunks and was shaking creases from the costumes, brushing down the garments, looking them over for stains that would need sponging, holes and tears that would need repairing. She hummed as she worked, an old air from Illyria. Violetta's eyes stung to hear it – it had been one of her mother's favourites – but she did not go in and join her. Maria had been made wardrobe mistress, but Violetta did not want to become her assistant. It seemed her obvious place, but she could not see herself patching and stitching, lengthening and shortening, letting in and letting out. Instead she sat on one of the stairs that led up to the gallery, watching the actors on the stage, learning the words as they spoke them, watching their gestures and movements. That is where she wanted to be. Women banished from the stage? What foolishness. They were short of players. Many parts had to be doubled. They were going to a deal of trouble coping with the lack, working out who should be onstage and who off it in order not to meet themselves coming back. She might have her chance yet.

The audience began to fill the yard and range themselves round the upper floors. Violetta stood at the entrance collecting the money: a penny for the yard, tuppence for the gallery. Soon the money bag was bulging and the place was full. Every space was taken. Boys climbed up on the roofs and perched there like rows of starlings. Violetta fought her way up the stairs to where George Price had saved a place for her. She smiled and thanked him.

'I saw you this morning,' she said.

'I've got a couple of men among Greenaway's carriers,' he said. 'Two more with the actors. We're here to keep an eye on you. Keep you safe.'

Violetta stared at him. The danger she was in had slowly been sliding out of view. She gripped the rail in front of her, searching the faces in the surrounding galleries, looking down at the crowd crammed into the inn yard.

'Do you think there could be men here? Now?'

'It's possible. It's best to assume so. I look for anything out of the ordinary way of things, like someone watching you instead of the play. Once it begins –' he nodded towards the stage – 'then we will know.'

Around her, the excited chatter began to lessen; the actors had yet to appear, but the audience seemed to know that the play was about to start. Violetta found herself watching the crowd, like George Price, but when the actors stepped out she forgot about that. She was down there with them. These were not boards set out on hogsheads, and this was not an inn yard in High Wycombe, and these were not Will, Tod, Ned, Tom, Henry and the rest, but this was Arden and these were dukes, their daughters, followers and courtiers, shepherds, shepherdesses and lost princes. Even Feste was transformed, splendid in a jester's cap and motley of green and yellow, rather than his battered hat and frayed and faded black.

'All the world's a stage,' the character Will played said, but to Violetta it seemed the other way round. The stage had become the world. Everything outside it ceased to exist. That was where the magic lay. That was why the people had parted with their hard-earned pennies today and would happily do so tomorrow, if the players could be persuaded to stay.

George Price sat by her side, immune to magic. He kept a sharp eye on what was happening in the audience, with the staff of the inn coming and going with food and ale. The players were known and trusted. He was not concerned about them. The play reached its conclusion and his practised eye noticed nothing out of the ordinary. The performance was over. He could reassure her. She was safe for the moment.

◆━◆

The players could not be persuaded to stay, no matter how much the townspeople begged them. Greenaway wanted to get away, and Will did too. He was not happy with the performance and wanted to put the town behind him. What pleased the crowd did not please him. What did they know, being starved of anything but half-remembered mummers' plays and Whit-tide interludes? These were the Lord Chamberlain's Men, yet they had stuttered and groped their way through the play, stumbling about and falling over each other like a cast made up from cobblers and blacksmiths. The next morning saw them packed up and on the road.

Violetta climbed on to the cart. Tod whipped the horses up and soon they had left the town behind them. Feste was sleeping, curled up like a cat in a space behind her. Tod was muttering lines to himself. Maria was busy with her needle, making a little jester's hat and costume of motley for Little Feste. They travelled on in companionable silence, Violetta drowsing a little, lulled by the sway of the wagon and the warm spring weather. She liked being back on the road. Ever since Feste rescued her from Venice, she had been infected by his restlessness. 'The road is no fixed abode, madonna,' he had said to her when they joined their first company. 'It winds between one place and another, between what lies in the past and what waits in the future, so you do not dwell in either. It is where you can be free.'

Feste did not like to stay in one place for long. Even in Illyria, he would wander off, his bag over his shoulder, his lute across his back. No one ever knew exactly where he went, or how long he would be gone. Eventually he would reappear, looking just the same, behaving as if he had never been away, except for the new tales he had to tell of the people he had met and the places he had been. Violetta remembered hearing his stories as a child, wanting to go with him, never guessing that one day her wish would be granted. *Be careful what you wish for.* Her mind was drifting, and she seemed to hear Marijita's voice calling to her from across the years, a distant sound, like a plaintive tune played by a shepherd on an old bone flute and brought down from the mountains on the wind. She woke with a start. *There are no mountains here.* She had been dreaming of her own country. She shivered, suddenly cold. *The past was here. We carry it with us. Feste was wrong.*

She had fallen against Tod in her dozing. She woke with her cheek against the rough wool of his doublet. It smelt faintly of lavender. Perhaps the herb had been strewn in his trunk by his mother. Violetta sat up quickly, tugging her cloak around her.

'You were shivering. It is still April,' Tod said as she pulled away from him. He withdrew the arm that he had put round her in what he hoped she would interpret as a protective, brotherly gesture. 'The breeze can strike chill.'

'I was dreaming of my country.'

'What's it like there?' Tod asked. He'd never been further east than Greenwich.

Violetta looked at the grey clouds lowering over the

rolling hills. Black birds wheeled over patches of woodland; sheep grazed in green fields divided by pale stone walls as bright as knife cuts; men worked in fields made up of long strips that looked like a counterpane stitched together from brown cord, rough woven stuff and stripes of bright green ribbon.

'Not like here,' she said.

Before long, Violetta was asleep on his shoulder again.

'Hup, hup!' Tod called softly. His thoughts ran on as the horses plodded up the next long hill. *Romeo and Juliet*. The play was very popular, being all about love and fighting. There was not a strong clown part, but the nurse was good and bawdy. Something in it for everybody. He would suggest to Master Shakespeare that it should be part of the tour. He could play Romeo and . . . he looked down at Violetta's dark head resting on his shoulder, the delicate arch of her brow, the sweep of her lashes, the curve of her lip, her cheek faintly flushed with sleep. She would make a perfect Juliet. And why not? The rest of the company might need a bit of persuading, but the audience need never know. The rehearsing would be particularly pleasant. Violetta stirred. Her eyes moved under their lids as if she was searching some dream landscape, and Tod sank into a reverie of his own.

◆→◆←◆

Will watched the girl lolling and the boy gather her to him, to prevent her from falling as much as anything, but Will could tell from the tender way he folded her cloak around her that it was more than that. He wondered if the girl realised the effect she had on the young player. Ever since he met her, Tod had been a changed man. For although he was young, he was one for the women. Not that it was difficult. Players could take their pick. The stage cast a glamour. The magic conjured there lingered long after the players had left the stage. It clung to them, disguising their ordinariness, deceiving the sight of the women, and men too, who sent them notes expressing their admiration, desiring to meet them. Violetta seemed immune to it. Perhaps that was because she had been a player herself. Just as wizards and witches are wise to the spells of others, the glamour could not work on her. Besides, she was promised to another. Her countryman Stephano. But that would just provoke Tod further. The more she held him off, the more irresistible he would find her. Will shook his head. Sometimes he was glad to be no longer young.

'Why do you smile, master?'

He looked down to see Feste jogging along beside him.

'I was just thinking how love makes us all into fools.'

'Aye.' Feste nodded. 'It does that. Feste is the only wise man.'

The next town was Oxford. They would lay over there, but would put on no performance. They were not ready, as last night had demonstrated. There was a difference between touring and appearing in a permanent playhouse with a full company. Most of the actors had never been on the road before, and it showed. Besides, the University took a dim view of plays and players alike, seeing both as inciting idleness and corrupting youth. Will did not want to get caught up in some broil.

He wanted to get back to Stratford, to his family, his new house, his life in the town. Perhaps he could get some writing done. He'd left the play he was working on like a field half-ploughed. But this time it would not be the same. What happens in London stays in London – that had always been his watchword – but now he was bringing that world with him. This matter that Cecil had laid upon him lay distant, like a dark line of forest smudging the horizon, but soon enough it would be all around. To write plays full of plotting and intrigue was one thing, to be caught up in them quite another. *All the world's a stage*. His own words were here to taunt him. If that was so, Will always cast himself as audience. He shivered and pulled his cloak about him. Clouds were running in from the west and the chill little wind that had sprung up had rain upon its breath.

19

'Besides that he's a fool, he's a great quarreller'

On Headington Hill, leading down into Oxford, Tod nearly lost control of the rig. The hill was long and steep. A dagging rain had been falling since noon and the road was greasy with dried ruts under the surface slime. About a quarter of the way down, the wheels began to slide. Tod hauled on the brakes until they smoked, but that just made things worse. The whole rig began to slew sideways, threatening to capsize and throw passengers and contents into the milky brown mud. Greenaway acted quickly to stop the descent before the wagon got completely out of Tod's control and involved his valuable line of packhorses in a disastrous spill. Tod resumed his seat, much shaken, blaming the road surface and the horses. Will considered the boy was quite as much at fault for paying too much attention to Violetta and none to his driving, but he did not say anything. The young actor had suffered fright enough.

They crossed the long bridge which spanned the divided streams of the Cherwell, passed the looming tower of Magdalen College and entered the city by the East Gate. At Carfax, the meeting of four ways, Greenaway turned the packhorses into Cornmarket. They were to put up at the inn used by the carriers. Will would stay at the tavern on the other side of the wide street, where Devenant, the landlord, had rooms that were quiet and away from the street. Violetta and Maria were to stay at the tavern with him, while the rest of the actors would put up at the carriers' inn.

There was concern about the cart. Tod was convinced that the slide had loosened one of the wheels and asked Greenaway to look it over with him. Will came back to the inn yard to find the cart up on blocks, a wheelwright and blacksmith in attendance. After further inspection, ale and conversation, it was decided that the trouble could be fixed but it would take a day or two. Will frowned at the delay and the expense involved.

'Hurry them on. Smiths and wheelwrights always lie about the time it will take them to do anything.'

'We could always put on a play,' Tod suggested. 'I've been thinking –'

'No.' Will cut him off. 'There will be no performance here. I have decided. That is an end of it.'

Will's decision was final. He did not intend to quibble. Oxford always seemed to bring him ill luck. He couldn't wait to leave the town.

◆➤◆◆

The next morning, Maria was not feeling well. She'd retired early last evening, the swaying of the cart and the near spill having made her feel queasy, and she still felt good for nothing and was suffering with her stomach.

Mistress Devenant directed Violetta to the nearest apothecary. Violetta was used to being alone in strange places. She had a good sense of direction. Besides, the ways were broad; she was unlikely to get lost. The grand buildings and wide streets, encompassed by a wall pierced through by gates, reminded her of her home city. The only thing missing was the sea.

The apothecary listen carefully as she explained what ailed Maria. He went off to make a fresh decoction and Violetta admired the crocodile dangling from the ceiling, the turtle-shells and the other strange objects that he had displayed about his shop.

She put the package in her basket and stepped on to the street. Up towards Carfax, there was a carriage drawn up causing an obstruction. The crowd thickened with people trying to get past it. She heard someone call her name, in greeting, or warning, but could see no one she recognised in the milling throng. The carriage door was open. Inside she could see a buckled foot, and above it a narrow ankle in black hose. She hesitated which way to go. Then a man appeared, blocking her way. He had one arm in a leather sling, which made it harder to get past him. She tried to back away, but the crowd was all around her, pushing her towards him. His other arm, matted with black hair, criss-crossed with half-healed scratches, reached out for her. She sensed rather than saw the other one coming up behind her. It was the two from the Hollander. They must have dragged themselves out of the river. Now they meant to bundle her into this carriage.

She had no time to struggle. Hands grabbed her and pushed her from behind, while others grasped her arm, dragging her inside. The door banged shut, the lock dropped into place. The driver cracked his whip over the horses and the carriage jolted away.

The window was covered by a leather flap, but there was enough light to see the man sitting opposite her. The carriage lurched as the driver whipped up the horses, and Violetta nearly fell into his lap. He had swapped his Jesuit black for the clothes of a gentleman of fashion, with a ruff about his neck and a high-crowned hat upon his head. The hat was adorned with a jewelled brooch and fine-plumed feather. His russet doublet was slashed to show the green silk lining; his puffed velvet breeches were the same shade of green, slashed to show red satin. They tied beneath the knee in the Venetian fashion and were trimmed with rows of lace.

'Malvolio!'

'I do not go under that name here.' He waved a jewelled hand as if to dismiss the past. 'I am now Signore Vendelino, a gentleman in the service of the Venetian Ambassador. I do not think that you have met my companion.'

He had not been alone in the carriage. There was another man with him, dressed more soberly, but in materials just as rich; his dark doublet glittered with rows of jet beads. He sat forward, his bony hands grasping the silver knob of an ebony stick. His large head looked too big for his narrow shoulders. The strands of thin grey hair that hung from under his hat were spread carefully over his shoulders and his fine lace collar as if to disguise their sparseness.

'This is my friend Sir Andrew. You do not know him, but he knows your family. Especially your mother, Viola. Very like, do you not agree?'

Sir Andrew nodded. 'Very like indeed. The spit of her, and I don't doubt as much of a vixen. She was no friend to me, young lady.'

'What a surprise to see you here, my dear.' Malvolio smiled, his eyes mocking her. 'We are visiting friends in the area and came into Oxford. We have friends here too, in certain of the colleges, and we wanted to visit the place where the blessed sons of the True Faith were lately martyred. I wanted to pay my respects. Make a pilgrimage of sorts. There should be a shrine to them. One day there will be. That day will be soon!' A different light showed in his eyes now. He wiped his mouth with a kerchief and paused to collect himself. 'We came to visit, as I say, and who do I see walking down High Street? What a lucky coincidence. Except I do not believe in coincidence. Our meeting was meant to be. I think you know my men, Crank and Gennings? You escaped them once. I was determined that you would not do so again. They have orders to scour the town for that wretch Feste. If you are here, he cannot be far away.'

'What do you want with me? With Feste? You have ruined our lives and ruined our country. You have taken everything from us. We have nothing. No home, no belongings. We live like vagabonds. What danger can we pose?'

'Soon, none at all,' he said, his smile laced with menace. 'You know what I want.'

'The stone? I don't have it. Neither does Feste.'

'Now, why should I believe you?'

Before he could say anything more, the carriage slowed and came to a halt. It rocked violently, jostled by the crowd. Malvolio pulled back his curtain as the driver cursed, yelling at people to get out of his road.

'There's always a throng going in and out of the South Gate.' Sir Andrew picked up the flap and peered out of his window. 'We will just have to wait.'

They were leaving the city. Violetta looked about,

frantic. She had to escape, or at least draw someone's attention to her capture. With both men turned away from her, she made a lunge for the door. Sir Andrew felt her sudden movement and turned back, changing his grip on the ebony stick. He gave the handle a quick twist and, with a flick of the wrist, a long thin blade hissed through the air between them. She withdrew her hand just in time to avoid being slashed and sat back as he angled the swordstick upwards so that the needle-sharp point was pricking at her throat.

'Not a blink, not a sound as we leave the town, or you will be choking on your own blood.' He regarded her with eyes as pale and colourless as glass. 'Do not think for a minute that I would not do it. The blow your mother dealt still rankles. I would enjoy doing to you what I should have done to her all those years ago.'

The knot of people around them seemed to loosen. They were on the move again. The horses' hoofs on the cobbles took on an echoing clatter and there was a difference in the noise of the wheels over the ground. They were going through the gate. Any hope of help was quickly fading, but Violetta did not move. The thin blade seemed to quiver as if quickened by its owner's malice. She did not make a sound.

The driver cracked his whip and called to the horses. They picked up speed. They were leaving the town behind. They were passing meadows; she could smell grass and river water. Still Sir Andrew did not drop his weapon. Violetta stayed as still as she had been before. She found it hard even to swallow. One look at his eyes told her what she knew already: at the slightest excuse, he would pin her to the back of the carriage, skewering her like a butterfly to a board.

20

'I shall be constrained in't to call thee knave, knight'

'**P**ut up your weapon, Sir Andrew.' Malvolio laid his gloved hand on the naked blade, pushing it away from Violetta. 'She is not going anywhere and it would not be wise, so near to the town.'

He drew back the curtain so that Violetta could see the countryside: meadows, marshland, the meandering course of a river. There were no people here, just long-horned cattle. She was careful to keep her face free of any expression. She was determined not to show any fear. Malvolio smiled as if he knew that the hopelessness pricking her heart was every bit as sharp as the point of the sword at her throat.

'She faces her future bravely, does she not?' He turned to Sir Andrew. 'Every bit her mother's daughter. Her mother . . .' he went on, speaking about her as if she was not there. 'There is a story. She arrived as if from nowhere, emerging from the sea, like Aphrodite. It was not natural – many said it at the time, I among them.'

'Witchcraft.' Sir Andrew spat the word out. 'Pure and simple. Her mother was a witch. She is one too.' He looked at Violetta. 'Do you deny it?'

'Certainly I deny it.' She looked from one to the other. 'Why do you insult me and my mother's memory with these foul untruths?'

'Untrue, you say?' Malvolio's eyebrows rose. 'Yet

you practise sorcery more or less openly.'

'I do not!'

'You carry the trappings about you. What is that you wear around your neck?'

'A charm, an amulet. Such as is worn by many in my country.'

'What of the shewstone?' Malvolio sat forward. 'What is that, if not sorcery?'

'And you would not use it?'

'For good. Not ill. To tell us who our enemies are, what they are planning. You will tell us where it is and you will help us, or you will burn at the stake.'

'They do not burn witches here,' Sir Andrew corrected him. 'They hang them instead.'

'That is a pity. Burning is much more fitting; but dead is dead, in any event.'

'I do not have it. I told you.'

'Oh, you have it. Although that vile rascal Feste seems an unlikely bearer. Why you should trust it to him is beyond me.' His small mouth twitched. He was a connoisseur of cruelty and could tell by her eyes that he had guessed right. 'Oxford is a small place. He will not elude my men for long. We will have it, and once we do . . .' He pressed together finger and thumb as if snuffing out a candle. 'Who will miss you? Your friends? The players? We saw their cart at High Wycombe.'

'They are not our friends. We are not travelling with them.'

Malvolio shrugged. 'You will sink from their memory like a pebble cast into a brook. No one will care if you die.' He smiled as he prepared to deliver the final blow. 'Loyal sons of Illyria know where their duty lies.'

The words chimed precisely with Feste's suspicions about Stephano and Guido. Feste was rarely wrong about people. Malvolio had been probing with great care, looking for the tenderest spot and he'd found it. Violetta had been careful to mask her feelings, but she could not hide her reaction to that.

'I thank the Lord and his Blessed Mother that Lord Stephano has seen the error of his ways,' he went on, his words as precise and measured as drops of poison slipped into a sleeper's ear. 'He is destined for greatness. The Venetian Ambassador has a daughter, Christiana. A girl both beautiful and accomplished, from one of Venice's oldest families, a cousin of Lady Francesca, who accompanies her. Their marriage will cement Illyria's alliance with Venice. In the fullness of time, she will become Duchessa. They will rule together under the protection of Venice. What true Illyrian would not want that for his country?'

He sat back, his eyes like clouded agate, the better to savour the pain he was inflicting. He was tempted to taunt her further, but thought better of it. The poison was slow-acting but sure; it would work its way down into her soul.

His satisfaction was short-lived. The carriage took a violent lurch to the right. There was a crash, as if something heavy had fallen, then it began to slow.

'What in the name of . . . !' Malvolio shouted as they came to stop. He drew back the curtain and looked down a rough bank at a waste of marsh and willows. 'Where are we? Why are we stopping here?'

'Looking for me, gents?' He started back as Feste's grinning face appeared at the window, upside down like a hanging devil. 'Well, you've found me!' The next moment, he was in the carriage. 'Don't you move,' he said to Sir Andrew, 'or I'll open his fat throat.'

Sir Andrew was struggling to draw his sword, but Violetta was too quick for him. She wrenched his stick away and soon had the sword pointed at his midriff.

'Out! Both of you, out!' Feste forced them from the carriage.

He was all for killing them and pushing them into the marsh. 'It looks good and boggy down there –' he craned over the edge of the causeway – 'and we are miles from anywhere. Who would think to look here? They'd sink right to the bottom. No one will ever find them. What could be better?'

'No!' Violetta shook her head. 'I'll have no killing.'

'Have it your way, madonna.' Feste sighed his disappointment as he turned to the two men. 'Take your shoes off, both of you!' he ordered. 'Throw them into the carriage. Now stand over there.'

He marched them in their stockinged feet to the edge of the causeway. The steep sides were tangled with willows and brambles. At the bottom, marshy ground spread away, dotted with dark pools, spiked with patches of reed and bright with moss and water buttercup. When he had them positioned to his satisfaction, he pushed them over, one at a time.

'Hear that, madonna?' He laughed at each cry and crash, peering over at the final splash. 'Up to their arses in muck! It'll take them a while to get out of that.'

There was the sound of hoofs on the road. George Price threw himself down off his horse.

'I saw them take you, but couldn't get to you,' he

panted. 'The crush was too great. Then I had to find a horse.' He looked to the open door of the carriage. 'What have you done with them?'

Feste pointed. The two men were splashing and wallowing, bellowing like calves caught in a mire. When they saw Price, they began waving and hollering, hoping that he would save them. It was a comic prospect, but Price was not laughing.

'Whose idea was that?' he asked.

'Hers.' Feste stood, arms folded. 'I would have killed them.'

'I will not have blood on my hands,' Violetta said. 'Theirs or any man's.'

'You should have killed them,' Price said. 'You may live to regret your kind-heartedness. There's a saying in my line of work: you should always kill those who would kill you.'

❖❧❖

Will surfaced slowly, coming to the present place and time as a man might exchange one element for another. He had been gazing out of the window at the roofs and chimney pots of Oxford, but not seeing them. He had been staring at a skull, clotted with earth, mossy with clumps of hair still attached here and there, smelling of the grave. The recently disinterred, dug up to make way for a fresh occupant, as often happened in the burying grounds in London. He had seen it many times, gravediggers throwing skulls about, using them as footballs, hitting them with thigh bones in games of stick ball. Dead is dead. What does it matter? But the grave disturbed, the corpse unearthed, filled him with a special horror. He had half slipped back into his reverie, when the knocking came again.

What was it now? Will ran his hands through his wiry dark hair; no wonder it was thinning by the day. He had given instructions not to be disturbed on any account. Why did no one ever heed what he said? He was tempted not to answer, but then thought it might be one of the lads with news of the cart – that they needed more money to pay the blacksmith, or the wheelwright, or even worse, that it could not be repaired and they would have to get another. He was already reaching for his strongbox and wondering what the rate would be for wagon hire as he called: 'Come in!'

The table in front of him was spread with papers: some neat, fair copies, others hatched and black with additions and crossings-out. He was in his shirtsleeves, a quill in his hand, his fingers stained with ink. He turned as Violetta entered. She could tell by his look of surprise that he had not been expecting her.

'Violetta?' His look was quizzical and enquiring. 'What has happened?' he asked, reading the trouble on her face. 'What is it?'

He put down his pen and wiped his ink-stained hand on his breeches. He listened, arms folded, until she had finished.

'How did they know I was here?'

'It could have been an accident.' Will shrugged. 'Perhaps he was visiting someone and saw you. There are plenty of papists in Oxford.'

'Perhaps, but what if they keep following?'

'We have George Price. He seems a useful fellow.'

'He is,' Violetta agreed. 'But he cannot look after

everyone. We are drawing danger to you like a tower draws lightning. I don't want to bring trouble into your home.'

'You won't be staying there for long. When we get to Stratford, I intend to hide you.'

'Hide me? Where?'

'I know a place. A place they will never find you. A place where you will be safe.' Whether she would ever get out again was a different matter, he almost crossed his fingers, but he would worry about that later. Present concerns were pressing harder. 'I'd better go down and see how the work on the cart goes on.'

He took one last look at the pages in front of him. He would get no more writing done today. He pushed his chair back from the desk and pulled on his jerkin. Unless that wheel was fixed on the wagon, they would not be going anywhere.

21

'O mistress mine, where are you roaming?'

They started early. The sun had barely risen above the rooftops and the inn yard was in deep shadow when the company assembled. Greenaway had left the day before. George Price and his men had shed their carriers' sheepskins for travelling cloaks. They would be joining their party as ordinary travellers. There was safety in numbers on the road. Will hired extra horses; he did not want anyone walking. It was more expense, and he had already dug deep to pay blacksmith, wheelwright and farrier, but it could not be helped. He wanted no more delay. If they got off smartly, and made good time on the road, they might be able to get as far as Shipston, perhaps even home to Stratford. His heart rose at the prospect, but there were many miles to go before they crossed Clopton Bridge. Anything could happen before then.

The first town they came to was Woodstock. The long main street was crowded. A tall maypole was being erected in the marketplace. Tomorrow was May Day. Will had not thought of that. He had completely lost track of the days since they had left London. He listened to Tod's chatter, telling Violetta about the celebrations that would follow on the morrow. He wondered what the custom was in her country; May Day was ever popular with the young.

They turned into the inn at the foot of the steep hill that wound out of Woodstock to rest and water the horses and take refreshment themselves. It would be a lengthy haul after that, with precious few places to stop. And lonely, with remnants of the ancient Wychwood Forest stretching off to the west as they took one long rise after another, sapping for men and horses alike.

The day was fine. The sun held the promise of summer. Jacinth crept from the edge of the wildwood and the party was infected with the mood of coming holiday. Maypoles were going up on the greens of each little hamlet they passed through, some brightly painted, others plain trunks still nubbed with lopped branches, but all garlanded with flowers, rosettes and hanging ribbons.

Tod explained the customs of the country to Violetta. Very early in the morning, youths and girls go out together to gather quickthorn blossom to decorate the lintels of houses and cottages. His fair skin coloured as he was telling her this, as though there was more to the early morning expeditions than picking flowers, but he was too careful of her to hint at anything like that. He went on hurriedly. Superstitions are as two-edged as swords. They are careful not to take too much from one tree, or to bring the blossoms inside. That would bring bad luck, and it's death to fell a thorn tree.

'Do you celebrate May Day in Illyria?' he asked her.

'We do,' she said, 'and it is a time of singing and dancing. Houses are decorated with flowers, the doors garlanded with bay. On the night before it, *this* night, witches are said to gather. It is a time of the year when the boundary thins between the dead and the living. Spirits and sprites walk and wander. Only the witches know which are good and which are evil. Other folk keep indoors.'

Tod looked up at the sky, reading the time from the sun: about three in the afternoon. Five hours to sundown, by his reckoning. He cracked his reins, urging the horses up yet another long rise.

◆►❂◄◆

They came down the long, steep hill that marked the Cotswolds' edge, almost under the shadow of the Rollright Stones. It was a place famous for witches, as notorious hereabouts as the Brocken Mountain in Germany. The rites held there were described in the little chapbook where Kit Marlowe found the story of Dr Faustus. Will did not have to read about them in books.

The sun was dropping away quickly now, below the rough edge of the horizon. Trees and coppices stood out, etched black against the red-and-orange sky. Night drew on and dark shapes filled the air, some trailing twigs and sticks, but they were only birds, lone crows and rooks whirling down in a clamour of harsh cries, returning to their nesting places before the last of the light disappeared.

Will did not believe that witches flew through the air, but everyone knew that they would be gathering. Most would be walking, some arriving on horseback, a very few by carriage. They would be coming from towns and villages, tiny hamlets and isolated cottages, travelling from many miles around, slipping away early to follow the old green ways and hollow ways, the salt roads and ancient tracks that passed through field and forest; guided from parish to parish by steeples, church towers and the old markers: standing stones, lone trees and coppices, notches in hillsides, the fingerposts of ancient memory that pointed them to the green paths that joined the ridgeway and brought them to the stones.

Then, as though thought had invited it, there was a sudden glow above them. It lay to the west, as if the sun had reignited. All around, from hill to hill, the Beltane fires sprang out, from the Rollrights to Lark Hill to Brailes and on across the county, as if fired by a spark born from this one beacon, carried on some spirit wind.

There was something in the very air, a kind of thickening, as if a storm was brewing, although the sky was a clear, deep blue. It was as though they were surrounded by unseen presences. The horses felt it. Although tired from a hard day's travelling, they grew nervous and skittish. One pulled harder than the other as they took the long slope from the hills to the plain. Tod had to fight to control them and to prevent the cart from spilling. His face was pale, rigid with concentration. The repair that they had made was only temporary. The whole thing could go again.

'We must make haste,' Will shouted.

'I know that, master,' Tod shouted back. 'It is just a thing of tale and story,' he muttered, trying hard to dismiss it, but he didn't quite believe it. Everybody knew: all things that flew, walked or crawled – elves, imps, fairies, sprites and boggarts – everything caught between Earth and Heaven would be out tonight.

People did not like to be out on this night in her

country either. Violetta sat by his side, caught up in the general unease.

They drove on, while the glow behind them grew and the woodland margins and hedgerows seemed to stir and move with life hidden from view. The village of Long Compton was in darkness. No dogs barked as they entered the winding main street. Blossom glimmered on the fruit trees in the gardens crowded close to the old church. The white petals of apple and pear drifted past the black yews and into the graveyard, to dance there like the spirits of those who were to die that year, old and young. This was a night when such things could happen. Or so country people believed. Long Compton had its share of witches, enough to pull a wagonload of hay up Harrow Hill, that's what they said. They would all be up at the stones this night, but all the doors were firmly shut, some with boughs of rowan above the lintel, sovereign at warding off evil spirits. Better to be safe. There was no one about and hardly a light showed through the shutters of any of the small stone houses and low thatched cottages that straggled along the sides of the road.

Will directed Tod to turn in off the main street to the inn that he always used. He had been here many times, accompanying his father's visits to the glove-makers here or in the old man's brogging days when he would go out buying fleeces for the illegal wool trade. Later, Will had often broken his journey here on his way to or from London.

At first the inn seemed as quiet and deserted as the houses. The door had a rowan bough above the lintel and they had to do a deal of knocking before the landlord appeared. Once he saw who was calling him, and the size of the company, he lost his wariness.

'Will Greenaway said to expect you. Come in! Welcome all!'

He called for boys to uncouple the cart and look after the horses, and sent girls to make rooms ready. The night was not cold, but there was a good fire in the grate. The landlady brought jugs of ale and cider and soon had a table laid for them with ham, cold fowl, cheeses and several kinds of pie.

Once they had eaten, the jugs were replenished, a space was cleared for dancing and someone called for a song. Instruments appeared as if from nowhere, and everyone took their places. It was a tradition, when they were out on the road, that each would take a turn to entertain the company. Tod began to sing in a strong high tenor, '*Oh, mistress mine, why do you roam?*'

As he began his song, he turned to Violetta. Will smiled. It was one of the boy's own songs. He had a good voice and fancied himself as something of a poet. He accompanied himself on the lute and it was a pretty tune, but the words were not quite right, too flowery and about nothing, bent to make the rhyme. He looked from the singer to the object of his song. Violetta's cheeks were swept with a delicate shade of madder at being the focus of the boy's attention. She looked so lovely. And so young.

Violetta was relieved when others took over the singing and she drank deep of the cup being passed round to cover her embarrassment. All day Tod had been flirting with her, his attentions becoming more and more obvious. One after another the players sang:

popular songs known to everyone, bawdy ditties that brought a belly laugh. The landlord kept them well supplied with strong ale of his own brewing. Word got round and the inn was soon crowded with people from the village. The players were good for business. The music was bringing them scurrying out of their houses and through the doors of the inn. Merry-making is an excellent antidote to fear.

'Everyone has to take a turn,' Tod said. 'Is that not so, Master Shakespeare?'

Violetta smiled, thinking that he was teasing her.

'Yes,' Will agreed, 'that is so. It is a rule of the company when we are on tour.'

'But I cannot sing!' Violetta protested. 'I do not know anything!'

'Yes, she can!' Feste grabbed her by the hand. 'And dance, too! Come, Violetta. Show them!'

He whirled her into the middle of the room, into the space cleared for dancing. Violetta pulled away from him. She had no intention of taking part, but he'd begun to beat on his drum. Maria picked up the familiar rhythm on spoons, clattering them against her thigh and humming. Violetta began stepping to a tune that she had known from childhood: an ancient song from the threshing floor. A piper began to play, a fiddler joined him. Feste's insistent rhythm was picked up by others, who clapped or beat out time on tables, stools, anything they could reach, and called her name: *Violetta! Violetta!* as she turned and turned in the dance. Then she began to sing.

Her voice was totally unexpected. So strong, so plaintive, so powerful that the other instruments fell silent; only Feste's drum continued its beat. The raucous company listened in wonder. Will felt the hairs stirring on the back of his neck as she sang of loss and longing, of joy and sorrowing, of the beginning and the end of things. It was the kind of song that made you laugh and be glad, while you cried at its sadness. It did not matter that the language was strange to him. He did not want to know the meaning of the words. The song spoke of mysteries, as if composed in a place beyond our world, by a people beyond our knowing.

Maria joined Violetta. They swayed and sang together, tears streaming down their faces, their voices going higher and higher, as if they would join some celestial chorus. Then the song ended, all on a sudden, as if there was nothing left to sing.

There was a brief silence; then everyone began clapping and cheering, drumming and stamping, shouting for more. Maria took her hand and curtsied to the company, while Violetta looked around her as if wondering who and why they were applauding.

'It is a song of my country, nothing more,' she said, refusing all entreaties to sing again. 'I am tired now. I will retire.'

Maria came with her and was soon snoring, but the roistering downstairs looked set to go on far into the night. Violetta could not settle into sleep. Perhaps the wildness of the night had infected her. Even after the last carousers had stumbled up the stairs, or had shouted their goodnights and staggered off to their homes, she was still awake. The inn was quiet now, except for the creaking of the old timbers, the skitter of mice in the rafters, the muffled chorus of snores coming from different rooms.

At length she got up, unable to lie still any longer waiting for sleep that would not come. She went to the window. The merest sliver of a moon looked down, a bright shaving of silver. The same indifferent moon gazed down on Illyria, while she stood, a stranger in a strange land, beset by uncertainties, unable to see anything, blind as a mole.

She stole from the room in search of the sleeping Feste and found him curled on a truckle bed outside her door. He chose to sleep there, close to her, as he had done to Lady Olivia. She smiled as she looked down at him. Despite their spats and quarrels, there was great affection between them and a loyalty unto death. He would give his life for her, she knew that, but would he ever wake in time to foil a potential assassin? That was the question. The killer would likely just step over him. When in drink, which was most nights, Feste slept like the dead. She marvelled at how like a child he looked, his pale face unlined, unmarked by any of his debaucheries. He held Little Feste clutched tight, as if it could comfort his troubled heart and still his restless dreams.

He did not stir as she took the folly stick from him, his arms closing on empty air. She carried it back to her room and twisted the carved cap to remove the top of the skull. The shewstone lay inside like a translucent egg. She took it out carefully and went over to the window. The faint silver light struck through the glass, igniting a golden glow deep in the milky blue depths of the stone. Violetta stood quite still, muttering an incantation to Hecate, goddess of the moon, queen of the witches. Ask, and she would answer. The stone hadn't worked here before, but this night belonged to her. Perhaps it would do now. The moon shone down on all.

At first she could see nothing, but Violetta knew she had to be patient, continue looking and the blankness would pass. Then she saw her mother smiling out at her. She felt the touch of her fingers on her cheek. Violetta was startled; she hadn't been thinking about her mother, but the stone showed many things, not all of them present in the forefront of the mind. Perhaps she was there all the time.

Violetta felt the old sensation, of being in the scene and out of it, like in a dream. She was standing on the shore now, like she had done as a young child. Her mother said no word, just turned away from her, towards the sea. She was wearing a thin summer shift, gathered at the shoulder. She undid the clasp and let her clothes drop from her on to the sand. Then she dived into the waves. It was night-time. The sea shone black and silver, like a tarnished shield. She swam away from the shore with long, strong strokes, out into the bay. Violetta was looking down at the scene now, as if she was a bird flying high above the wrinkling waves. There was a ship anchored in the next bay, a pirate vessel, its sails as red as blood. A long boat waited, close to the headland; it began to slip through the water. Antonio, Sebastian's friend, the Uskok pirate, stood in the prow. She saw the glint of steel from the rings in his ears, his trailing mustachios, his iron-grey hair spread over his shoulders like lengths of twisted wire. One blow from his long, curving oar and the swimmer was stopped in her motion. Her pale body glimmered as it slipped beneath the surface waves and drifted down to the black depths. The boat rowed back. The ship flew the flag of Senj. She had been killed on the orders of her own brother. Violetta turned away from the stone. Some things you do not have to see to know.

When she turned back, the scene had changed. She was in a chapel, small and intimate, Mass was being said by a priest. Beneath the ornate vestments, Violetta recognised Malvolio. He was served by the thin young Jesuit. The congregation was small. Those at the front were nobly and richly dressed, with servants and people of a lower sort at the back. The atmosphere was tense and furtive. Violetta suddenly knew that this was an English house, where to hear Mass was against the law and to serve it was treason.

The heads were bent and devout. Sir Andrew was sitting in the front row. Violetta looked along from him and found Stephano and Guido. A lady sat between them. She wore a gown of rose brocade, slashed at the sleeves and all embroidered in silver. Her thick wheaten hair was caught up under a caul of gold netting, decorated with pearls. Violetta did not have to see her face; she could tell that she was beautiful by the colour of her hair, the narrowness of her waist, the set of her shoulders, the richness of her clothes. They were sitting close, so close as to be actually touching, even though their eyes were closed, their fingers locked in prayer. Near to her sat Lady Francesca, head bowed, similarly devout. She appeared somehow diminished. Her elaborately coiffed hair looked thin and lustreless, her slender frame merely bony, her pale allure insipid. Her carefully conjured beauty had been quite eclipsed by the girl's youth and bloom.

Violetta's attention was caught by a movement from the priest as he turned to face something that had been placed on the altar between the candles: a domed reliquary, intricately worked, chased and embossed to show the scenes of the Epiphany, silver on gold, bright with enamel and gleaming with precious stones. The doors were closed, but Violetta knew that inside lay the holy vessel that had contained the myrrh used to embalm the body of Our Lord.

What was it doing here? It had been put in great jeopardy: taken from its rightful place, brought to a country that counted such things as baubles, with no more worth than the value of their metal, to be venerated in a chapel no bigger than a closet.

Violetta looked on as fair head leaned towards darker and the two whispered together under the breath of prayer. She remembered those games well. Their promises to each other had not been blessed by the Church, but in Violetta's mind they were just as abiding. Had he not held her in his arms, whispered of his love as they walked by the soft flowing Thames? Had he not pledged first his help and then, taking her in his arms again, himself? They would take the blessed relic back to Illyria; they would return in triumph; they would be married in the cathedral and their true love would make up for their parents' failures. They would restore peace and prosperity to their country and rule as one. Had he not said all that to her only a few days ago? Was he betraying her with the daughter of the Venetian Ambassador, sitting so close a knife could hardly be fitted between them? Malvolio had insinuated as much. He knew how to wound, and he knew too that truth cut deeper than lies. Stephano had been all on fire for them to be married, to go to the Ambassador and be restored to Illyria by Venice's power. How much did he want to be Duke? Feste had been right to doubt Stephano. He had been right and she hadn't believed him. Who was the fool now?

She turned away, no longer able to see. Maria had warned her not to trust the stone, but what did she know? Violetta blinked the tears away and then returned her gaze, clear-eyed, the showing in the stone replaced by her own vision. The relic would be returned to Illyria, set in its rightful place in the cathedral there. Malvolio would be punished for what he had done, even if she had to do it with her own hand. As for Stephano, if he thought that he could replace *her*, Violetta, with a Venetian whore, he could think again. She would rule as the Duchessa, and she would rule alone.

She stood rapt, lost in her thoughts, roused only when the cock crowed. She opened her eyes to the first grey light of dawn. The stone in her hands was once again just that, a stone. She looked out to see a young man standing in the yard below, looking up at her window. She thought she was still dreaming. Stranger by far than anything that the stone had revealed to her. It was if she had conjured him. One last gift from Hecate.

'Come down!' he mouthed, his arm beckoning. 'Come down!'

She pulled her gown over her head and ran barefoot to meet him, giving the folly stick back to a sleeping Feste on her way.

She approached Stephano slowly. She reached up and touched his face, hardly trusting that he was real.

'I saw you. I saw you with another,' she said when she could find her voice.

'In a dream?' he asked.

'Yes, in a kind of a dream.'

'Who was the lady?'

'I only saw her from the back, but I could tell that she was beautiful,' she said reluctantly. 'Richly dressed with wheaten hair caught up in a golden net all embroidered with pearls. You were in a chapel sitting close to her.'

'Dreams can be false. At least that one was.' He laughed. 'That is Christiana, the Ambassador's daughter. She's promised to Guido. If I was sitting close, he was sitting closer. There's not much room in those chapels – they're hardly bigger than cupboards.' He took her hands in his. 'I've ridden all day and all night to find you. I am true to you and you only.'

'What I saw . . .' She looked away from him. 'It chimed with something Malvolio said.'

'Malvolio?' Stephano frowned. 'When did you see him?'

'He was in Oxford,' Violetta said. 'He took me captive, him and Sir Andrew. Feste rescued me. Tipped them out of the carriage into a mire.'

'So *that's* what happened.' Stephano smiled. 'They tried to twist it about, said they had been set about by rogues, not a clown and a girl.' His face grew serious. 'Don't believe any foulness that comes from his mouth. He takes delight in hurting people – you said so yourself.'

'Don't let's talk about him now. It's May morning. They have a custom here . . .'

She took his hand and they walked out into

meadows heavy with dew. The sun made every blade glisten, as if each one was studded with crystal.

They went up to the ridge behind the village. The air was quite still, with no wind to chill the skin. Violetta stood between the land and the sky and closed her eyes. The strengthening sun held the promise of warmth during that day, and in all the days to come. She breathed in and felt as though she had drunk a great draught of fine Rhenish wine. The air was heady with the scents of earth, trampled grass and pollen, green growing things. She held Stephano's hand and did not let go of it. He drew her to him and they kissed as larks rose about them and the belling call of the cuckoo welcomed in the spring.

They met other couples coming from the woods laden with armfuls of blossom and garlands of wild flowers: jacinth, cowslips, oxslips, fritillary, lady's smock and buttercups. Violetta and Stephano joined them. They came back together, bearing boughs of May blossom for the innkeeper to decorate his lintel, garlands for the horses and wagon.

'Where have you been?' Maria demanded. 'I've been looking for you everywhere.'

'It is May Day morning,' Violetta replied. 'I have been out in the fields collecting flowers. It is the custom.'

Stephano had left her to find Master Shakespeare. Violetta had wandered out into the yard, feeling dazed, strange, detached from the bustle going on about her.

'For unmarried maids to go to the woods with men before the sun has fairly risen?' Maria frowned. 'Is that what they do here?'

'So it seems. They go out to pick flowers.'

'Is that what they're calling it now?' Feste chipped in from the back of the cart.

He had been listening to the conversation with interest while munching on bread and bacon.

Violetta looked at him. 'That's what we were doing. Gathering blossom and plucking flowers for garlands. They say it is good luck.'

'I bet they do!' Feste cackled. 'There was plucking going on, I'd wager, and not just flowers. I wonder where Stephano is on this bright May morning.' He cupped a hand to his ear. 'Does he hear the cuckoo, d'you think?'

'That's enough from you, Feste!' Maria scolded. 'You are no more than a vulgar, bawdy mischief-maker. Go your ways. Find something useful to do!'

'Vulgar? Bawdy? Mischief-maker?' Feste threw the rest of his bread to the dogs in the yard. 'I'm a jester, mistress. That's why folk pay me. It's my job!'

Violetta laughed. They hadn't seen Stephano yet.

'I don't know what you are laughing about.' Maria turned on her. 'I'm the nearest thing you have to a mother, so I will take the liberty. He's a fine young fellow, no mistaking that. But he's a player, with a girl in every town and hamlet, I shouldn't wonder, and who knows how many in London. He's not for you. Do not forget who you are and that you are promised.'

'You think I was with Tod?' Violetta laughed again. 'Oh, Maria!' She took her hands. 'It was Stephano!' She turned to Feste. 'And yes, he did hear the cuckoo. So did I. We heard it together. Up on the ridge.'

'Lord Stephano!' Maria's face was transformed. 'Here? Now?'

'Yes. He's inside talking to Master Shakespeare. He rode all night to get here.'

'Well, that changes things.' Maria tore off her apron, tidying her hair as she made for the inn door.

Feste hopped off the back of the cart.

'Rode all night to pick flowers? Now I've heard everything.'

<hr />

Will was talking to Stephano, but the boy was hardly listening. He had given a good account of himself, the information he brought was valuable, but his first intent was to be with the girl. His eyes kept straying to the window to catch a glimpse of her, or to the door to see if she was entering the room. Will had seen them returning together, laughing, arms linked, Violetta's hair laced with flowers, the boy's dark head crowned with buttercups. He had not seen her look like that before. She looked younger, all the worry and care gone from her face. Yet older too. If the girl was the image of her mother, then Viola must have been very beautiful.

The lad had followed them from Oxford, riding through the night, yet he looked as fresh as if he had just risen from his bed, while Will's head ached from the night before and his back pained him from sleeping on hard boards and a thin mattress. He'd crossed the great divide, begun the long slide from youth to age. He thanked Stephano and let him go out to find his girl. They were young. Let them enjoy it while they could.

22

'More matter for a May morning'

There was no hope of an early start. The cart was left in the inn yard. The whole village was parading down the long main street, with drummers drumming and pipers piping to welcome in the merry morning of May. They were led by the Queen of the May, the prettiest girl in the village, crowned with flowers, borne shoulder high with her attendants around her. She was accompanied by Jack o' the Green, a young man caged all in leaves. The Morris sides were out, their faces blacked, many-coloured ribbons fluttering on their tatter coats, bells jingling, kerchiefs waving, accompanied by hobby hoss and clown. Feste broke away to join them, greeted by shouts of welcome. Will led his company, joining in at the end of the procession to go to the celebrations round the Maypole on the green.

Violetta, still wearing the garland of flowers fashioned that morning, took Stephano's hand and led him into the dance. The steps were simple, like the circle dances of their native land. Stephano cut an exotic figure in the intricate courtship of the dance. He had stripped off his doublet, and his fine cambric shirt billowed as he danced, showing glimpses of burnished, golden skin, so different from the poultry-white local boys. His long dark hair flew out as he turned, and his earring flashed. All the girls looked in his direction. Every maid, every matron, wanted a turn with him, but his gaze never left Violetta. He wove through the dancers with grace and energy, but his only aim was to return to her. She was his Queen of the May. None more beautiful would be crowned that day.

Ever the watcher, Will stood to one side, supping his ale, refusing all entreaties to join the dancers. He was impatient to get home, but he would let them dance yet awhile. It was a perfect day for it. No chilling rain, as in recent years, or rough winds to spoil the promised arrival of summer. He'd been wondering how young Tod would take the sudden appearance of a rival, but Violetta did not seem to have bruised his heart too much. One minute he was dancing with the Queen of the May; the next, Will saw them slipping away.

Stephano left them and they went on, a merry party. Some of the villagers were coming along with them to visit other towns and villages on the way to Stratford, the Queen of the May among them, riding on a pony, her crowning garland slightly askew. Not far to go now. Will felt his heart quicken in both dread and anticipation as he noted the landmarks that meant he was nearing home, crossing the Stour at Newbold, sighting the windmill above Alderminster. A few miles on, just off the road on the left, stood the lone boundary oak. Behind the antler-spread of its bare upper branches lay the long back of Meon Hill. Woods cloaked its slopes like a dark mantle. At the summit, a lone thorn tree stood stark against the sky. Another witches' hill. It was several miles across country, but he could almost smell the smouldering embers of the Beltane fire that had blazed there last night.

It was late afternoon before they came to the bridge that would take them across the Avon into Stratford. The sun was bright, but Violetta shivered.

'It is always cold down by the river,' Will said to her as the cart began to rumble over the nine spans of the bridge.

He felt a chill of his own as boys left off fishing and messing on the bank and came to run alongside them, attracted by the painted wagon. He caught himself looking for his own lad, Hamnet, among them, although he'd have been too old to play by the river. He was eleven when he was taken by a sudden fever. He lay in Holy Trinity churchyard now, eleven for ever. There was a fair at the bridge foot and up Bridge Street. Will directed Tod along Waterside, up Sheep Street and into High Street. Chapel Lane would be too narrow for the cart.

New Place occupied the corner plot, opposite the Guild Church. It was an impressive building of brick and timber, built on three storeys with five gables. News of their arrival had already spread and Anne and his daughters were standing outside ready to greet them, with caps straightened and aprons hastily discarded. His wife was a tall woman, still handsome, with fine grey eyes. Her face was smooth, but lines of care and worry were beginning to show about her mouth and across her forehead. She was already casting an eye over the company, calculating how many beds they would need, how many mouths there would be to feed. Next to her stood two girls of about sixteen and eighteen; the younger was shorter in stature, with an open, pretty face. She darted forward to embrace her father as soon as he had dismounted. The older and taller of the two held back, looking on with her father's dark eyes and watchful expression, waiting for her mother to make her husband welcome, as was seemly. Anne Shakespeare did not look to be a woman who wore her emotions for the world to see, but there was a tear in her eye as Will came forward and put his arms round his family. After a moment's quiet, they were all talking at once, countering one question with another as they walked through the gate and to the door of the house. Violetta could barely look at them. No matter where she went or how far she travelled, she would never again feel a mother's hand on her shoulder, a father's arms gathering her into his embrace.

❖❯❳❰❖

Violetta wandered the garden, shooed out of the kitchen by the other women. Maria was making herself useful, but Violetta was more hindrance than help. She had many talents, but cooking and sewing were not among them. Will had gone off to visit his father, who was sick, Mistress Anne said, and to see the town council, to seek permission to perform in the guildhall. He had known most of them since boyhood, so did not anticipate any problems with that. The company had repaired to the Bear. Mistress Anne was glad of that. She didn't want players cluttering up the place, eating them out of house and home.

Mistress Anne told Violetta not to go out on her own. She did not know who this girl was, but there was more to her than Will was saying at the moment. He'd tell her in his good time, no doubt.

'This is a small town,' she'd said, wiping her hands

on her apron. 'You'll stick out like a jay in a flock of starlings. So no further than the garden gate.'

Mistress Anne had a frank way of speaking and a stern manner. Violetta had no intention of disobeying her. She looked round the garden. Mistress Anne had already started her planting. It was a fine plot, with sunny walls for vines and fruit trees. There was an orchard off to one side, with the apples and pears, cherries and plums all in blossom.

'It's a good garden and will come better.' Mistress Anne had come out in search of herbs for the stew she was preparing. 'Once the builders have gone.' Half the land was trampled and piled with blocks of stone, stacks of bricks and lengths of timber. 'No sooner do they finish one thing, then they find something else needs doing. I want Will to have a word with them. Here he comes now. Tell young Lambert,' she said to her husband, 'I want this lot cleared up and I want them out within the month.'

She went back into the house with her bunch of herbs. When Will had talked to the builder, he came back to Violetta. They walked about, Will asking her opinion on where they should have flower beds.

'After I'd been to father's house, I went to the Swan,' he said as they walked from one part of the garden to another. 'I found my old friends there. They welcomed me in, making room in their circle as if I'd never been away. We talked of this and that – they are important men in the town now and I had favours to ask – then Richard Quiney said, "I hear you travel with a princess from a foreign land and her clown. A droll little fellow, by all accounts." I near choked on my ale.'

'Who told him that?' Violetta looked at Will, alarmed. 'How could he know?'

Will shrugged. 'News travels quicker than fire through straw round here. Some sparks fly east, some fly west, some down to London and some t'other way.' Will had felt the town close round him. 'No man's business is his own in a place like this. Cecil's spies have nothing on the good people of Stratford. I told them that there was a young woman who joined us for safety, travelling north to visit kin, but I don't like it. I have to get you away.' He was silent for a while, thinking. 'When I come home, I like to go to the churchyard,' he said. 'Put some flowers on my lad Hamnet's grave. Perhaps you would care to come with me? There's someone there that I think you should meet.'

Violetta helped him pick flowers to make a posy. A graveyard was a strange place to meet someone. Who could this be?

❧

They walked down a long avenue of limes towards an old woman sweeping winter leaves from the porch. She left off sweeping as they approached and leaned on her broomstick to watch.

'Old Meg.' Will nodded to her. 'She sweeps the church porch and keeps the paths tidy. She'll be over shortly. You'll see.'

Will found the little mound that marked his son's grave and bent down to lay his flowers.

'He lies next to my sisters,' he said, reaching out to pass a hand over the short growing grass that covered three other mounds. 'They all died young.'

The graves were near the river, under the church elms. Will stood looking down at the brown swirling water. He was thinking about poor Kate Hamlett. She'd been in his mind lately, partly to do with the play he'd been writing. She'd drowned near here while gathering flowers, or that's what the family put out, but they might well have said that to get her a Christian burial. The gossips whispered that she had drowned herself, in grief over a lost lover. Will saw her drifting, buoyed up by her billowing skirts, her hair spreading out, mixing with the weed, starred by the white flowers of crowsfoot, her posy slipping from her slackening grasp. Flowers of the water margin: daisies, white nettle, flag iris, purple loosestrife . . .

'What are you thinking?' Violetta looked at him.

He thought of her drowned mother, the bodies she'd seen floating in the harbour.

'Nothing. A poet's fancy,' he said.

'Master Shakespeare.' A voice came from behind them. 'Back from London. Who's this young miss?'

'This is Violetta.' Will introduced her. 'Meet Old Meg – she keeps the graveyard.'

'Mother Margaret to you, Will Shakespeare. Let's have a bit more respect.' She turned to Violetta. 'Not from round here, are you?' She eyed the cimaruta around her neck, and her eyes sparked with recognition. 'Long way from home, I'd say.' She turned back to Will. 'Your old man's grievous sick, so I hear. Sexton will be making space for him before the leaves turn.' She nodded to the plot that contained the other Shakespeare graves. 'Damp down this part,' she added. 'Safer in the chancel.' She nodded towards the church behind them. 'Bones don't last long out here.'

'He won't be planted in there,' Will remarked. Only gentry and men of importance were buried inside the church.

'He might not, maister, but you might be. Don't touch him. He scratches,' she said to Violetta as a grey-striped, hollow-sided, lop-eared cat began to rub himself about her legs. She looked up at Will. 'What do you want then?'

'I want a message taken to the lord and lady.' He nodded towards Violetta. 'I need their help.'

'Don't know if they're about. Might have gone travelling. Could be anywhere from here to the Severn.' Will gave her one coin, then another. 'I'll see what I can do. My cousin Janet and her lass Eliza, visiting from Balsall way, going back tomorrer. They might oblige.'

She nodded to two women who had sprung from nowhere. The girl regarded them boldly, with large black eyes. She was one of them, learning the craft. They weren't all old hags.

'We'll let you know.'

Old Meg hobbled off, her silent companions in attendance, followed by the brindled cat.

'Who are these people you want to get a message to?' Violetta asked.

'Lord and Lady Eldon. I want you to go and stay with them.'

'Why don't you send Tod or Ned, or George Price?'

Will looked over to where the women had turned to watch them again.

'That's not how these things are done. If you will excuse me, I have to see the sexton. Here's Master Price to see you back safe.'

23

'Not to be abed after midnight is to be up betimes'

'I didn't even know you were there,' Violetta said.

'My job is to watch you, so I watch. *You* might not have noticed, but those old beldames did.' George Price laughed. 'My master's spies have got nothing on this place.' He offered her his arm. 'Would you care to see something of the place? There's a May fair down by the river.'

The fair spread up from the Waterside, branching into the main streets of the town. Tod was there with his May Queen, buying her ribbons from a chapman, a pretty comb for her hair. It was a cheap thing made from horn, the jewels upon it coloured glass, but the girl looked on it as if it was turtle-shell and crusted with rubies and emeralds. Next they saw him at the sideshows, making a great deal of noise about winning things for his new girl.

'He's got a good eye,' George Price said. 'For a target and for a girl.'

'Yes,' Violetta agreed. 'She is very pretty.'

'I don't mean the May Queen.' George looked over to where the young actor was trying feats of strength, making a show of himself. 'He's not doing all this for her.'

On their way back to Master Shakespeare's house, Violetta had a strong feeling that she was being watched.

George's eyes took in the street: doorways, alleyways, up and down. He looked from there to the faces of the crowd. Then he looked up at the windows. A stirring in a casement window; a movement behind a diamond pane. Could be a face there, it was hard to tell. He could see nothing out of the ordinary, but he did not dismiss Violetta's feeling. Intuition was right more times than it was wrong. It was probably nothing, but Shakespeare should know about it. Either side could be watching her. The town would host spies of both stripes. Cecil would have his informants; so would the Catholics. Even if they did not do so openly, many in the town still held to the Old Religion. The trick was to know who reported to whom; being a local man, Shakespeare should know.

❖❖❖

'I cannot be sure,' Violetta said to Will, 'not certain. It was growing dark, and the street was crowded, but I felt . . . I felt eyes upon me.' She shuddered. 'It was as though malice followed me all the way down the street.'

'And you saw nothing?'

Price shook his head. 'A movement at a window, that's all. I didn't see anyone obvious hanging about.'

'Where was this?'

'The street that runs up from the river, parallel to this.'

'Sheep Street,' Mistress Anne suggested.

They were all sitting in the kitchen, as they often did in the Shakespeare household. The long, low room smelt of the sweet rushes strewn over the flagstones, drying clothes, baking bread and the dried herbs and hops which hung, looped and garlanded, along the beams. Will and Anne sat at the big scrubbed table, Maria on the settle by the wide fireplace. She'd picked up sewing from the mending box without being asked. Anne had declared her a 'useful little body' and they were already on the way to becoming friends. Feste was sitting with her, staring into the falling ashes of the fire. He did not turn as Violetta and Price came in and offered no word of greeting. It was a surprise to see him there; a fair was as good excuse as any for drinking and making merry. He must be in one of the glooms that sometimes took him and rendered everything too much trouble, any effort pointless.

Mistress Shakespeare frowned and looked up from the lists of figures that she had been showing to Will.

'There's more sources of malice in Sheep Street than loitering louts,' she said, pushing a straying strand of dark hair, threaded with grey, back beneath her cap.

'We met Old Meg in the churchyard today.' Will crossed his arms.

'She's one of them. The best of the bunch, I'll grant you, but I'd have no truck with any of them. They are not to be trusted.'

Will shrugged. 'Not in many things, I agree. But they are to be trusted in this when others are not.'

'Be wary, then.' She looked up at Violetta, her grey eyes shrewd and sharp. 'I haven't asked, but I'm asking now. What is it with this lass? Will she bring trouble to my house?'

'It is a long story, but don't worry, Nan,' Will could see the concern in his wife's eyes. 'She is no threat. She stands in need of help and I've pledged to give it. I'd hope that such kindness would be offered to our own daughters if the position was reversed.'

'Truly, mistress –' Violetta could keep quiet no longer – 'I do not want to bring trouble to you and yours. I will leave straightway. Tomorrow. As soon as it can be arranged –'

'That will not be necessary. I don't know what's going on here – he'll tell me in his good time – but if he's offered his protection, I offer mine.' Anne Shakespeare took the girl's hand in friendship. 'You can stay as long as you like.' She looked to her husband. 'I know he would not willingly bring trouble to my door. It grows late. We rise early here.'

This was the signal for them all to retire. George Price bade them goodnight. Will tidied the papers from the table, while Anne took the bread from the cooling oven to be ready for the morrow. Violetta and Maria lit candles to light the way to their chamber. Only Feste was left. He took a long time to respond to the knocking at the door.

'I thought you were staying at the Bear.' He walked back to his settle, leaving the boy to shut the door behind him.

'I want to be, have to be, under the same roof as her!' Tod turned, arms thrown wide, nearly over-balancing. He'd had a drink, and Stratford ale was strong.

'What happened to the Queen of the May?'

Tod slumped down next to Feste. 'Gone back to Long Compton on a cart.'

Feste grunted and stared at the fire. He did not relish this interruption.

'I really love her,' Tod said. 'I realise that now.'

The clown rolled his eyes. Tod wasn't talking about

the trull in the cart. Perhaps if he ignored him and gave the fire his full attention, the boy would go away.

'You don't understand! I have to be under the same roof as her!'

'You said that before.'

'I see her in all her aspects: laughing, smiling, thoughtful . . .'

Feste barely listened, but when a log collapsed, sending out heat and sparks, and Tod fell to making up verses about the new-kindled fire that burned in his heart, that was too much. To make it even worse, the boy had picked up the lute and was trying to tune it.

'By the rood! Stop that infernal twangling! Who said you could play that?' Feste snatched the instrument from him. 'It's mine!'

'I'm sorry, Master Feste.' Tod set to drumming with his fingers and humming the tune instead. 'Do you think I have any chance?'

Feste did not reply.

'You have great influence with her. You know her better than any. Could you speak to her on my behalf?'

Feste rubbed at the silvering stubble on his chin. He was seeing a way to enjoy this. Tod's handsome young face had lost its look of smooth confidence. The poet in him was failing to find the words that would rightly express his feelings; the actor was stumbling through lack of a script.

'See where good Mistress Anne keeps her ale,' he said, 'and I'll tell you what I think.'

Tod came back with a stone flagon and two horn beakers.

Feste drank deep and wiped his mouth. 'This is good stuff. She knows how to brew, I'll give her that.'

He waved his empty cup. 'Where did you find this? You could get more in Maria's thimble. Fill it up! That's more like it.'

'So,' Tod asked again, 'do you think I have a chance?'

'Pour and I'll tell you.' Feste was relishing the sudden power he had over the arrogant, cocksure youth-turned-boy again, full of uncertainty.

'Her countryman Stephano . . .' Tod filled Feste's cup. 'What of him? I hear that they are promised and . . . and love often grows stronger in separation. Does she still have feelings for him?'

'That I cannot say. You must ask the lady.' By Jove, Mistress Anne's ale was strong. His tongue was growing thick. 'They were promised as children, and although there was affection between them, lad and girl love often withers as first fruits fall to be replaced by others more robust,' he added with a wink.

'So you think I have a chance?'

'Well, now,' said Feste, pouring himself another cupful. His aim was unsteady; a good portion splashed on the floor. 'I'd say, in all truthfulness . . .'

'Yes, master,' Tod leaned forward, nearly slipping off his settle in his eagerness.

'Well now. I'd say . . .' Feste began. Young men in love were ever tedious, this could go on all night and his head suddenly felt impossibly heavy. He put down his cup. He was too drunk for fooling. Time to end it. 'I'd say . . .' he went on. 'I'd say, you don't stand a chance. She's promised to Stephano. Good as married. That's an end to it. She *likes* you well enough, but liking is not love, is it?' He spread his hands. 'She won't ever love you. She loves another. '

'I see . . .' Tod stared at him. 'No hope, you say?'

'No hope at all.' Feste said with finality. 'She'll be leaving soon, anyway. So you can go back to your other young wenches and village girls. Now I'm going to sleep.'

He fell over sideways and began to snore. Tod stayed for a while, finishing his ale, then he let himself out. He went back to the Bear, where he ordered more ale and sat brooding, turning the heavy gold ring that he wore on his left hand. It was a gift from an admirer, a noble lord. The stone could pass as ruby. It had been sent in appreciation of his Juliet. He was not used to rejection. Quite the opposite.

There were those there willing to join him, buy more ale and lend a sympathetic ear to a young player who was smarting from the unaccustomed slight and filled with sudden bitterness, feeling sad and sorry for himself.

24

'A witchcraft drew me hither'

'Get up and get washed before I dump you in the horse trough!'

Anne Shakespeare banged about with her broom, threatening to sweep Feste off the settle, none too pleased to find him asleep by the ashes of the fire, surrounded by empty flagons of her precious October ale. She would have words with Will about this.

Feste staggered off, his place at the hearth taken by Old Meg. She sat down heavily, spreading her skirts, her gnarled old hands, seamed with dirt, as brown and twisted as tree roots as she clutched the handle of her basket of herbs.

'Been out before sun rising, gathering plants. 'Tis the best time.' She sorted through the sweet-smelling froth of flowers, dark tubers and tender green leaves just beginning to wilt from being picked. 'I got comfrey, lady's smock, a tossie of cowslips, fumitory and hyssop from my own garden. I got a good bit of burdock root.' She pulled out a thick, crusted length and snapped it in half to show the pinkish white flesh. 'Look at that. Sweet as a nut.' She broke off a piece, popped it in her mouth, earth and all, and chewed it before spitting the wad into the fire.

Anne looked over the contents of the basket. Nothing she couldn't gather between here and Shottery, or find growing in her own garden. She began counting out the pennies nonetheless. It did not do to offend Old Meg and her kind, or the fire would not burn, the ale would not brew, the butter would not come in the churn, so they said. She wouldn't like to put it to the test.

'A word with your man, if I may,' Old Meg added from her place by the fire. 'And a drop of ale while I'm waiting wouldn't go amiss, lass. I'm that dry. And a bit of bread and cheese if you have it. Or a bit of pie.' She sniffed, as though scenting out the nature of last night's meal. Old Meg had a rare ability to nose out leftovers. 'I've not eaten since yesterday's supper and I'm that famished.'

Anne drew her a mug of ale. Then she went to the pantry and cut a piece of pie, a hunk of bread and a chunk of cheese, loading them on to a wooden platter.

'Thanks kindly, dear.' She took the platter in her gnarled hand. The cheese disappeared into the pocket she wore round her waist. 'Save that'un for later.'

Having seen to the needs of her guest, Anne went to tell Will of her arrival. He had risen early and had settled down at the table in their room, hoping to get a bit of peace to write before the household was properly stirring.

'I'm sorry, love,' she said as she went into him. 'Old Meg is here. She wants a word.'

Will sighed. He'd hardly started. He had only just taken ink and paper from his writing box, set the table out how he wanted it and sharpened his quills. He had been gazing down into Chapel Street, watching the town rise and come alive, when he'd seen Old Meg hobbling round the corner from Scholar's Lane. She had glanced up as she crossed the road and he'd caught her look, furtive but determined. He was already rising from his chair when Anne came into the room.

'How do, maister.' Old Meg looked up from her breakfast. She dunked a chunk of bread into the ale before beginning to chew. 'Teeth ent what they were.'

'I do well, Meg,' Will answered her. 'And you?'

'Well enough. I've a message. I were out gathering early. Some herbs is better, stronger in their action, when picked by the light of the moon with the first sweat of dew newly upon them. Guess who I met.'

Will stood in front of her, arms folded. He nodded; he knew already or she wouldn't be here.

'Him and her.'

Old Meg answered her own question. It didn't do to name them. Will nodded again. He knew who she was talking about. Anne's broom stilled. Will felt his wife's attention shift towards them.

'He says for you to come tonight in the evening while,' Old Meg said. 'You know the place. You know the tree. Best be off now.' She drained her mug and put the uneaten crust of the pie in her pocket. 'You don't trust me,' she said as Anne handed her the basket, 'but I never forget a kindness. Keep this.' She gave her a slip of rowan. 'Put it above the fireplace and may misfortune fly up your chimbley while luck walks in through your door.'

Anne took the sprig and accepted the singsong charm gracefully. She'd heard similar rhymes recited many times before. On the surface she regarded all such as superstitious nonsense, but belief ran deep. Better to be safe than sorry. She preferred to keep all sides happy. She would not want one of them to have a hank of her, she was certain of that.

'What was that about?' she asked as Old Meg hobbled out. 'Did she mean who I think she means?'

'I've got to get the girl out of the town. The clown too. What safer place could there be? Come, Nan.' He put his arms around her. 'They served us well once.'

'There's a strangeness about them. They never come into town, and folk do say –'

'That's all superstition.'

'They are thick with Meg and her kind.'

'They follow the old ways. Their estate is hard to find. I want to keep the girl secret. What better place?'

❦

Will went off to find Violetta and Feste, warn them to be ready to travel. Then he gave out to the rest of the company that the pair would be leaving them.

'Where are they going?' Tod wanted to know.

'I don't know exactly,' Will replied, which was no lie. 'Moving on.'

'Near or far?'

'Far,' Will said without offering more.

He did not invite Tod to see them on their way, but what did that matter? Tod intended to follow. There were those in town who would be interested to know where she had gone.

❦

Violetta and Feste collected their things together and made ready for their journey. They set out just as the day was moving towards evening, taking the road north out of Stratford towards Henley-in-Arden. They passed close to Wilmcote, the home of Will's mother's

248

family. The farm lay on the edge of the great Forest of Arden. As a boy, Will had often been sent to the farm in the summer, to escape the contagions of the town or when his mother was brought to bed with the birth of a child. He knew the country for miles around.

Long before they reached Henley, Will indicated that they should turn off and take a lesser road. Trees grew close on either side, the leaves on their lower branches layered in drifts like a pale green mist. The track saw little wheeled traffic. The way was smooth and unrutted, the horses' hoofs muffled by moss, grass and wild flowers. The lane branched and branched again, all the time leading them deeper into the woods. The trees grew taller, their trunks thicker, their over-arching branches meshed above their heads, making the lane into a kind of tunnel.

'Where exactly are we going?' Violetta asked him as they left the track and ventured under the shifting eaves of the spreading trees.

'I'm taking you to some people I know. You will be safe with them.'

'Who are these people?'

'They live deep in the forest. The Arden. They have always lived here.'

They were in the ancient part of the forest. The ground was thick with leaves of gold and copper, their horses treading over the litter of centuries. There was no discernible path. The ground rose and fell like the swell of the sea.

Eventually they came to a wide clearing, a slight depression surrounded by towering beeches, their smooth grey trunks soaring upwards into a tumbling filigree of delicate leaves. Markings like long-healed scars showed in the blank smoothness of their bark.

Will signalled for them to stop and dismount. The sun's rays slanted across the clearing, broken into long fingers by the canopy. The glancing beams held motes of dust, silken threads of spiders' webs, flickering fragments of chaff and other shining stuff. Insects swarmed, the light catching the glitter of their wings, the metallic glint of their tiny bodies, as they rose and fell. A man and a woman were entering the clearing from the opposite side, stepping through the shafts of light.

'Will! Well met! It has been a long time since we have seen you.' He held Will by the arms and looked him up and down. 'No longer the boy who used to haunt my woods, carving verses into the trees.'

Will glanced up at the space where time had erased his rhymes from the smooth parchment of the bark. He looked back, aware of how he had aged, how he must seem changed with his sallow, city complexion, his sunken eyes, his thinning hair receding from his lined forehead.

Lord and Lady Eldon were as he remembered them, dressed in hunting habit, both carrying bows. Red-and-white spotted dogs milled round their feet. Two keepers followed behind them, bearing a hart tied to a pole, game bags dripping blood. Lord Eldon's face was weathered, as leathery as the battered jerkin he wore. His full beard was touched with grey, curled like frosted holly leaves. He wore a battered old hat stuck with pheasant tail feathers and his long dark hair flowed thickly down his back, a dull greenish black, like ivy veined with white.

His lady was thin as a willow wand. She wore a

leather jerkin over her dark green riding habit, a quiver of arrows on her back. Her long hair was silvery, falling over her shoulders. Her face was lined but finely wrought, with high cheekbones and pale tilted eyes set wide apart.

'I have a favour to ask, my lord, my lady.' Will spoke to them with as much formality as if he was addressing Secretary Cecil and the Queen herself. 'These people –' he waved towards Violetta and Feste – 'stand in need of your protection. I ask you to keep them hidden.'

'Hidden?' Lord Eldon smiled, intrigued. 'From whom, may I ask?'

'An enemy who would do them harm. You know him, I think. Sir Andrew Agnew.'

At the name, the lord's face darkened as if there was no love lost between them. He looked to his lady, who nodded.

'You are welcome.' He put out his hand to Violetta and Feste. 'You will be safe with me. I give you my word.'

'We thank you, sir, madam.' Violetta curtsied to one, then the other.

The lord smiled at her. His face was open, even kind, but there was fierceness in his blue eyes. He was like the mountain chieftains who had sometimes come to see her father. Men who lived by the old ways and whose word, once given, would not be broken. Next to her, Feste gave his best bow.

There was a rustle in the branches above them and a boy dropped down from a tree to land at their feet. At least, he appeared at first glance to be a boy. He was small and slender. He looked at Violetta, his odd eyes different colours, one as green as the leaves above them, the other light brown and streaked, like a hazelnut. His stare expressed mild interest, mixed with amusement that could easily tip into malice. Despite his slight stature, he was no boy. His brown mossy hair was braided and wound with threads of different colours, hung with beads and shells. He wore necklaces made from beads of bone, tiny skulls, rough dark stones like petrified snails.

'This is Robin,' the lady said.

'They were followed.' Robin looked up at his mistress. 'A young one, unshaven, pretty as a girl.'

'It's one of our company,' Will said. 'He's in love with Violetta. Likely he's followed to see where we are taking her.'

'It might not be lovesickness.' Feste looked shifty. He turned to Violetta. 'I told him about Stephano, told him he didn't have a chance with you. He might not have taken it very well.'

'He might be following for other reasons, then,' Will considered. 'He's been acting strangely.'

Robin looked from one to the other and then at his master and mistress. 'Shall I see to it?'

'Don't hurt him,' Violetta said quickly.

'No. No bloodshed,' the lady told him. 'Just send him a different way.'

Robin nodded and disappeared back into the branches.

◆❥◆

Will did not go with them. He took the horses back to Stratford and left Violetta and Feste with their new hosts. Violetta did not feel the need to ask questions.

As she walked with the lady, deeper into the woods, she was filled with a feeling of great quiet, of peace spreading through her after so many days, months, years of anguish and turmoil. They went on in silence, their feet making no sound on the forest floor. She had no way of knowing where they were going, and knew that she could never find her way back by herself, but that did not matter. No enemy would find her here.

A broad way opened before them, a wide ride through the majesty of trees. A faint mist was rising and the last of the sun, shining through the branches, made it seem as though they were walking on a cloth of gold. The ride rose by degrees, until they were standing on top of a ridge. Below them lay a hidden valley, a lost combe. Smoke drifted from the wide chimney of a low house just visible through creeping layers of mist, the thatched roof so thick and ancient and moss-covered that it looked like part of the landscape.

The house grew from a base of soft, grey eroded stone that could have been carved from bedrock. Great oak timbers, silvered by time, formed crucks, branching upwards, following the shape of the forest trees from which they had been fashioned, curving round irregular panels washed with ochre and umber, the colours of the earth. Ivy and climbing roses grew all about the front of the house, curling and twining round a great stone-lintelled door, which stood open like the mouth of a cave.

'Welcome to our home.'

The lord led them into a great hall, lit by high, unglazed windows. The roof beams were supported by huge pillars fashioned from whole tree trunks. A log fire burned in the wide fireplace. An old red-and-white hunting dog, long-legged, narrow-flanked, heavy-jawed and deep-chested, lay stretched out by the hearth. He scrambled to his feet at the sound of his master's approach and came forward, tail wagging, claws clicking on the stone floor.

The lord bent down to stroke the dog's grizzled muzzle.

'He's too old to hunt now.' He stood up and laughed. 'Sometimes I feel like him, tempted to stay in and doze by the fire, but I do like to hunt.' He handed his game bag to a serving man. 'We will have some of these fowl roasted for supper. We live in a simple way, but while you are with us, this is your home. Rest, refresh yourselves, then we will eat.'

25

'What is love? 'Tis not hereafter'

Time was slippery. There were no clocks and the valley was deep, surrounded by trees, impossible to tell the hour by the sun. The days went slipping by, each one passing in a golden haze.

The lord went out hunting with his hounds. Sometimes the lady went with him but usually Violetta found her in the garden or in her solar at her loom. Violetta liked to sit with her. The loom stood under high pointed windows, and the stone walls were hung with her tapestries. It reminded Violetta of Marijita's room in Illyria.

'Your mother used to weave?' the lady asked her when she first came to watch her work.

'No.' Violetta shook her head. 'A friend. She gave me this.' She offered the cimaruta for the lady's inspection.

'A powerful charm,' the lady said. 'May it protect you. Do you want to learn the loom?'

Violetta shook her head. 'I would not have the patience. I'm content to sit and watch you.'

She came to the solar most days, but how many days had it been? One day was so like another. She tried to keep track but kept getting muddled and losing her count.

'My husband regards clocks as dangerously newfangled notions.' Lady Eldon laughed when she explained her confusion. 'We go by the sun and the seasons. They do say time passes differently here. Sometimes slower, sometimes faster. The country people regard us with deep superstition. Some will not venture into the valley, in case they never return. They call us the Lord and Lady of the Wood. Some won't even name us – we are just Him and Her. They leave gifts: a round of cheese, a pail of berries, baskets of nuts or mushrooms as if we were the fairy folk. It is nonsense, of course. We are all too mortal. My sight is not as keen as it was, and sometimes my hands pain me so much that I can hardly throw the shuttle. I can't vouch for Robin though.'

'He is not kin to you?'

'Oh, no. Although he has become like a son. We don't know where he came from. My husband found him one morning curled up asleep with the dogs. He had been living wild in the woods. He spoke no language, or none known to us, although the dogs seemed to understand him well enough. He went on all fours for years and is still happier up in the trees than on the ground. Whether he had been abandoned in the forest, or left behind by the travelling people, or had always been there, we've never found out. We cannot have children, so we took him as our own. My husband has done his best with him, but he's only half civilized.' She laughed. 'I couldn't introduce him into company. He doesn't take to people as a rule, apart from anything else. He seems to like your man, Feste. I hope he doesn't lead him into mischief.'

'He's not my man,' Violetta said absently. 'He's my friend, and he's quite capable of getting into mischief on his own.'

She could see them below her, in the garden. Robin was teaching Feste how to use a slingshot. They were like a pair of boys. She hoped they were not aiming at birds. A thrush plummeted to the ground in mid-song, its fall greeted by howls of laughter. There would be words.

'We have been here for such a long time,' the lady went on, timing her talk to the rhythm of her loom. 'My husband's family have owned this land since the time of King Arthur, when the forest was everywhere and they say that a squirrel could travel from one side of the country to the other without touching the ground. Now the woods ring with the sound of axes, and the heathland is turned by ploughs. That's why my lord hates Sir Andrew. He lives not so very far from here, but his land is very different. The trees have all been cleared. Every year our world dwindles and grows smaller, thanks to him and his kind. The forest dwellers, charcoal burners, woodsmen and furze cutters who have lived in and about the woods time out of mind are driven from their shelters, and the travelling people, who find refuge here, have nowhere to go.'

Violetta sat by the window, listening to the clack of the loom, the hiss of the shuttle being passed back and forth, watching the tapestry grow one strand after another, until the picture came clear. The lady did not ask her anything about herself, her past, but bit by bit she began pouring out her heart.

◆━◆━◆

If time seemed to move slowly for Violetta, it was moving swiftly for Will. Too swiftly. Performances meant every day was busy. Apart from the guildhall in Stratford, the company had been travelling about, setting up anywhere within a day's ride: guildhalls, marketplaces and inn yards in towns large and small, village inns, village greens, private houses – anywhere that would let them perform.

Touring from a centre was easier than travelling from place to place, and it brought in just as much money. More importantly, it established their presence here. There were a number of great houses in the neighbourhood, as well as halls, manor houses and substantial private dwellings. Many of their owners were deserting London now that summer was coming, with its heat, stench, flies and rising bills of mortality. Once in the country, they were desperate for diversion. Those that stayed year round were *always* desperate for diversions. The local gentry were hungry for the kinds of entertainments available in London. The provinces had been starved of amusement since the companies had left off touring, and there was none to equal the Lord Chamberlain's Men, inside or outside the capital.

Touring was very different from being in a proper playhouse with a whole company to call on, but Will was beginning to enjoy it. There were eight of them, all good men, with Mistress Maria in charge of properties, costumes and tiring. He had cut and sliced the parts to fit the available cast and devised a playlist pleasing to all. Although most of the actors had not been touring before, they seemed to relish the opportunity it gave for wit and ingenuity. The audiences were, for the most part, uncritically adoring, making a pleasant change from the surly

London crowd, who had their pick of playhouses.

They performed in halls, in courtyards, in gardens, on lawns and had engagements from here to Michaelmas. The money was pouring in. Burbage would be proud of him, but that was not the sole reason for all this industry. If they appeared at one house, then they were invited to others, as the local families tried to outdo one another. Soon it would be obligatory for any household of note to invite Master Shakespeare and his men to entertain the company.

One day, towards the middle of June, Will came home to find the yard transformed into a grove. A cart stood in Chapel Lane, causing quite an obstruction to traffic coming up from Waterside, while men trooped back and forth, unloading trees and all manner of plants.

He hurried into the house to see what this was all about, to be met by Anne in a state of unaccustomed agitation.

'Nan? What's the matter? What is all this?'

'There's plums, cherries, apricots and quinces,' Anne said, counting them off on her fingers. 'Enough to stock the orchards of half the town. There are different kinds of berries, vines and mulberries, red and white. There are seeds of all kinds of things, and look at this!'

She held out a small bowl, a cluster of pale shoots just breaking the surface of the fine white sand. Anne delicately extracted a tear-shaped bulb covered in papery brown skin. She held it on her fingertips as if it were fashioned from gold and ivory.

'Tulips,' she said. 'The first in Stratford!'

The first anywhere, outside a few great gardens.

These were very rare. Will knew who had sent them.

'Did any message come with them?' he asked Anne. 'Or a messenger?'

'He's in the parlour. George Price – the man who was with you when you first arrived.'

Will hoped Price appreciated the honour. The parlour was the best room in the house. The walls were covered in painted cloths that had come all the way from Oxford. They had cost Will deep in the purse, but they were Anne's pride. The furniture gleamed, polished with beeswax, and the plate on the sideboard shone.

George Price stood up when Will came into the room. He was dressed as a gentleman today, in a black velvet doublet and silk hose.

'I've come with plants for your wife and a message from my master.'

'I thank him for his kindness,' Will said. 'He could not have sent a better gift. My wife values her garden and orchard above all things.'

'Are our friends still safe?'

'They are.'

'The boy actor, Tod – when I left, he seemed less than happy with how things had turned out. I was worried he might do something rash.'

'He did try to follow, but was misdirected. It has worked to our advantage. If he was in touch with Sir Andrew's agents, he will have told them that Violetta and Feste travel north.'

Robin could be very persuasive. He was famous for the way he could beguile dogs and horses. Young men presented even less of a challenge.

'How goes the other thing?'

'It goes well. We have performed at nearly every house in the neighbourhood. That should be enough for Sir Andrew's guests at Bardsley to demand that we entertain them too.' Will smiled. 'No one likes to feel left out.'

'Are you sure?'

'Sir Andrew will want to match his neighbours in the quality of entertainment he can provide. The families hereabouts jockey endlessly for position and are ever ready to do each other down. Besides, young Stephano is our agent. We will get our invitation. The Venetian Ambassador was in daily attendance at the Globe. Stephano will make sure he knows that we are here and ready to perform. Sir Andrew cannot refuse a request from so important a guest.'

'Sir Andrew and his guests are due any day now. The other conspirators will arrive hard on their heels. This is the message from my master: He hopes your garden grows well and would have you know that by midsummer all should be ready for plucking.' Price began to pull on his gloves. 'You'd best get ready for the call.'

26

'Present mirth hath present laughter'

'There she is . . .'

Robin pointed towards the place where Violetta lay sleeping. She had found a shaded bank, fragrant with thyme and violets. She had meant to settle there to read while the lady tended her hives nearby, but the warmth of the sun, the scent of the flowers, the buzzing of the bees had sent her into reverie and then into sleep. Night was coming on, shadows were lengthening across the lawn, but the evening was warm and Violetta did not wake.

'Come!' Robin beckoned the young man forward. He had no idea why his lady had ordered this, the human heart was a mystery, but she would have the girl happy.

Stephano crossed the close-cropped emerald sward, releasing the scent of chamomile as he walked. He sat down on the bank, breathing in the tang of herbs and the sweet perfume of flowers. Violets for Violetta. He plucked a handful of purple petals and scattered them over her sleeping form. He leaned over her, studying her face, brushing back a lock of hair that had fallen across her cheek. Then he lay down beside her.

Violetta woke to find him next to her and blinked, sure that she was still dreaming. His face was open, unguarded in sleep, allowing her a chance to study him: the arching curve of his brow, the sweep of his dark lashes, the straightness of his nose, the softness of his lips. His mouth curled up at the corners, as if he smiled in his sleep. He had shaved off his beard and she stroked a finger down the smooth skin of his cheek and traced the slight cleft in his chin. She could bear it no longer. She kissed the delicate lids and his eyes fluttered open. He lay bewildered for a moment, wondering where he was, what was happening, then her lips were on his.

'What spell is it?' Robin breathed. 'What mystery? It always amazes me. What fools they are, if fools they be.'

He would have stayed on, to see what would happen next, but Feste pulled him away. It was not for them to see.

❖❖❖

Stephano came to see her every night. He marvelled at how close they were to Sir Andrew's house. It was hardly any distance at all, once you knew the way, although without a guide Lord Eldon's estate might as well be in Illyria.

Robin had appeared in the stables at Bardsley the day after they arrived. The stable boys were wary of him, but the horses had all set to whinnying, wanting his attention. Robin was stroking the muzzle of a fine stallion that Sir Andrew found too mettlesome to ride. Stephano had offered to exercise the horse for him. He was swift but temperamental, shying at the slightest thing. The stable boys found it hard to even get a saddle on him; now here he was as docile as a nun's palfrey, nuzzling at the strange boy's shoulder, taking titbits from his palm.

Robin finished sharing a carrot with the horse, threw the reins to Stephano and said:

'There's a lady wants to see you,' he said. 'Come with me.'

◆➤❈◀◆

Violetta bathed and dressed as the sun went down and prepared to go out. She slipped across the garden while bats flitted overhead and white moths fluttered, attracted by the heady scent of flowers. She followed the path into the woods and found him, always in the same place, the open glade where the trees had once held Master Shakespeare's verses.

Stephano left the roan stallion there, tethered, and they wandered off, hand in hand, through the black and silver of the moonlit woods, until they found a place under the spreading boughs of some great tree, or in a hollow filled with dried leaves, or on some mossy bank next to a stream, or in a meadow bleached of colour, the grasses still warm and fragrant from the day's heat. They would sit and listen to the nightingales and the endless hushed whisper of the wind in the leaves. Sometimes they sat in silence, hands clasped, finding themselves in each other's eyes, speaking soul to soul, or they would talk in murmurs, as if the woods were full of eavesdroppers, whispering of their love for each other, the life they would have together when they returned to Illyria.

'It won't be long now,' Stephano whispered. It was almost midsummer. The stars barely showed through the canopy of leaves above them; the sky was still washed with the paleness of day. 'I ride to Stratford tomorrow to tell Master Shakespeare that we are in need of entertainment and if his company would care to visit Bardsley Hall, they will be welcomed. All is ready . . .'

Violetta nodded. She knew. Feste and Robin had been rehearsing with Will's players. They both had parts in the play. There was one for her too. 'Only small,' Feste had said. 'No talking.' But he had been taking her through it, as strict as Will.

Stephano's grey eyes sparked excitement as he described what would occur on Midsummer Night, but Violetta felt a creeping sense of dread. That was the day after tomorrow. Who knew what it would bring? She did not want to think about that now. For all that time had seemed to move slowly here, now its passage was swift. Too swift. Whatever happened in the future, Violetta knew that the time that she'd spent with him here in the woods' midsummer quiet would always be there, just beneath the surface of her mind, to be conjured like a summoning, and they would be young again, their love new and growing. No matter how old, she would be able to close her eyes and see again the oak leaves turned to silver, smell the delicate scent of wood sorrel, feel the warmth of his lips in the coolness of the night air. Violetta put her hand up to stop the prattle about numbers of guards and men-at-arms, the layout of the house. Men always talked as if success was already theirs, but this enterprise was filled with danger. This might be the last night together. Ever. A chill ran through her. She wanted his arms around her. Enough time had been wasted.

27

'This is very midsummer madness'

This was the day. Will was up early. There was much to prepare. He went out into the yard. Swifts and martins shrilled above his head, swooping through the milky air, diving in and out of nests tucked into the eaves of the buildings. The mist from the river would soon burn away. It promised to be a hot day. Anne was already out with a watering pot, tending to the latest batch of tubs and little trees. They were coming faster than she could plant them, each consignment accompanied by a message from Cecil.

'I have not questioned you about these gifts,' she said as she tended the plants, 'where they come from, who is sending them, but I am no fool. There's talk.'

Wasn't there always? Will frowned. 'What do they say?'

'That you are the favourite of a great lord. That he does you favours.' Anne's face grew flushed. She was flustered. 'And . . . and much else besides.'

'Let them think that.' Will began to laugh with relief at the town's foolishness. He took her in his arms and swung her round. 'Let them think what they will. What would such a one want with me? A poor player. There's no truth in it, but the further from the truth they stray, the better.'

'Even so.' Anne would not be mollified, despite his comforting. She had too much common sense for that.

'Only a great man would have the kind of garden that grows such as these, and great men generally want something in return . . .'

He nodded solemnly. That they do.

'So?' She looked up at him. 'What is expected of you?'

'A favour. A performance. Tonight. At Bardsley Hall.'

'Sir Andrew Agnew's place?'

'A party has gathered there. They are in want of entertainment. We are to offer our services.'

Anne shrugged. It seemed a little thing compared with all this.

'You are to be paid in plants instead of money?'

Will smiled. 'Something like that.'

'What will you do?'

'*The Dream*, of course.' He laughed. 'On this day, what else would we do?'

➤◆◄

Violetta took one last look back at the hidden valley, the place where she had been so happy, and turned her pony's head to what the future held.

They left by way of a wide ride through the forest that led down to a deep greenway, the path cushioned with bright, soft moss, the high banks thick with ferns. Lord and Lady Eldon would accompany them as far as the road; the lady was mounted on a white horse, the lord on a bay. Feste and Robin would be coming with her.

Eventually the path branched, the broader way going on in a straight line, disappearing into blue haze, the other becoming a country lane, with trees on either side. The surface was well trodden, full of dips and hollows from passing cattle, crusted and splattered with cowpats. The setting sun cast long shadows. A faint moon showed sketched white in the deepening blue of the sky. Up ahead, a boy whistled as he wielded a long hazel stick to drive his herd towards home.

'This is where we leave you.' The lord slipped from his horse and took her into his embrace. He smelt of horses and leather, like her father when he returned from hunting. Violetta felt her eyes prick with tears. 'Fare you well.'

The lady held her for longer, and when she finally released her there were tears in her grey eyes too. She took the charm that Violetta wore and held it for a moment.

'May she help and guide you,' she said. 'May you be blessed.

'Robin will make sure no harm comes to you,' she called as she rode off. 'He has promised us both.'

◆►◄◆

They found Will and the company waiting for them at the crossroads.

'Are you a player now, Master Price?' Violetta asked as George Price gave her a hand up into the cart.

'Not I.' He laughed. 'I'm here to help with the scenery and such. This place has proved a devil of a job to get in to. No new men taken on, only trusted servants of known families. Just as well we have Master Shakespeare's help.'

Maria was ready with a headscarf for her and a shapeless gown. Violetta was a tiring woman again.

'I'm so glad to see you!' Maria exclaimed as she tied

the scarf tightly, making sure no hair escaped. 'I've been that worried! Master Shakespeare wouldn't say where you were, just that you were safe, but that could mean anything. Here, put a bit of this on.'

Maria daubed some brown greasepaint on to her face. 'You are so pale. Where have they been keeping you? In a cellar? The days have been so sunny, yet you look like you've only been out at night! Are you ready?' She held Violetta's hands tightly. 'I have another costume for you in the hamper. No need to worry. Master Shakespeare knows you are used to performing. He will have a word with you as soon as we get to the place.'

Maria talked on as the cart rumbled towards Bardsley Hall, her chatter hiding her anxiety. Tod had left the company, gone back to London. He had been replaced by Edmond, Master Shakespeare's brother, who had come back home because the theatres were shut. Violetta was only half listening. Her growing nervousness had nothing to do with acting a part in a play. Stephano said everything was planned, but nothing was sure. Her fear was building, but she knew that she had to control it. She had to use it, just like an actor before a performance, or she would be a liability, leading others into danger if they had to look after her. That she could never bear . . .

'Who's that strange little fellow?' Maria suddenly asked, pulling her out of her thoughts.

'His name is Robin.'

'He looks as bad as Feste.' Maria sniffed. 'They're as thick as thieves, by the look of it. Don't tell me he's in the play.'

'They both are.' Violetta leaned back in the cart.

'And keep an eye out for their tricks. They make terrible mischief when they are together. Robin is even worse than Feste.'

❖❖❖

They drew up in front of a grey building surrounded by a wide dark moat. It had battlements running round it and turrets at the corners and looked more like a small castle than a private house. The massive oak doors were shut against them.

'What's going on, master?' Ned looked doubtful. 'Are we expected? We don't usually just turn up on the off chance they want to see us, like some group of travelling players.'

'What else would you call us?' Will gestured to the loaded cart, with its painted boards, piled up with properties and cloths, the crew of actors perched on the back or tagging along behind. 'I will announce us myself.'

The house stood perfectly mirrored in the still, black water as Will walked across the bridge that led to the gatehouse. The stone was streaked with green moss and powdery mildew. He passed into the shadow of the house and felt a chill as he caught the tang of damp and decay. The massive studded wooden doors were shut fast. He looked round for a bell pull, any means to announce their presence. He lifted the great knocker, shaped like a curled serpent, and let it fall a couple of times, then stepped back as the sound boomed from him, muffled by the thickness of the door. He looked up at the windows, sunk deep into their stone mullions, wondering if there was anyone even here. The leaded lozenges of green glass, dotted with faded coats of arms, winked back at him like tiny mirrors, giving nothing away.

After what seemed like a very long time, a servant looked out, his narrow face hostile and suspicious.

'Yes?' he enquired. 'What do you want?'

'Compliments to your master,' Will said with a slight nod of the head. 'Tell him the Lord Chamberlain's Men are here and beg leave to appear for him and his guests.'

The man shut the door without any reply, leaving Will standing there, caught between the expectant scrutiny from the cart and the blank door. Had the boy Stephano played his part? The door opened again.

'The master is not here at present,' the servant announced.

'Masters! Welcome!' Stephano thrust the man aside. 'We are desperate for diversion.' He was accompanied by a pretty young woman, her hair dressed in a foreign fashion, who nodded and clapped her hands at the prospect of entertainment. 'You are expected. Come in!' He beckoned for the cart to cross the bridge. 'Come in!'

The servant's protests were drowned by the excited chatter from the Ambassador's daughter and the other ladies.

'Is our welcome secure?' Will asked, as he shook Stephano's hand.

'Oh, yes. Sir Andrew is out hunting with some of the other gentlemen, but my Lady Christiana has gone off to tell her father, the Ambassador, who has been looking forward to your visit. Come in, masters,' Stephano's voice rose in welcome. 'We are in want of entertainment. Guests have been arriving from near and far.'

The cart rumbled into the courtyard. The Ambassador came forward with his daughter to meet the players. Christiana is beautiful, Violetta thought, but from the way she is hanging on to Guido's arm it is clear where her love lies.

Her father was tall and spare, handsome and vigorous, although his hair was silver white. He was exquisitely dressed in the Venetian style, with an elegant rapier dangling at his side. He was very proud of his position and his station, Stephano had told her. His family was one of the oldest in Venice, their name in the Golden Book, but he was not all surface conceit and vanity. In his youth he had been a renowned swordsman, impetuous and quick to action. Now he preferred to play the statesman, but he was no coward. He'd been into battle on Venice's behalf and would not shrink from a fight. He'd become something of a hero to Stephano. A man he could admire and who would teach him the ways of statecraft and diplomacy in place of the father who had disowned him.

'I'm surprised he's still here,' Will said to her quietly. 'I can't see Secretary Cecil putting himself in the middle of something like this.'

'He's Italian,' Violetta replied. 'Stephano says it is a matter of honour.'

Will looked round, as nervous and restless as she was.

'There is no need to go through the part with me,' she said. 'I've been rehearsing with Feste. He played the Fairy Queen.'

Normally Will would have laughed at that, but neither of them smiled.

'I'd better go and check on things,' he said. 'And you should get ready.'

Only a few of the actors, his most trusted men, knew anything about the real reason for their visit. Price had advised that the fewer who knew the better. It was safer that way. Will had told Nat Hartley and one or two others. Nat was a useful man in a fight, if it came to that. He'd been a sword thrower, and the dirk he would be wearing wouldn't be just for show.

George Price stood by the cart, directing the unloading. He felt a tiny stirring of apprehension. They'd got in all right, but would they be able to get out? He had plenty of men on the outside, but this place was heavily fortified. He had brought some with him, disguised as players and helpers, but they were few. He felt the hairs on the back of his neck prickle and turned to catch a movement at an upstairs window. Behind him the big door banged shut. He twisted about to see a bar the size of a tree trunk drop into place. He thought he heard chains, the sound of machinery. Was the drawbridge still in use?

Malvolio watched from a window. At his nod, the door was shut and barred. The Ambassador wanted the players to come. Well, here they were. He hoped His Excellency would enjoy the performance. It would be the last one these players would give. They were all together now. All his enemies. He counted them off. Chief among them were Violetta, Stephano and Feste. Count Sebastian would be safer without them. Maria would be here somewhere. Now they had found each other, they stuck together. He'd get rid of her too. For good measure. The players who had harboured them, Cecil's agents who travelled with them – they would be punished too. And the Venetian Ambassador. He had proved false, pretending to help them, while all the time conspiring with Cecil. He had tried to play both sides, as Venetians are wont to do. His Excellency had involved himself in one too many intrigues. Let him enjoy the play. It was the last one he would ever see.

◆━◆━◆

The house was set in a hollow, surrounded by woods. The company was to perform in the courtyard. It was a good space, surrounded on three sides by the wings of the house. The chairs were set in rows against the walls; the actors would play in the central area, the backdrop provided by the waters of the moat, the trees and the sky. Ivy, rose and woody vines climbing the sides of the house, removed the need for too much scenery and created the feeling of being in a forest. It was the longest day of the year, but under the trees the darkness was gathering. The stage would be lit by lantern, torch and candlelight, moon and stars.

There is a time, just before a performance begins, when players and audience alike take pause and ready themselves to turn from their own thoughts to the matter of the play. Will stood with Edmond in the shadows of the gatehouse, watching the audience ranged round their three sides of the playing floor. On the fourth side, a thin moon rode high and the first of the stars were showing as the blue of the sky darkened towards night. Everything was ready. Candles, torches and lanterns were lit. Will waited for the chatter to die down and for each person to sink into that moment of silence, their attention turned inward, their thoughts flashing and turning like shoals of fish about to be caught by the net of the play.

Malvolio sat in the middle of the row in front of the house. The Ambassador sat at his side. Next to him was a space, Sir Andrew's place. There were other empty seats. Malvolio waited until the audience had taken their places, the play about to start, before he announced that their host and certain other gentlemen had not yet returned from hunting, but the performance would go on. They had even applauded. Malvolio smiled as he took his seat.

George Price leaned against the side of the gatehouse, looking on. He was puzzled by Sir Andrew's absence, and the other empty places, and not a little annoyed. Outside, his forces were gathering, while those inside were lulled by the play. That was how the plan went. Somehow Sir Andrew must have got wind of it. There was nothing he could do about it now. The play was about to begin.

Will saw Price frown. Something was wrong. He squeezed Edmond's hand so tight that the bones ground together. Inside he winced, but his actor's face remained calm and happy as his brother led him out on to the playing floor. Will turned him round to face each side of the audience. Then he spoke:

'*Now, fair Hippolyta, our nuptial hour*
Draws on apace . . .'

The play had begun.

Stephano watched attentively, arms folded. He sat on one side of a door; Guido on the other. He saw the players come on, one after the other. Under the disguise of their characters, he recognised Master Shakespeare, then Feste as one of the mechanicals. He didn't look anything like his usual self, but he was making them laugh. Then he saw Robin as Puck. He had no costume, just looked as he ever was. He appeared to be playing himself. When would Violetta appear? He tried not to fidget, but he was finding it difficult. He was tempted to stand up and go and seek her, but that would give everything away. Then one fairy attendant in particular drew his attention. She looked in no way like Violetta, yet he knew it was her. He sat forward in his seat, all concentration now.

Violetta was in the train of the Fairy Queen, tricked out in a gossamer gown, her skin gilded; her hair powdered with glitter dust and teased out about her head like a cloud. She made herself look away from Stephano. She must concentrate on what she was supposed to do. She must not give herself away. She did not have any lines to say, but she had been reminded by Master Shakespeare on no account to look at the audience. They might be near enough to touch, but players had to go about their business as if they did not exist.

Malvolio found such low entertainment loathsome and tedious in equal measure. He failed to see what His Excellency the Ambassador saw in it. The theme managed to be both trivial and offensive at the same time. The antics of the mechanicals were crude, while the Fairy King and Queen were ludicrous and fantastical. Who could believe in such things? The whole thing was not only foolish, but it had the reek of paganism about it and the story was immoral: couples wandering about in a wood, lying down to sleep not yards from each other without the sanctity of marriage. That character Puck was particularly odious. There was very little between him and an imp of the Devil, capering about, making spells, distributing potions, singing nonsense: '*On the ground, Sleep sound* . . .' Like some silly children's rhyme. Still, no matter; it would be over soon, one way or another.

Malvolio fell into a reverie, dreaming of triumphs to come. All around, the audience sat lost in their own thoughts or entranced by the play. Puck stole away. He could beguile many as easily as one. No one noticed when the least of the fairy attendants slipped through an open door and into the house.

Stephano was waiting inside. He took Violetta's hand and led her up a winding wooden staircase, Guido following behind. They reached the first landing, and then stole along a shadowy, candlelit corridor. They stopped in front of a wall hung with a faded tapestry. There was no door that Violetta could see. They appeared to have reached the end of the building.

'This house is full of surprises,' Stephano whispered.

He pulled the tapestry aside and passed his hand lightly along the panels behind until he came to a hidden spring. A low door swung open under the slightest pressure. They each took a candle and Stephano led Violetta into the secret chapel.

The room was in darkness, lit only by their candles and a red light above the altar. There was a strong smell of incense and Violetta saw that the walls were thickly covered in icons and religious paintings: diptychs and triptychs rescued from churches and abbeys all over the country. A statue of the Virgin Mary holding the Christ Child stood at the side of the altar, her hand raised in benediction. Below her, an iron stand held rows of thin tapers ready to be lit in prayer to her. Out of old habit Violetta touched her candle to one of the tapers. The flame glittered on the ornate crucifix that hung on the wall behind the altar and was caught in tiny reflection, flaring on the gold and silver reliquaries that stood above the richly embroidered silk and damask frontal cloth.

Two large candlesticks stood at either end of the altar, the thick white candles unlit. Between them stood the reliquaries made from precious metal, crystal, ivory, carved box and ebony. They contained relics of every kind – fragments of the true cross, phials of holy blood, bones of saints, pieces of cloth – anything and everything held to be holy, collected from across this country and beyond, symbolic emblems to rally the faithful and lead them in Holy War. In the centre lay the thing that had brought her all this way: the Magi's gift contained within its Byzantine reliquary, the finest work of the finest goldsmiths, the golden casket glinting with precious stones.

As she stepped forward to claim it, there was a click behind her. A hidden door opened and three men stepped out of the shadows. Two of them were armed like soldiers; the other was dressed in the black cassock of a Jesuit priest.

'Did you think that such things would be left unguarded?' he asked.

He was unarmed, but the others had drawn their swords.

Guido and Stephano moved forward to shield Violetta. They hesitated, neither of them wanting to fight in a place consecrated for holy worship, but their enemies had no such qualms. They came from either side, cutting off any hope of escape, their weapons poised for the kill. Guido and Stephano drew their swords reluctantly, but neither was prepared to be slaughtered where he stood.

'Kill them,' the priest said. 'Kill them all.'

Stephano dropped back to protect Violetta, while Guido engaged the first of the swordsmen. He caught the boy with a blow to the shoulder and Guido's sword clattered to the floor. The man stepped over it and came towards Stephano, while his partner circled round to seize the girl.

Violetta retreated towards the altar and lit one taper after another until she held a fistful, their flames merging together into a flaring torch. She held the smoking bundle close to the lace hem of the long linen altar cloth.

'Call your men off,' she shouted to the priest, 'or I'll set it afire.'

'Then you will burn with it, like the witch you are. There is no escape from here.'

'I'm dead anyway, on your orders.' She moved the tapers closer. The chapel filled with the stench of singed linen. 'What do I care?'

The priest signalled for the men to back away. Stephano did not take his eyes off them. He called the wounded Guido to him and beckoned for Violetta to join him. He changed position, angling himself to protect their retreat towards the hidden door, but Violetta would not go without the relic. She had not come halfway across the world and risked her life, and the lives of others, to leave it here. She reached up and took the precious reliquary from its place on the altar.

As soon as she moved, the taller of the two men lunged towards her. He moved fast, swerving to avoid the sweep of Stephano's sword. He was nearly upon her, his sword arm above his head, ready to deal a killing blow.

Violetta held the casket in front of her like a shield. Her back was against the altar. There was nowhere to go. She dodged as the sword fell. The blade missed her by a hair. It sliced through the coverings, clanging on the stone beneath. Violetta was forced back towards the statue of the Virgin Mary as he raised the sword again. She moved to the side and the blade sliced an arm off the statue, striking sparks from the granite plinth. She was trapped now, between the altar and the pulpit. The man was so near she could feel his breath on her cheek. His body blocked off any retreat. He drew his sword arm back, able to take his time. Violetta clutched the reliquary to her chest and bowed her head. She was determined to die well.

The blow never came. He fell to his knees, his eyes rolling upwards. A tiny little arrow, no bigger than a dart, lodged in his upper arm. He pitched forward, dead before he hit the ground. Stephano was fighting his way back to her, desperately holding off the other swordsman. One arm trailed useless, but Guido could still use his other hand. He took up his yataghan and brought the man down with a sideways, scything blow to the hamstrings.

There was no sign of the priest. Just Robin, bow by his side.

'My lady said to take special care of you,' he said. He cocked his head, listening. 'You'd better get downstairs. The play has stopped.'

28

'And thus the whirligig of time brings in his revenges'

Nobody was moving. The players stood frozen in mid-action. The audience sat rigid in their seats. Malvolio stood in the centre of the courtyard as though king in a play of his own devising. The young Jesuit stood by his side like an attendant courtier. Men-at-arms were ranged around the turreted rooftops, their crossbows ready to fire.

Will signalled to the players to remain in their places, to do nothing to draw attention. He had brought them into the most terrible danger. He had to try to keep them safe. They were all at the mercy of a madman. He watched the drama being played out before him. It became clearer, as moment followed moment, that this man, Malvolio, was insane. Perhaps he had been for a long time.

Malvolio beckoned Violetta and Stephano forward. Robin sidled back to the players unnoticed. He went to stand next to Feste, his short bow like a toy in his hand.

'Come and join us.' Malvolio made a mocking gesture of welcome. 'Did you really think that we would not see through your little plot? Did you think that we were that stupid? This is a sideshow. A sham. Devised as a decoy to draw attention away from our true intent. Sir Andrew and a few brave companions are even now riding through the night so that they can be ready to ambush Her Majesty.'

'They will not get near her!' George Price stepped out of the shadows. 'Many have tried. All have failed.'

'That is because of the methods they used.' Malvolio was fairly crowing, carried away by his own cleverness. 'She will be travelling by barge tomorrow. Is that not so? There are cannons hidden either side of the river ready to blow her to the infernal realm where she belongs.'

'Not if I can get there first!'

George Price strode towards the gatehouse. An arrow splintered the wood on the door; another bedded itself in the lintel of the window by his side.

'No one is leaving.' Malvolio turned about in the middle of the courtyard. 'Drop your weapons or my men start shooting. They have orders to pick off the players and the women first, then dispose of the rest of you.'

Arrows thudded, reinforcing the warning. George Price dropped his knife, nodding to the men he had brought in with him to do the same. Stephano stood defiant.

'Do what I say,' Malvolio hissed at him, 'or I will put your friend out of his misery.'

He pointed towards where Guido stood, his arm hanging useless, blood dripping from his fingertips on to the flagstones. Stephano's sword clattered to the ground. A group of Venetian gentlemen had sprung up to defend the Ambassador, swords drawn. The Ambassador signalled to them to sit down. He would see how this thing played out. Two of them remained standing, their swords now pointing at their master's throat. So that was the way of it. The Ambassador stared at Malvolio with undisguised hatred.

Violetta looked around, trying to control the first flutterings of panic. The men of Venice were playing false, or else they had given up their swords. The players were unarmed or carried weapons that were mere props, useless for fighting. This was a stout house, surrounded by a moat. It was impossible to get out once the gates were shut, the bridge drawn up – impossible to get in either. So there could be no help from outside. But there was one way . . . She caught George Price's eye. He had seen it too.

'I know what you are thinking: we are trapped in here with you.' Malvolio gave her a look almost of pity. 'Not so. Sir Andrew's house is well equipped with the means of escape – as long as you know where to find them. We will be leaving soon. Our work here is done. I would love to take Your Excellency –' he bowed to the Venetian Ambassador – 'but I fear our alliance is over. I serve other masters now. The gold we have collected from the Faithful across the country is going to Spain. As is the relic. Spain has long wanted a base in the Adriatic. Illyria will provide that service. We no longer need the help of Venice. You betrayed us to Cecil. The intelligence you fed him was false, but it was a betrayal none the less. Betrayal has to be punished.'

He signalled to the young Jesuit to take the reliquary from Violetta. She held on to her precious burden, resisting the attempts of the priest to take it from her. She would not give it up now, even if it meant her life.

'Unhand her!'

Stephano leaped to her side, dragging the priest

away from her. Malvolio nodded to one of the bowman on the roof. He loosed the bolt of his crossbow. Stephano's arms flew out and he fell face down. Violetta dropped to her knees beside him, the relic forgotten.

George Price took advantage of the confusion, setting off at a run and jumping up on to the low wall that served as the fourth side of the courtyard. Arrows showered around him as he dived into the moat. A couple of his men tried to circle round and seize Malvolio. They were picked off by the men on the roof, but how many more might be lurking? Things were not going as Malvolio had planned. It was all the girl's doing. He would finish this once and for all. As he stepped towards Violetta he slipped a long knife out from under his cloak. The boy was dead. Now it was her turn. He crouched over Violetta, seized her by her hair, pulling her head back and angling the thin blade of the knife inwards towards her exposed throat.

'I want for one more thing. The shewstone. Did you think I had forgotten it? Step forward, Feste. I know you are here and I know you bear it.' He tugged Violetta's hair harder, the point of the blade nicking the whiteness of her neck. 'Bring it to me, or I spill her blood.'

Feste took Little Feste from inside his jerkin. He'd been using him as padding for his part as Bottom the weaver.

'Here, master,' he said. He offered the folly stick to Malvolio. 'The stone's in the head.'

'Hidden inside the Devil's doll. How very appropriate.'

He passed Violetta into the priest's care and took Little Feste in both hands, meaning to dash the head against the pavement.

'No!' Feste turned away, unable to bear it.

Malvolio began to laugh. It was a rehearsal for what he would do to Feste after he had disposed of the girl. Then he would be rid of the whole nest of them. He swung the folly stick up, intending to crack it against the ground, but there was no forward momentum, he continued to fall backwards, gargling and choking on his own blood. He tore at his throat, unable to breathe, his groping fingers failing to find the little arrow buried so deep only the fletching showed.

He fell on his back, fighting for breath.

The men guarding the Ambassador had orders to kill him and his daughter, but the game was over. Malvolio was as good as dead. They lowered their swords, but it was too late for that. One died from a rapier thrust to the heart, the other fell with a dirk in his back. His Excellency wiped his sword on his pale satin sleeve and turned to comfort the girl who wept by his side.

Up on the rooftops, the men-at-arms faltered. First one crumpled where he stood, then another toppled from the turrets to the ground below, felled by little arrows or stones from a slingshot. From across the moat came the roar and flash of gunfire. Most of the balls missed their targets, but the firing was enough for the remaining men-at-arms. They left their posts and went scrambling over the roofs.

The young priest seized the reliquary and backed away, uncertain what to do now that his master was dead. He had not taken two steps when his knees went from under him. By the time he hit the ground he was already dead, felled by a slingshot to the forehead.

When the trouble started, the players had dived behind any bit of scenery that could provide cover. Will called them out now and sent them to help Price's remaining men to open the gates and lower the drawbridge. Maria came from where she had been sheltering, already tearing a cloak into strips to tend to Guido. The Ambassador's daughter ran to him, offering her silk scarf to bind his shoulder. But there seemed little anyone could do for the young man lying by Violetta. Robin was there beside her, probing for the place where the crossbow bolt was lodged. He brought his hand away and looked at his fingers. There was no blood. He pulled at the bolt. It was not lodged in flesh, but caught in the rings of the mail shirt he was wearing under his clothes. Violetta touched the slippery close-textured metal, exploring to see if it had been penetrated. There was no break in the fine mesh. Marijita's shirt had held. It had saved him. She sat back on her heels hardly knowing if she would laugh or cry.

Will helped Robin to turn Stephano over. There was a livid bruise forming on his forehead where he had fallen and he was deathly pale, but his eyes were moving under the lids. Will called for water and dashed some on to his face. The eyes fluttered open. He was alive.

Robin left the boy and looked to where the other one dripped blood on the ground. He swarmed up the woody vines that had spread themselves over the sides of the house, crawled along under the eaves of the house, then swung himself back down again.

'Here.' He gave a ball of moss and cobwebs to Maria. 'Sovereign for wounds, my lady says. Pack the cut with it and bind it tight.'

He walked over to Malvolio and reached down to wrench his flint-tipped arrow out of the dead man's throat.

'They are hard to fashion.' He twirled the bloody shaft between his fingers, wiped it on his jerkin and put it back into the quiver he wore on his hip. He took the folly stick from the dead man's grip. 'And here.' He handed it to Feste. 'I know how fond you are of the little man.'

There was a clatter of hoofs and the sound of marching feet. George Price was leading his men across the drawbridge and into the house.

'Give me the folly stick!' Violetta ordered. 'Quickly now!'

She took it from Feste, twisting the head to release the hidden chamber. She took the stone in her hand. The milky surface reflected the blackness of the sky, the thin crescent of the moon, the sprinkle of stars around it. She did not look further. She did not look into its depths, to seek to know what would happen next. She hefted its weight in her hand before throwing it as far as she could. There was a distant splash as it hit the dark, still waters of the moat.

'Let them seek it there,' she said.

'I have sent riders to warn Sir Robert of this attempt on Her Majesty's life,' Price said as he came towards them. 'My master will be grateful to you both. I'm sure he would like to thank you in person and I think

Master Shakespeare can look forward to a performance before the court.' He looked at Violetta. 'There is
the matter of the shewstone . . .'

'You're too late, master,' Feste gave him a wry
smile. 'She's thrown it in the moat.'

'Perhaps that is for the best.' Price looked out
towards the black glitter of the waters that
surrounded them. 'These things only bring trouble.' It
would certainly bring trouble to the young woman
standing before him, and he did not want his master
putting faith in such things. His superiors might have
other ideas. He wanted her out of here. 'I will tell my
master that it was lost in the melee. I know that you
have pressing business in your homeland. We will deal
with all this here and get the Ambassador safe away. I
don't see any reason to delay you any further.'

The cart was already packed and ready. The actors
were scrambling on board, still in their costumes.

When they were out on the road and under the
shelter of the trees, Robin put his fingers to his mouth
and whistled. No sound came out, or none that
anyone could hear, but out of the darkness trotted two
horses, one white, one black.

'My lord and lady have sent their horses for you.'
Robin brought them forward by their bridles. 'They
are a gift.' He looked up at Violetta. 'My lady sends
her blessing with them. She would like you to ride
them in triumph, when you reclaim your country.'

Violetta mounted the lady's grey, the precious relic
stowed behind her. Stephano took the bay.

'Come, Feste.' Stephano reached down. 'Ride up
with me.'

'No.' Feste shook his head. 'Let Guido ride with

you.' He looked from Stephano to Violetta, as if to say: *She's in your care now.* 'I want to stay here awhile. There's things I want to do.'

He went off down the road with Robin, singing a little tune.

'*With hey, ho, the wind and the rain . . .*'

◆➤◼◀◆

Will arrived back in Stratford tired to the marrow of his bones, but he could not rest. He got up from Anne's side and went to his writing table. He could not sleep for the need to write. He would start this very night. He sat for a while in reverie. He thought of the girl riding through the night, on her way to London, there to take ship for her homeland and who knew what fate. He thought of the events that had brought her here and all that had happened from that time to this. He sat for a while longer, viewing how it might be. He would go back to the beginning of the story. The play would start with music and continue in mirth and joyous humour that would banish unhappiness and dispel all the misery that lay between that time and this.

He cleared away the papers that had been occupying him. They could wait. He took up his quill and used his little knife to cut a new nib. Then he took out a ream of fresh paper, squaring it in front of him. When everything was arranged to his satisfaction, he began to write.

EPILOGUE

'But that's all one, our play is done'

6th January 1602

Cecil was a man of his word. The night was bitter cold, with flurries of snow falling and starring their cloaks as they set off from the Globe. The Thames was flowing black and slow and had the look of ice upon it as they crossed the bridge. They rode in ranks of three, the whole company, some twenty or so of them. Under their riding cloaks they wore their official livery, blue coats marked on the shoulder with the Lord Chamberlain's insignia, a silver swan flying. They were accompanied by a pair of outriders, each with a staff torch in a stirrup holder, to light their way. Behind them came a group of attendants, their sturdy ponies burdened with cloak bags and hampers. Maria rode with them. It was unusual for a woman to attend the company, but she had been up nights brushing, ironing, sponging, repairing, embroidering and sewing until her hands shook from exhaustion and her fingers bled. The costumes were costly and she would not see them creased and mauled, or her wigs and head tires mangled by clumsy boys and men. Besides, she would not miss this performance for worlds.

Will and Burbage rode at the head of the column, with Robert Armin between them. The diminutive actor perched on his broad-backed cob, his stirrups as short as a child's, his chin tucked into the collar of his cloak. He was clean-shaved, at Will's insistence, and it was mighty cold. They were outside the city walls now, climbing the long incline of Fleet Street, the mud frozen into ruts under their horse's hoofs. They bunched together to pass under the wooden archway of Temple Bar.

'I hope it goes well,' Will said, almost to himself.

'Well? Well?' Burbage boomed back at him over Armin's head. 'Of course it will. To think other will bring bad luck. It will be a sensation. It's good, Will, very good. A change from the last gloomy piece, although that went better than I thought it would. Ghosts are always popular, as are graveyards and drownings. That fight, too, at the end – excellent! But this is different. What do you think, Armin?'

'Good. Good.' The actor looked from one to the other. 'Excellent stuff. Best Fool's part ever written.'

Will smiled and thanked him. 'Are you happy with the arrangement?' he asked.

'Of course.'

Armin waved a gloved hand as if the favour asked was of no moment. Will smiled. Armin was not only a great clown, he was also a good and generous man.

They passed the great mansions set along the Strand: Essex House stood darkened, its courtyard empty, while Somerset House was ablaze with lights. Cecil's new house was finished now, the gates and court full of activity, the elegant frontage lit with torches. Burbage signalled for the company to close ranks as they stepped on to the King's Road, which would take them to Whitehall.

When they got to the Court Gate they threw back their cloaks to show their livery and announced themselves as 'My Lord Chamberlain's Players'. They knew the way. They had been before. Wide stone steps led up to the great hall where they would be appearing, but they turned off, drew rein and dismounted under the adjacent archway that led to the stables, where the Lord Chamberlain's man and a Groom of the Revels stood waiting for them. They shouldered the baggage and hampers and made their way to the chamber where they would get ready. They left their baggage there and followed the Groom to the Buttery Bar to get their *bever*, a measure of the special revel ale.

'Good stuff.' Burbage toasted Will. 'But not as good as Mistress Anne's October brew.'

Will gulped down one cup and took up another. He had hardly tasted it. He waited for the liquor to plane the edge from his anxiety. He wanted it to begin, and soon, but the court moved at its own pace. Feasting was still going on in various chambers and then there would be dancing. They were due to perform at nine o'clock and there was no hastening time. He listened as the Groom of the Revels reeled off a list of the assembled guests: My Lord this and My Lady that, His Grace, *Her* Grace, His Excellency the Archduke, His Royal Highness, Prince of some other place . . .

'Anyone would think that he had invited them himself,' Armin muttered as he poured more ale.

Will smiled. His smile broadened when the Groom mentioned a young duke and duchess from a small country bordering the Middle Sea.

It was time to go and check that the properties and

scenery had arrived and that the scene men knew what to do with them. The great hall, the Noon Hall, where they would play, was brightly lit with hundreds of candles set in branches hung from wires strung across from one side of the room to the other. There was a huge coal fire in the wide chimney place, and the high windows were hung with rich tapestries to keep out the draughts. At one end of the room stood a great dais for the Queen's canopied throne. All around, tiered seats rose in ranks up above the floor where they would perform. Will stood alone, measuring the room with his eyes. It was big, ninety feet by forty, but with the seating the playing floor was reduced to twenty feet wide or less. He went through the play in his mind, the movements, exits and entrances.

Trumpets were sounding, announcing the end of the feasting and the beginning of the dancing. They could hear voices, laughter, people were coming. Time that had seemed to trickle, grain by grain, was now pouring through the glass.

The dancing over, the dancers honoured the throne and returned to their places. Will saw Burbage reach out to softly knock wood for luck and, in the momentary hush before their master, Lord Chamberlain Hunsdon, held up his white staff of office, he was sure that the whole assembly, including the Queen, would hear the thudding of his heart. Hunsdon's signal sent the scene men scurrying. Within seconds they were back, the scene set. Hunsdon's staff went up again. Trumpets rang out, making Will start. It was the signal for Will and Burbage to step out and lead the company up the chamber. The high ranks of tiers seemed very close, the floor even smaller. They advanced towards Her Majesty, every eye upon them. The jewels she wore, from her delicate crown to the hem of her gown, picked up the light from the blaze of candles so she seemed all a-glitter. She seemed impossibly distant, her dark, hooded eyes looking down from far above. Her face, devoid of expression, a white mask under the vivid red of her hair, seemed to float above the delicate layers of her wide ruff. Will tried not to let his eyes linger as he and Burbage bowed low three times. To do so would be to risk being caught by the awe of being in her presence and frozen, as if by the basilisk.

Obeisances done, Will followed Burbage into the left-hand mansion. They would emerge as Duke Orsino and his gentleman, Curio. The play had begun.

◆➤◆◆

Violetta sat with Stephano, watching from the third tier. She gripped Stephano's hand more tightly than ever, her eyes wide, and watched, fascinated, as the story that she had told Master Shakespeare, the story of her mother's arrival in Illyria, took place before her eyes.

A rolling, rumbling crash broke from the thunder sheet and brought her back to the play. From out of billowing blue-green folds stepped Viola.

Violetta felt the catch of tears in her throat. He had taken the story that she had woven for him, and he had cut and stitched and made it his own. Here was her mother. Alive again for all to see. As long as the play had life, then so did she.

'*What country, friends, is this?*'
'*This is Illyria, lady.*'

'And what should I do in Illyria?'

Her mother had come from the sea. Violetta had returned to her country by the same means, but not to be wrecked on the shore. She had sailed from Venice with a powerful fleet of galleys. They had defeated the usurper Sebastian and the pirate Antonio in a great sea battle. She and Stephano, riding on the splendid horses given to them by the Lord and Lady of the Wood, had been welcomed into Illyria. They had gone straight to the cathedral, where they had returned the relic to its rightful place on the high altar. A few days later they had knelt before it to be united in marriage and been anointed as the rightful Duke and Duchess of Illyria, the coronets of office placed on their heads.

But that was a story for another day. Violetta's attention was claimed by the play.

Will stepped forward, dressed as a sea captain in salt-stained gabardine, a battered hat pulled low. He turned as he spoke, his arm outstretched, circling slowly round as if to describe Illyria was to indicate the world. Usually he looked for nobody, not even the Queen, but his eyes searched each tier until he found Violetta. She was sitting next to her handsome young husband and was much changed from the wandering girl in a stained blue dress of poor stuff, darned at the elbow, frayed at the cuffs. She was now a duchessa, as rich in apparel as any lady there, excepting the Queen. She wore silk and velvet, with ermine on her collar. Her dark hair was caught up in a golden net crusted with gems. His eyes met hers and held them. He expressed his thanks and begged a poet's forgiveness for using her life to feed his art. She gave it freely and in turn thanked him for the grace of his choice.

Then his gaze moved on. The moment was gone.

Maria watched, peeping round the tiers of seating, almost forgetting to hand out the props she had ready, to help the actors in and out of their cloaks and gowns. She heard Feste's words again: *Do you remember, Maria, when we were young?* And here they all were: herself when she was full of fun and mischief, Sir Toby when he was hale and strong, Sir Andrew a gullible fool again, not a traitor with his head on the gatehouse of London Bridge.

The play went on, scene after scene. Even the Queen was laughing, until the end when all eyes were on the joining of the couples.

No one noticed when one clown was replaced by another of similar height and stature. It was as easy as passing on a coat of motley. Suddenly it was over. All the other actors were gone, melted to the margins, or into one of the mansions. The floor was empty, except for Feste. He sat cross-legged, his lute across his knees, to begin his last song.

'*When that I was and a little tiny boy,*
With hey, ho, the wind and the rain . . .'

He rose slowly to his feet, still singing, his long coat trailing behind him and Little Feste dangling from his belt in his own little coat and jester's cap. He wandered as he sang, circling the mansions of Duke Orsino and Countess Olivia, their curtains closed now, weaving about the miniature shrubs and trees of the make-believe garden as though treading a maze. Sometimes he sang loud and danced as he went; sometimes he sang soft, his voice as light as his step. At length, he stopped and looked up to where Violetta was sitting with Stephano, and she knew it was the real Feste. Her Feste. Her eyes filled with tears as he began the last verse of his song and she knew how very much she had missed him.

> *A great while ago the world began,*
> *With hey, ho, the wind and the rain;*
> *But that's all one, our play is done,*
> *And we'll strive to please you every day.*

He turned, sweeping down low before the Queen. Violetta smiled as, behind his back, Little Feste gave her a little bow.

ACKNOWLEDGEMENTS

I am most grateful to the Shakespeare Birthplace Trust and the Globe Theatre for their thoughtful and illuminating displays of Shakespeare's life and work and for the helpfulness of their staff. Further afield, I would like to thank the staff at the Museum in Dubrovnik and the Ducal Palace in Mantua. I have seen some wonderful productions of *Twelfth Night* over the years staged by the Royal Shakespeare Company, but I am most indebted to York University Drama Society for their exuberant and spirited outdoor production, which I saw one hot summer day by the river in Stratford and started me thinking, *what if . . .*

There are very few indisputable facts known about the life of William Shakespeare. Even the date of his birth is uncertain. I have ventured an explanation that, since nobody knows, is as valid as any. Much of his life is open to speculation in this way, which leaves the writer a certain latitude. Despite this lack of documented detail, very many books have been written about him. It is impossible to list all the books that I have consulted, but I am grateful for the scholarship and insights offered by the following writers: Germaine Greer, *Shakespeare's Wife* (Bloomsbury, 2007), Jonathan Bate, *Soul of the Age* (Viking, 2008), Peter Ackroyd, *Shakespeare: The Biography* (Chatto and Windus, 2005) and James Shapiro, *1599* (Faber and Faber, 2003). Also, Leslie Hotson, *The First Night of Twelfth Night* (Rupert Hart-Davis, 1954), George

Morley, *Shakespeare's Greenwood,* (David Nutt – At the Sign of the Phoenix, 1900). For other aspects of Elizabethan life: Judith Cook's *Roaring Boys – Shakespeare's Rat Pack* and her book on Doctor Simon Forman. The *A to Z of Elizabethan London*, compiled by Adrian Proctor and Robert Taylor, was as invaluable as its modern counterpart. For Illyria, I made considerable use of guidebooks for Croatia and Dubrovnik, Venice and the Italian City States, but I also found Jan Morris's *The Venetian Empire* very helpful, Mary McCarthy's *Florence and Venice Observed* (Penguin Classics, 2006) and Rebecca West's account of her travels in Yugoslavia: *Black Lamb and Grey Falcon* (Macmillan, 1942).

Author Note

Twelfth Night is my favourite Shakespeare play. The plot has similarities to *Gl'Ingannati*, a story by Matteo Bandello, but it is not quite the same. If Shakespeare did borrow the tale, he turned it into something else, with different characters, in a different time and setting. I was caught by the idea of Illyria, not just as a fantasy world, but as an actual place. What could happen to these people if Illyria was a real country on the Adriatic Sea? What might happen in Illyria after the end of Shakespeare's play?

To tell the story in the way I wanted, Shakespeare would have to be in the book. In the past I have avoided including real historical figures, especially the very famous, who have libraries of books written about them. There are few absolute facts about Shakespeare's life. This allowed me to think that I could include him in the story. I wanted to write about Shakespeare *before* he was Shakespeare, when he was just Will from Warwickshire, trying to make a living in the competitive and precarious world of Elizabethan Theatre.

To write a book that includes such a revered and famous figure is still a daunting prospect. My agent, Rosemary Sandberg, gave me the extra impetus to do it. She loves *Twelfth Night* as much as I do and loved the idea. I am grateful for her enthusiasm and encouragement, not just for this book, but for all the others. This book is for her.